BARBED-WIRE EMPIRE

BARBED-WIRE EMPIRE

WILL ERMINE

M. EVANS
Lanham • Boulder • New York • Toronto • Plymouth, UK

Published by M. Evans
An imprint of The Rowman & Littlefield Publishing Group, Inc.
4501 Forbes Boulevard, Suite 200, Lanham, Maryland 20706
www.rowman.com

16 Carlisle Street, London W1D 3BT, United Kingdom

Distributed by NATIONAL BOOK NETWORK

British Library Cataloguing in Publication Information Available

Library of Congress Cataloging-in-Publication Data

Library of Congress Control Number: 2014939197

ISBN: 978-1-59077-414-4 (pbk. : alk. paper)
ISBN: 978-1-59077-415-1 (electronic)

BARBED-WIRE EMPIRE

I

THE south-bound flyer bored wailing down a tunnel of wind as it fled by, drawing the quick clatter of rail-joints across the easy peace outside the White Oaks Hotel. Rusty Maxwell did not glance toward the window, but his leonine head took an intolerant and sharp tilt. There was a wild light in his fierce old eye. He hated that sound.

It was the symbol of his trouble—the trouble he had come here today to fight. That he should come at all showed how seriously he took it; he, master of a hundred thousand acres, a barbed-wire empire; he, who time out of mind had always waited for trouble to come to him.

Here, with a remarkable completeness, were the protagonists in this struggle; seasoned warriors, standing in the hotel office, a strained civility holding them momentarily in check: Rusty Maxwell himself, big, full-blooded, forthright—Major Jubal Pickett, the railroad builder, spare and quiet—and Ben Sharp.

All three were above fifty, experience bitten deep in the lines about trap-like mouths. But there resemblance quit. Maxwell was red-skinned, white-haired, bulky; while Jube Pickett showed grizzled hair and thin, clever hands. Ben Sharp had not this honesty about him, at least physically. His high cheek bones were sallow, his stringy hair still black. His bony hands had a habit of hiding, and then flashing out, taloned even in repose.

Lance Kincaid, the fourth member of the group—he stood at Rusty Maxwell's side, a tall reserved force of youth in this room—also played a part. He was not thinking of that now, however, listening to the brooding summer silence flow back to the room, from which an oppressive warmth had not gone at all. His deep eyes rested on the three faces while he waited.

Maxwell rumbled angrily: "I'm looking to you, Ben. Word that your damned South Western Pacific has been granted permission to condemn a right-of-way followin' the thirty-fourth parallel west to the State-line is no bolt from the blue! I don't ask what you mean by it." He stared incriminatingly. "You did it! That's enough for me!"

"You always was a vindictive cuss, Rusty. Don't try to make me say," said Ben Sharp smoothly, "that I approve or disapprove of the Governor's action. This condemnation grant is a fact." The smugness in him brought ar immediate craft to the severe face. "There's a bigger question involved than your desires, or mine. The railroad's a fine thing." He was in his stride now, conviction somehow boiling up out of his enormous guile. "No man can get anywheres by flyin' in the face of progress. You can't compare cows with women and children——"

"Don't hide behind the barn!" Rusty Maxwell cut across his talk dominantly. "You engineered this thing, with the help of your lead-rope Governor! While I've been raisin' cows and tending to my own business, on my own ground, you've been playin' politics all over the state, with your knife out! I know what's goin' on!"

Pickett listened in plain discomfort. All this was bitterly personal. From Nashville and from a mannered past he had brought to the West a delicacy against standing between other men at such a time. He wanted to stay; but he wanted to leave more. A glance at Kincaid's unmoved face gave him no cue.

He began stiffly: "Well, gentlemen, I——"

Maxwell read him without effort and held up a detaining hand. "Pickett, this concerns you too."

Jubal murmured, with dry submissiveness: "It does indeed;" and Kincaid's long flat lips stirred at some thought of his own.

Firmer men than Jube Pickett stepped warily in the cross fire of words between these two. Now they had reached the climax of forty years of enmity; forty years of chicanery and sharp dealing from old Ben, which Rusty had everywhere put down as a browsing steer tramples weeds.

Maxwell's logic was never more sound than in this hour, in this accusation that Ben Sharp had manipulated the right-of-way condemnation proceedings in a manner which threatened to lay Rusty's huge 2 M ranch in two broken halves. It was a shrewd blow, long sought and longer planned, aimed at an otherwise invulnerable foe.

It was the end. Long conferences had smoldered and then flamed over the railroad Rusty hated with an intensity which alone could raise him to such heights. This was the last. Words were powerless to support the tension of struggle which throbbed here. It was not so much words, as the full weight of his imperious rage, that Rusty hurled over against Ben Sharp now, rumbling like a cornered grizzly.

"No statement of yours will hold water a full second," he told Sharp, with baleful intent; "or you could explain this thirty-fourth parallel business, instead of walkin' wide and treating me to your damned progress. There's no towns to be served west of White Oaks; no reason why your road has got to go just there, instead of twenty miles above or as much below!"

If he was to smoke Ben out, it would not be this way. "Everybody knows what you're coverin' up, Rusty," Sharp said, infuriatingly assured. "You've kept every other kind of a road out of Santa Bonita County. Your dummy organization has worked smooth up to now, I'll hand you that. It's got you thinking you're a king."

"What goes on on land you don't own is none of your business!" Maxwell thundered.

"That ain't the point. The Governor knows you're about everything from commissioners to coroner out there; I've heard him say you've been it so long, you think it's your right. I suppose, along with the troubles of pilin' up a million or two, you've done the best you could. But your day is past."

Rusty choked. Restraint mottled his quivering cheeks; but it was alone a restraint of the immediate impulse to smash Ben Sharp where he stood. His gushing response grew to a roar:

"You'd chop me down like that, eh? I'll break you for this!"

High words, these. But Sharp rubbed his hands. "That's a threat, Maxwell," he pointed out, not at all displeased that it should have come. In his obsidian eyes flickered a glint Kincaid read to its end; but Maxwell fastened on to its sly defiance.

"I put my meanin' into plain words, Ben: You're ridin' for a fall! Any of your understrappers that get in the way will go down too! There needn't be any doubts— when somethin' hits you, it'll be me."

Silence drew out, in which Kincaid stood tall and immobile, backing Old Rusty with sure support. Ben Sharp might have been receiving the news of a minor irritation, instead of an ultimatum that could seal his fate. He said, forgivingly:

"Well, Rusty, you'll have to go your way. It's the wrong way, you'll find." His voice thinned off in a sinister bite at the end. It said plainer than anything that his stake was on the cards as they lay.

Rusty had been sure of his ground for forty years. He could only meet this man's words now with a colossal contempt.

"You fully agree with him, it goes without sayin'," he snapped abruptly to Pickett.

The railroad man—an ex-army-contractor and engineer —dropped a briefly courteous nod.

"I do, Maxwell. In my opinion you are out of order. There may have been some color of justice to your stand at one time; but all that has changed. You can't stop railroads out of spite, man!" he declared, something of their sacredness to him getting into his words. "The South Western Pacific has been held up here, due to your stubbornness. But certainly now the writing is plain, even to you. It must and will be built!"

No other subject could bring this ring to his diction, Kincaid reflected. A soft-spoken, resolute man, in his way. Glancing at Ben Sharp, Kincaid mused, rolling a thin cigaret: "Buildin' railroad certainly makes strange bedfellows." He filed this disparity of men away in his store of knowledge.

"It must and will be built!" Pickett repeated, his eyes bright with belief.

Rusty retorted: "That's all right from your point of view." He put a hand on Kincaid's arm and added sharply: "But let me tell you this—your railroad will never cross my ranch. That's my answer!" His voice trembled with heat, not doubt, nor indecision.

Talk quit. Inability to go on this way stiffened them all. Kincaid's cigaret smoke roped upward without a break, and the pause that lay here was deeper than silence. It was raw suspense. Rusty Maxwell's continuing rumble only succeeded in emphasizing it:

"All I want is to be left alone. And I'm goin' to be left alone!" It was the essence of finality, ringing down the corridors of the mind. His square chin jerked down, eyes biting into Sharp and Major Pickett alike. He put pressure on Kincaid's arm then and said, in a heavy undertone: "All right, Lance."

Turning his big shoulders, Kincaid's flicking glance embraced their audience: The desk man, fussing at the mail boxes, needlessly; hotel loafers here and there in corners, all studiously self-concerned, but smirking over Rusty Maxwell's gusty vehemence; awaiting the violence of which he was capable. They left no residue in Kincaid's impressions beyond shallow observation. There was something of Rusty in him, he learned, without wonder; the older man's words and actions echoed in his approval as they had done, more or less, for a dozen years.

They moved toward the porch, Kincaid and Old Rusty. A horse thudded softly by in the sun-dyed dust beyond and Kincaid was aware that Ben Sharp and the Major, who had been sitting together in the office before this talk started, were following them out.

They stopped on the porch. Maxwell arrested himself there, solid, his breathing loud in his nostrils. Ben Sharp was saying to Pickett, with deliberate clarity: "A way will be found to persuade Maxwell, Major."

They passed Rusty and Kincaid and descended the steps. Looking down from his vantage, red veining his florid cheeks, Rusty fired out: "You be thankful for a whole hide and two legs, you hound! Now get out of my sight!"

The authority of half a lifetime rolled out from him, striking them both: a potent intent that sharply clouded the clear warm-wine amber of the afternoon.

Kincaid's comprehension swept the street, the wooden railroad depot opposite and not far from it on a siding, the Pickett car. They meant nothing to him. The thing that mattered was Rusty Maxwell's law, which had to be cruel, reaching out to strengthen the thin wire hedge surrounding the 2 M. He saw clearly, of a sudden, that Rusty Maxwell was himself the 2 M. They sought to amputate a part of him with his half-mile-wide right-of-way. Rusty would not let them. And Kincaid knew that he too would not.

"Maxwell," Jube Pickett broke in, and his high face was suddenly thin and harsh; "we've said all we've got to say to you!"

"Hold that." Kincaid did not shoulder up beside Rusty, speaking flat words. He did not have to. Something evil and spontaneous raised its head here, cording his muscles. Whatever he knew of Jube Pickett was put aside now.

Gray hairs and youth were alike caught in a mortal pinch of wills. He said: "You men are bringin' a fight to him. Don't forget it."

Kincaid could only just remember a time when his every serious impulse had not been somehow fashioned by the will or the interests of Rusty Maxwell. Sliding into the saddle a raw cub, he had carried a rope that worked for 2 M.

Long before that, his father had stood shoulder to shoulder with Rusty, more a partner than a wagon boss. But Mort Kincaid had ridden luck like he did horses. And that was hard. Riding to Baxter Springs on a trail drive, he had not come back: Killed in the line of duty. It was an incident of the Old Trail still told in bunkhouses; but Rusty Maxwell had made it a living memory. No pains to make Lance Kincaid into a cattleman had been overlooked. Lance had pretended to step into his father's sizeable boots. He had come a long ways since then. By dying, Mort had bequeathed his son a position he could never have earned in life. Someday Lance would control 2 M, Rusty said; and it was true that this high and driving man was more firmly than ever cemented to his origins.

Pickett stood firm. "Young fellow, bluff will get us nowhere. Must I tell you that?"

A high tension lifted and shook the moment, sultry with unseen lightning. Kincaid, never an expressive man, felt wrapped in a fog of purposes. Moving carefully, he sheared to the bone. "Whatever saves Rusty trouble will not be too much trouble for me."

Someone came across the street swiftly, attacking Kincaid from that side. "Save your proud talk for a younger man, Kincaid," a tense voice rasped, insolent with exasperation. Trace Pickett was built like his father, but there was a rash virility about his carved brows; a spurious depth to his chest that spoke of school sports and university training. The clothes of a field engineer gave him an air of swagger.

Kincaid held him off with his gaze, but Trace had furious words in him.

"I've got a bone to pick with you! You're responsible for holding up my surveyors out on your county-line! Your land—and your rights! Do you know what they've cost us in a month? Thousands! Idle men to feed and herd like kids! Time going to waste! God damn it——!"

Outwardly unmoved, the 2 M range boss was beginning to feel the freshening bite of fire along his veins. His even brows narrowed, knitting the strong face to a focus of command. "Pickett, that'll be a plenty."

Echo slapped against the depot's squat side and came back freighted with possibility. Up this street the breeze ran hot and heady, like thick blood in the nostrils.

"It's too damned much!" Trace flamed. "But you haven't done anything about it—and I will! Lift your finger and by God, I'll take you apart!"

Kincaid quit listening. His thin cheeks showed the firm outline of teeth and his mouth was a finely-drawn cord. What he was going to do about this was the burden of his dark musing. He moved toward Trace resistlessly. In his hands was already a fierce desire, the feel of sweaty skin giving before the impact of clean, finishing blows; the rubbery snap of breaking bones. . . .

There occurred a diversion. A girl came forward with a quick step and said clearly: "Hello, Father." She laid a hand on Jube Pickett's wrist and turned expectantly, firmly ignoring the odor of hostility here. Her smile at Trace Pickett was a serene thing, taking no account of his flushed heat.

Such unswerving ease came with an impact of its own to Kincaid. He looked at her incuriously, as the accidental barrier to a street fight; and suddenly he forgot everything but her.

She had light chestnut hair, outlining with orderly rebellion the even tan of regular features, azure eyes, and a strong mouth. The wing collar of her linen suit was caught by an old-gold brooch at the smooth column of throat. There was a suggestion of full chest and freedom of graceful movement.

"You know Mr. Sharp, Valerie," said Major Pickett. Animosities were behind him now, and his dryness was meant. "Mr. Maxwell." Rusty bowed stiffly. "And Mr. . . ."

"Kincaid," said Kincaid. His hat came off, wide.

"Thank you," Jube Pickett responded, with dropping inflection; and Valerie Pickett smiled warmly.

The light of the afternoon, for Kincaid, returned instantly. He felt the electric quality of untasted impressions lighten the set of his flat muscles. Here was more satisfaction in one thing to look at than he had ever experienced. There was something improbable in her clear charm and he waited for it to flaw as she turned her head. It did not.

She spoke easily, including them all; and was graceful with Rusty Maxwell. His weathered face softened. But no one was inclined to prolong this moment. Ben Sharp suavely excused himself and walked off, to step presently into the Cattlemen's Exchange.

Kincaid, his hat still in his big hand, stood looking after the Picketts until Rusty Maxwell's grunt aroused him.

"I am glad to have made your acquaintance, Mr. Kincaid," Valerie Pickett had said. He weighed the words with care, and knew there was in him the desire that they had been meant.

II

I'LL go and see Gavin," said Rusty Maxwell. Fred Gavin was his attorney.

He was as solid as rock, stating his intention. The heat had gone out of him, leaving its temper. His blocky shape was a citadel still. Fred Gavin would have an exasperating half-hour; for Rusty made the same unreasonable demands on the law, at times, that he made on himself, and couldn't see why it was impossible that they should be fulfilled. It was no accident of chance that this man, as master of 2 M, was the bulwark who stood between circumstance and scores of his kind.

Kincaid waited while Rusty said where he would be found later. Then Kincaid nodded and swung away. Starting for Len Hagen's Maverick saloon, he did not get far.

"I'll not believe you mean to ignore me," a feminine voice floated out to him from Voght's store-porch, in gentle derision. Kincaid's head turned casually; it was his eyes that snapped to the speaker. He got the impression that Donita Sharp had waited for this opportunity.

"Hello, Donita."

She came down to him familiarly, glowing and fresh in snowy muslin, rich with ruffles. Donita was a martyr to style, yet appeared never to suffer for it. Kincaid wasn't so sure. Humor tugged at his firm brown cheeks.

There was a self-possessed roguery behind the dancing hazel eyes which met his own.

"I flattered myself you had come to White Oaks because I existed," she said lightly.

He knew then that she had witnessed the passage before the hotel. "I came because the South Western Pacific exists," he retorted good-naturedly.

Ben Sharp's grand-daughter disposed of this airily. "I haven't a crumb of jealousy in me," she declared without petulance, and began to pick up the strands they had snapped casually weeks before at their last meeting.

They walked down Peach Street to Sycamore. A man in a delivery wagon turned to gaze after them long. Three shrill-voiced youngsters at a fence waited silently while they passed, freckled, knowing faces turned up. A woman at a window flounced back to remark acidly: "I declare, Donita Sharp's always with a man! Now it's Kincaid, of 2 M. I wonder what Buck Ewing will have to say to that!"

Kincaid was not unaware of the couple they made. Donita, he thought idly, was the best catch in town. And yet it was true enough that this was words without significance; himself, he had no intention of——

"You're not listening to a thing I say!" she exclaimed, tapping his hard arm.

"Pretty sure, are you?"

"Of course. Scowling like that!" Vexation edged her indulgent manner.

He turned deliberately, looking down. Lively hazel eyes, with a dash of unconscious supplication in them. Uncompromising trim chin. Honey-colored hair, wastrel and appealing. Donita loved the nickname of Honey, which he never used. There was a thoroughbred pride in those square, small shoulders and in the whole gay carriage of her.

"I'll confess to being provoked." His tone now was faintly dogged.

She said swiftly: "I have no effect on you whatever."

His lips smiled at this wistfulness. "That's right. Old Ben gets in between. He's a kind of sliver."

Donita gave over abruptly as they reached the gate of her home. She confronted him. Her words were crisp: "Lance, can you think of nothing else? . . . I have no more patience with Grandfather than with Rusty Maxwell himself. The crusty old fools have been at each other's throats long enough to have settled it!" She gave him a steady look, strong with admonishment, and dropped without jar into equability once more.

"Come in, Lance." Although he swung the gate accommodatingly she waited.

He knew it for an invitation to forgetfulness.

"No . . . Thanks."

Ben Sharp, besides his Jingle-bob ranch adjoining 2 M, forty miles west, had built a spacious, ginger-breaded house in White Oaks. Donita successfully claimed it and was its mistress; she spent only her summers at the ranch. School in Dallas had given her a taste for town. But she was saddle-wise; and perhaps by this time man-wise as well.

"I'll be returning to the ranch in two weeks. I hoped you couldn't wait," she said demurely.

Kincaid smilingly removed his hat. "Of course you'll hurry." He liked her best in this mood.

Her glance was on his Stetson. It was the second time

she had seen him remove it today and the memory of the first time impelled her to feather-light malice.

"Tell me you'll not hurry back to the—railroad station, Lance."

Impetuosity from her didn't bother him. "I was going back that way," he acknowledged with apparent reluctance, and watched the velvet of her eyes give way to something different. Donita, he saw, wasn't going to like Valerie Pickett. And her reasons would be frank ones.

Donita's small nose twisted comically and ruefully. "You're as ornery as old Rusty!" she asserted with brusque honesty, and dropped it there. "Lance . . . are you going to take me to the dance tonight?" She made a lingering plea of her asking.

He had forgotten the dance, his mind freighted with Rusty Maxwell's cares. But he said simply: "I'll be pleased." A Daughters of the Confederacy dance and basket party was not to be taken lightly. A day ago he had discussed the scheduled affair with interest. Then word had reached 2 M of the Governor's action.

Donita spilled quick, rippling words of arrangement, her face bright again; at the end of it she was already hastening up the walk to the gallery. On the top step she turned to watch Kincaid move off, her expression sobered, drawn to some inward question; her hurry forgotten.

On the corner of Chattanooga and Main a tall, quietly-dressed figure under a flat-brimmed hat attracted Kincaid's definite notice. Buck Ewing stood with his back turned, arms folded; but Kincaid, penetrating that unique identity of his without effort, somehow felt his attention strike this way, a thin thing, rapier-pointed. It was odd, and more than odd: this feeling that their meeting so was not wholly accidental.

"Hello, Buck."

Ewing turned deliberately. His strongly formed face offered no change. An experienced face, intelligence shining under the bushy brows. The rest of him was like that. A black mustache, blending with mahogany skin; broad shoulders, as high as Kincaid's; an angular freedom of powerful body. For a brief moment his arms held, locked, and then came down. As they shook hands, Kincaid said: "Didn't expect to find you here."

Ewing's presence was a matter of some surprise on any grounds. A frontier marshal, with more than one yoked and broken hell-town behind him, he had an unenviable reputation with a gun: headboards scattered throughout the Southwest were monuments to it. He never referred to his smoky past. This added to his stature; for the stories about him were in no danger of being forgotten. Kincaid had invariably found him pleasant, quiet-spoken, controlled. It was the thoughts of other men which gave him an indelible aura of dark repute; but he wrapped himself in remoteness, like a man who had experienced too much.

The two had shared a casual acquaintance since they came through a saloon fight together, on one of Kincaid's trips to El Paso, several years ago now.

Ewing's palpable glance rested on Kincaid's lips, and was removed, and Kincaid added: "How long have you been in town?"

Ewing always appeared to think before he spoke. He said: "Couple of weeks."

"Sounds like a woman," Kincaid smiled. "I guess you'll have a clear field, as far as I'm concerned."

Buck Ewing's weighing pause could no longer be considered accidental, so long was it. "I was wondering," he said dryly.

A clock stopped somewhere in Kincaid's brain. Alertness carved his posture to finer poise in a moment. What lay here—and it was naked jealousy—he took in his stride, and as quickly rejected. Softness put a keen edge on his talk for Ewing's ear:

"Give me the rest of it, Buck."

Ewing, notably unmoved by the lesser disturbances of storm and earthquake, was rocked now by some inward gust. Kincaid, cocked, watched him master it with iron will. Ewing's utterance was a sliding exaction: "Stay away from her, Kincaid."

No more than that. But in a twinkling Donita Sharp stood here, with wilful power to drag these two toward the thing all sensible men avoided how they could.

"Maybe," murmured Kincaid, "we'll leave it up to the lady."

Their eyes locked like twining blades, and there was a clashing in the stillness. Low sunshine ran their shadows over the deep dust in heroic stature, and even these were quick with waiting. The rattle of a freight wagon a block down had a commonplace sound but here the footfall of an approaching man was marked with distinctness. This man stepped swiftly aside and then backed away.

"Well," said Ewing; and Kincaid was aware of ease without softness: "think it over."

"I will."

Buck Ewing would know what to make of that answer. Kincaid left him with it, moving calmly away from there.

Afternoon shadows were draped from the buildings on the west side of Main. Thick dust puffed under the soundless hoof-pads of passing riders. Bar K lifted collective hands and chins to Kincaid. He nodded.

"Oh, Kin!"

Andy Stroud ambled out to join him and at once dropped his voice. "The old man breathin' fire?" he wanted to know, a larger question in his tone.

Kincaid, watching a yellowhammer soar over the roofs, said that Rusy wasn't. But his eyes twinkled. "If you don't believe me——"

"No thanks," Stroud responded hastily. He gave his friend a thrust. "You old Injun!" Then he was serious again. "You get anywheres with the big bugs? . . . Kin, there's a bunch of bad ones in town—rough and tough hombres," he went on without awaiting an answer.

"Railroad riffraff."

"That make it any better?" said Stroud shrewdly.

Kincaid thought about it. He said, "Well . . ." and lapsed into silence again.

The Maverick hid behind the deep shadow of a wooden awning. They turned in there. Old Kize, the bartender, fussing at the upper end of the bar, ignored these two customers. Scenting untoward coolness in this place Andy Stroud delayed, his eye coasting.

Nearly a dozen 2 M hands were grouped at the bar's lower end, looking one way. The tin hanging-lamp above the battered green pool table threw shadows down the hard faces of seven men who faced them. Kincaid pushed to the fore. By half a head the tallest, he paused there.

"What's this?" he grunted.

Tautness lifted the moment to something vaguely ugly. No foot scraped accidentally and the high words which had fallen off were ringing here yet. Kincaid measured the seven callous visages and found not one innocent of intent. Two he recognized, without any pleasure. Turning then, closing them out by that simple act, he fixed 2 M with an interrogative regard.

"Dammit, Kin! If you'd only stayed out of here five minutes!" Jake Kernan blurted.

"Who're you?"

The strident challenge slashed across the little space from the pool table: noise, touched with the prudence a shift of set-up always brings at such a time. Kincaid ignored it, and the answer was mixed in with mutterings: "He's Maxwell's range boss."

Kernan tore some invisible bond loose. "Oh, hell! Stand aside, Kin. We'll show you somethin'!"

He was no more rashly belligerent than his companions. Blood boiled turbulently up, hovering at the brim. But Kincaid raised a mastering hand. Marking Jake Kernan with his gaze he jerked his thumb toward the door. It was plain enough. Kernan choked. He turned, cursing.

"All right, boys," Kincaid persuaded tersely.

His men wavered. But now they looked to him. Kincaid's look shifted as one of the strangers rasped: "Mebby you'd like to take this up!" He made no immediate answer but his cool delay did something to them all that was unexpected.

"Maybe I would."

Andy Stroud was at his side now, bristling. His jaw was long, and it looked whittled. "Wave them cues a little," he invited; "and watch the roof come down!" He was ready for anything; he had been ready for years.

Kincaid pushed him back with an elbow.

Clearly unused to baiting and not entertained by it, these men spread out. An abandoned cue rapped the floor smartly. Tangible menace rolled out from them and the silence was long.

"Well?"

That was all. There were too many here, as Kincaid had known there were. No man out of seven leads unless he is expected to, and plainly none had found himself in this position.

"Let's drift." The scorning words dropped like a curtain between what was, and what might have been.

2 M moved out, definitely casual. Kincaid turned also, while Andy Stroud backed away behind him; hoping for the worst. A wave of belated rage followed them like a creeping thunder-head.

In the open talk came easier. Jake Kernan told Kincaid: "Dang it, Kin! What's behind all this? The Maverick's always been our headquarters. We've bought Len's pool table six times over, and that bunch wouldn't let us git a shot at it . . . hangin' on, spendin' their last two-bits, out of miserable cussedness! That's what riled us."

Kincaid saw the thing, mercilessly clear. A cool rebuff to 2 M, on ground tacitly their own in White Oaks, moved by an obscure but not unknown purpose. An ominous similarity linked it with other things that had moved in the open today; robbed it of the casual face it sought to wear.

Another puncher spoke up: "Them fellers are gun-slingers, Kincaid! I'm hep to three-four of 'em."

"I know." Kincaid's calm wore a curious grimness, a resignation and a waiting. "We don't want any trouble here."

Stroud insisted, over Kincaid's shoulder: "All the same, it's no accident that that bunch showed up. Town's plumb full of 'em!"

"We'll be ready for that too," was the smooth answer.

III

NIGHT powdered the dimly lit street with palpable softness. Carriages, spring-wagons, lined the walks around Mullen's Opera House, and strains of music rolled out to claim this soft obscurity. Donita Sharp's light and energetic step quickened. Her oval face, Kincaid saw in a patch of light, was eager.

He pushed a way through the ranks of murmuring onlookers: punchers, burly railroad paddies, Mexicans, an Indian or two. A wave of thick warm air struck them at the door. Recognizing voices broke from the stir here. Instead of awaiting attention Donita hurried off with her wrap.

On the floor a heavy press swayed and turned. A violin, a banjo, two guitars, a muted cornet, lifted the throb of a piano into measured waltz music. Kincaid's eyes touched all this gaiety with awareness but he found time for a word with two smiling elderly ranchers from up north, on the fringe of the crowd.

Donita came back breathless. Her hazel irises danced in anticipation; she said, "Oh, pshaw!" as the music stopped. Kincaid's quizzical glance answered her report of who had so far arrived.

Gallantry claimed the hall as partners were changed. A happy murmur ran through the rafters. The music started and Donita expectantly put up her arms. . . .

"I love a tall man to dance with," she murmured, floating to his sure guidance. Her lifted glance was luminous with approval.

"I should have brought in Short McGrath tonight. He has buck-teeth and keeps his ears warm with his hair; but he's six foot seven."

"Too bad you didn't—or does he dance with his eyes on the door too?" She raked him once with mock rage, then leaned sidewise swiftly to touch the arm of a friend. Nothing damped her animation.

She made friends with him again casually. Two dances later he stung her afresh. Valerie Pickett entered with her brother. Kincaid missed a figure. Donita jerked her head up, following the direction of his attention. For an unguarded moment her eyes flamed.

Valerie was dressed in flowing lines, falling away from a whispy waist. Breast and neck were a froth of tulle from which emerged round, smooth arms and that erect head.

Donita pointedly avoided Kincaid's heedless foot. He came back to her with a jar and thought her perverse.

They ended the dance perfunctorily. A slow flush of anger fought its way into Donita's cheeks. To hide it she called to acquaintances and gave him scant attention, and it was only his amused guess that she watched him closely. He looked over the heads.

Valerie Pickett was not in sight. But as the new dance was about to start a high-shouldered form sided Kincaid. Buck Ewing said:

"Isn't this my dance, Miss Sharp?"

His dark smile flashed, reaching beyond Kincaid as if he wasn't there. Stiffness froze this moment. Ewing swept

Donita gracefully into the step. Kincaid lifted his brows as he glanced after them. Donita, of course, couldn't know what she did. Despite his words of the afternoon, this thing had already gone past that. It lay between Buck Ewing and himself and it would ripen there.

He walked toward the door, but turned his back to it and so stood, not intending to dance. Valerie Pickett glided past, near, but she was speaking to Trace.

A man brushed in at the door whose spurs had not been removed. His face touched with an alien concern, he paused to scan the dancers. A step took him, presently, to Trace Pickett's elbow and he spoke briefly. Trace frowned. Kincaid saw an expression drawn across Valerie Pickett's features, in the overlaid beams of lamplight, which he had not beheld before; she was provoked, then smiling.

Trace started for the door. Valerie looked up to find Kincaid at her side.

"May I——?"

"Certainly, Mr. Kincaid," she accepted, the smile laying behind her lips.

Kincaid, dancing, thought of clouds and the soft kiss of the night wind, and rejected them. He looked into Valerie Pickett's frank face and reflected, "She's like nothing I've ever known."

Valerie spoke with quiet gravity of White Oaks society; of other railroad towns, vastly different. Kincaid found time to muse how odd it was, what dancing would let a man do. His arm circled this remote girl, wanting to contract; bringing him softness and fresh life, and more still. Probably other men felt this way with her, imbued with unpredictable zest. . . .

Intermission found them amongst the older folks on the fringe of the floor. Kincaid had no words. Her eyes asked a question.

"I was trying to describe you to myself—without much success," he answered.

Her increase of attention was a light thing. "Why bother?"

"I'm curious—and interested," he said without hesitation.

It was not the expected answer. Color came into her face. His big shoulders cut off much of the room; his gray eyes were friendly. They could be depended on to see only what they were meant to, she felt. She said thoughtfully, "I'm afraid I am going to need cattlemen described for me again . . . I seem to have mistaken the picture somewhere," she pursued. "I believe I like it better this way."

He couldn't quarrel with that. "Maybe you see too deep," he remarked. He had always distrusted talk about himself. Now, curiously, he didn't; and the memory of Trace Pickett's departure, which had lain across his thoughts, was for this moment gone.

"Choose 'em, boys!"

The music began. Valerie Pickett's dancing was a rediscovery. Kincaid might have waited long for this hour, but it wasn't everything; something waited beyond too. Something he wasn't going to get, it was pretty sure. More than an aroma and a desire.

Donita, still with Buck Ewing, danced as though her body needed this freedom. But touching Kincaid with a lift of opaque eyes, she lost fire.

At the end of that dance Gail Childress, the post-master, claimed Kincaid's partner. Kincaid strolled out for a smoke. It was as he pressed in once more that Charley May, a 2 M dandy, joined him for a moment. May had drifted up the street when Trace Pickett went out.

"Pickett hasn't come back yet," Kincaid said.

Charley brushed back yellow hair, his luminous eyes cognizant. "No," he said. "Ben Sharp and some others are gatherin' down at the hotel."

"So." This was plain reading. Kincaid hadn't considered the dance without understanding that things would go inexorably on outside during its progress. What those things were precisely was another matter. He said quietly: "Rusty?"

"He's in the Maverick. Or was." The music, tugging at Charley May's heels, pulled them apart.

Kincaid thought it over, dancing with Donita again. She was silent, even when Buck Ewing firmly intervened. Kincaid sought Valerie, found her surrounded. . . .

It was after eleven when the luncheon baskets were auctioned. Gideon Wall, the genial clergyman, made a carnival of it. Skirts fluttered and bright eyes talked. The music platform was cleared, an array of napkined baskets bustled forward. The men maneuvered table trestles.

Gaiety accompanied Gideon Wall's spirited imitation of the manner of Randolph Rhodes, a White Oaks auctioneer, here present. Baskets were knocked down with celerity to grinning gallants for excessive levies. Gideon Wall was a good manager.

A wicker-work container with carved handle was held aloft. "Miss Donita Sharp!" Wall intoned. His patter began.

"Five dollars," Kincaid made himself heard.

"Six," said a voice. "Seven!" Feminine eyes followed the bids.

"Ten," Buck Ewing interposed, harshly solid.

A hearing ear or two was cocked at that tone. That some unexpected thing was happening of a sudden was as certain as that there would be more of it. "Eleven," said Kincaid. He did not look at Ewing or Donita.

"Fifteen."

A flutter of envious excitement greeted the rise. Ewing glanced across at Kincaid with flat black eyes; and suddenly something was sharp and plain in this room that could not be missed. A line melted open between them. A dropped coin would have sounded noisy in this hush.

"Fifteen! Fifteen! Who'll make it sixteen?" Gideon Wall droned, trying with determined aplomb to get beyond the moment. "Miss Donita Sharp, gentlemen! Who'll give me sixteen?"

"Fifteen," Buck Ewing repeated distinctly, in a blunt invitation to find it an approachable price.

"Sixteen," said Kincaid instantly. Crawling stubbornness pinched his nostrils and the faces, except one, had faded for him.

No child in the hall would have said the stake here was a luncheon basket. Bitter wills braced in meeting and the swirl of struggle washed outward to the walls. It might easily carry the result of this night's doing beyond them, to end in fire and violence in outer darkness.

"Eighteen!" Ewing barked forbiddingly. He stood, feet apart and braced, coat hanging open, his shoulders squared; and the eyes that clung to him saw an iron hardness.

Wrath, long sleeping and now aroused, tugged at the lips Kincaid opened to top that bid. Gideon Wall, flustered and unseeing, his back turned to this volcano, was ahead of him. The borrowed gavel came down with an accent of haste. "Sold! to Mr. Ewing," the ecclesiastical voice declared, with a finality that seemed also borrowed and improbable. Donita's basket, a moment later, was handed down to Buck Ewing in silence for eighteen dollars.

Chance had it that Valerie Pickett's basket appeared immediately afterward. Courtesy ran the demand briskly to eight dollars, to ten, and Kincaid emerged abruptly from encasing anger to rap out a top bid of eleven dollars. An earnest field engineer for the railroad jockeyed him up. But here Kincaid was firm and quick and not to be gainsaid. The engineer dropped out and Kincaid claimed Valerie Pickett's basket for sixteen dollars.

Couples were finding their places along the trestle-tables. Valerie, as they sat down, said reprovingly: "I would have accused you of more common-sense," and turned to wrinkle her nose at the smiling engineer, three seats away.

"Burn the candle at both ends," Kincaid responded lightly, "and you're bound to have light."

The supper progressed. From the other table Donita threw daggers without fatality, for Kincaid was unnoticing. Buck Ewing's ease now was marked.

The fast eaters were beginning to rise when Trace Pickett walked in, hat in hand. He went directly to Ewing and bent beside him, speaking guardedly. Kincaid caught Buck's surprise and then dissent. Trace spoke further and Ewing, his brooding look at rest on Donita's hands, at length reluctantly nodded.

Speculation, for Kincaid, ran hungrily ahead of knowledge. Forgetfulness of the hotel meeting Charley May had spoken of was not in him. What Valerie Pickett's brother represented, moreover, was so clear that his movements molded themselves to but one meaning. But where Buck Ewing—that redoubtable and dangerously able man—fitted in this picture was a matter of nettled imaginings.

Trace rounded the tables toward Valerie. He came to a halt and said to his sister apologetically: "You won't mind getting back to the car alone? Something's come up."

Kincaid promised him: "I'll see that she gets back to the car."

Pickett apparently had to be satisfied. He spared no more words, nodding, his bold brows giving him an impatient look. He and Ewing swung out.

Donita didn't want to move, fastening to friends; but Kincaid brought her over to his table. She and Valerie acknowledged introductions and then talk languished. It was that way later, when, the affair breaking up, Kincaid saw that the baskets and silver were taken care of and walked with the two girls along sleeping Sycamore Street.

One or two lights, a green block, picked out the depot. Kincaid, disturbed by a foreign current that seemed to flow from Donita's side, noted the Pickett coach still lighted up. Cinders crunched under their feet in the soft night and near the car steps a cracked voice said:

"Evening, Miss Valerie!"

It was Limpy Smail, Jubal Pickett's pensioned watchman.

Good-nights were said, with Valerie's thanks. Her trim head, above the wrap, rose against the glow of the vestibule. Disappearing, she took something with her from the minute which Donita, in wise silence, forebore to emphasize.

They left the car diagonally and Kincaid glanced carefully back. Under yellow light, Major Pickett, his son, Ben Sharp and Buck Ewing sat with heads together in the car, a cigar angling Ben Sharp's shrewd features. Kincaid broke step, stared, and then went thoughtfully on.

"It doesn't surprise me," he mused aloud.

Donita caught him up hotly: "What do you mean?" She had not forgiven him the evening.

He turned soberly, absorbed. "The way things are shaping up here. These gunmen in town—bad ones. Working for the railroad. I saw one or two outside at the dance. It looks now as though they were getting the most dangerous man of their kind to head them. There's only one reading to that."

"I suppose you mean Mr. Ewing."

He couldn't find anything obscure in the situation. For him, at once, Buck Ewing and the South Western Pacific were one thing, and that thing dark with swelling menace.

Donita didn't want to talk about it. "Lance," she demanded, short with him; "has it occurred to you that you treated me shabbily tonight?"

"I?" He was surprised, and then direct. "Not at all. I've had things on my mind—unavoidable things, if that's what you're referring to——"

"You made taking me to the dance a chore," she told him coldly. "You danced with your mind at the hotel— or anywhere else. When it was convenient, you forgot you already had a partner." She stood before him, taut, convicting him beyond appeal. "Buck Ewing bluffed you," she ended flatly.

He couldn't tell her how wrong she was. She had the power to dredge up some disturbing influence that muddled his intentions. Anger left her as clean as flame, and as dangerous. Her swift thrusts he couldn't meet, now that he saw he had hurt her.

They stepped up to the Sharp gallery and sank on a swing, settling this thing. Donita slipped off her cloak and verbena perfume on the still night thickened his talk and his indifference. In diluted dusk her swelling chest was round; her cheeks were soft, her murmuring tone was soft. Kincaid, frowning, leaned back away from that contradictory invitation.

The gate creaked and Kincaid, turning hard, saw two high forms on the walk. Ben Sharp had his own stoop; but that other man, under the flat hat-brim, could only be Buck Ewing. Kincaid and Donita rose with one accord and found the shadowed side steps into the garden. If Donita took no note of the cold face turned this way it was because she preferred not to.

The garden was redolent of blossoms and growing things. It breathed its own soft insistence, and in it, Donita's murmured words were like a sweeping, tumbling current. Her mood had suffered one of those complete changes that had made her so difficult for Kincaid in the past. These two, arm in arm, might never have quarreled or known differences; except that Kincaid's solicitude was a deeper thing, fully warned.

"You're excited. Nervous as a cat. All that dancing—— Get hold of yourself."

"Lance, how little you know me!" she said. "The dance—and all that—meant less than nothing. It's you I want." Urgency was riding in her tone; an intensity that was its own promise. "If you could only share my wanting, feel it sweep and tumble you! It's glorious, and terrible sometimes." She was quickly sad, her voice a plaintive thread. "Terrible to think: what if you don't win—when it seems that only an hour, a minute, would do forever——" She halted him, looking up. And now this was the look of confident expectancy, the look of a child.

He said, faintly puzzled: "You can be hard on a man;" but it didn't reach her. Her waiting was a peremptory command.

Kincaid, taking a deep breath, brought her forward in his hard arms—and found an explosion of violent emotion in his embrace that shook and confounded him. Her lips burnt with a possessive fire, eager and wild and happy. Something came through from her to reach him; for the moment it swept and tumbled and had its way with him, even as she had said. In that one moment he savagely wanted to forget, to rush on headlong toward oblivion. Then, with a wrench of the deepest instinct in him, he came to himself—and not too soon. His lingering amazement with this girl and with himself was still greater than his immediate feeling about a step which rasped the gravel behind them.

Donita sighed her relinquishment and withdrew and

faded to vagueness. But Buck Ewing's face was plain above the black coat.

Softness and surety went out of this garden with plummet swiftness. Ewing's steel hard mien edged the balmy air with a sudden chill and the chasm of raw potentiality gaped between them.

"Kincaid, this needn't wait," Buck said with a blurred force, like the leashed evidence of a sharp and bitter impulse; and Kincaid met him on that ground.

"I was expecting it, Buck."

"You're getting it. From now on, don't trade on the past." Ewing's intention snapped the words off clean. If more was needed to proclaim right, Kincaid's guess as to his purpose here, Buck supplied it: "This is a warning —if you want to take it that way."

So it had come, what Kincaid had expected. A dry weather fly rasped sleepily and the ticking of Buck Ewing's watch was a quickening pulse in the silence.

"The South Western Pacific should pay high," Kincaid said dryly. He felt the hatred of this man, and knew it would not end here. "When do you start to work, Ewing?"

"I'm working this minute, if that means anything to you." Having delivered himself thus, Ewing heeled around, and his dark shoulders merged with the shadows of the house. Kincaid looked after him and didn't like it at all. In him was the knowledge that where Buck Ewing was concerned, forewarned was a far cry from being forearmed.

IV

IN the broad light of mid-morning the rugged backbone of Comanche Mountain stood up boldly against blue space. The peak dominated tumbled miles of high range, darkened with pine forest. Southward under this eminence the hills fell away for miles to the parked meadows and the rolling sweep of Rusty Maxwell's vast 2 M ranch.

Adjoining the lower half of Maxwell's domain, which the South Western Pacific expected to bisect, lay Ben Sharp's Jingle-bob, carved with shallow canyons and edging the flat-lands which stretched away to White Oaks.

Everywhere the lines of this country carried the eye upward to that mountain to which the Indians had given a name. And it was up there in a welter of canyons and wild land deep in the Santa Bonita forest that the Standing Stone, a brawling mountain stream in its first downward plunges, had its hidden birth in the glades where deer drank and above which bald eagles circled.

The river twisted down in a curving path diagonally through Rusty Maxwell's acres, until, beyond the spillway of Maxwell's Low Lake dam at the foot of the Basin, it escaped westward to the plains. It was a natural path into the hills and paralleling it an upward-winding trail ran through the trees from Maxwell's ranch buildings to the point where Slide Canyon prohibited farther passage. Here the trail looped back over the first ridge to grazing ground beyond.

Charley May, fresh from another trip to White Oaks since the dance of a week ago, climbed the last pitch to the crest of the ridge on an indolent horse. Having arrived there, Charley's cheerful eye roved over and down and picked up the angular form of Quill Hoskins, approaching on his slow way to the ranch. Young Rankin was with him. But it was Old Quill on whom Charley May's attention rested with wise affection; Old Quill for whom, sitting there, he waited.

Hoskins rode forward with lowering, deep-carved hatchet face, unseeing: the embodiment of an earlier day, threatened time and again, but remaining sturdy, implacable, self-sufficient. He seemed likely to brush Charley May physically aside, lost in a brooding world of his own; but suddenly bombing into animation, he gave May a tremendous slap on the shoulder and bellowed:

"Heyah, Chuck! How's the road commissioner this mornin'?"

Charley grunted: "Roads, hell! I'm in the ammunition department now."

"Good thing," Hoskins retorted, "you know how to buy shells, anyway. Ain't seen you do nothin' else for your country for the past two weeks. I was about to git you hauled up before the board."

Charley May had held various courtesy offices in Rusty Maxwell's Santa Bonita County organization from time to time. Like Maxwell's other straw-bosses, he came in for his share of ribbing on these vicarious honors. Every county office was filled from the 2 M crews because there were no other residents within its borders who mattered, despite the fact that Rusty's holdings did not absorb the county's entire area.

"I been plenty busy," Charley assured austerely. "And I ain't the only one either . . . Have you got all the stock pushed away from the line, finally?"

"Sure." Old Quill and Rankin were on their way back from an extensive stock movement. "But Charley, what else is goin' on, or about to? Dummed if it seems like I ever git to know!"

"We're doubling the wire, over against Ben Sharp's range," said Charley thoughtfully. "And if you haven't seen any night fence-riding yet, you will. I'm to tell you to amble that way now. Lance has been workin' out from the Spring camp. You'll find somebody there." He brushed cigaret ashes tidily from the doe-skin vest, of which he was proud.

Hoskins' slitted eyes ran musingly over the scope of range outspread below the ridge—2 M land as far as sight could plumb. "Bound to bring steel over that line, are they?" he grumbled, and broke out angrily: "Let 'em try! Let 'em bring on their tough-nuts, if they think they can take this away from us!" His loyalty to 2 M, and his belligerence, were fierce. Hoskins had sweated saddle-leather for fifty years. This was the last haven of the old range he was ever to know, the last undivided bit of prodigal baronry any of them would ever see.

"You dead right," said Rankin, touched with sullenness; and Charley May nodded.

"We'll have somethin' to say about it." He looked across and said: "Pete, you go back. Tell Jake Kernan Rusty wants his whole crew down on the line. Then swing through the Gap and give Gurley the same word. Tell 'em Lance says today."

Rankin ejaculated: "Hell, Chuck! I want to get down there myself." Hot, resentful youth colored his talk with begging impatience.

"All right, Pete."

Charley May knew the right intonation to throw into the words. Young Rankin heeled around sharply and galloped away. May's eyes followed him only a moment. He turned his pony then and dropped down the ridge ranchward at a shambling trot, listening to Quill Hoskins' mutterings.

"Cow ranch!" Hoskins pretended to grumble, fishing for information in his own wily way; "why, accordin' to your tell, Rusty'll have sixty-seventy of the boys down on that line t'day. Punchers ain't what they used to be."

Charley grinned. "This fence trouble we got ain't like always, neither. You can look for it to be right brisk."

"I sh'd hope so!" But Hoskins was catching at crumbs, studying Charley May's inflection like a primer. Something gathering in the air today and for days past smelt ominous, and more than ominous. Old Quill scented the biggest and the toughest fight of his stormy knowing.

They entered the pines. Shadows lay here, a cool gray trimmed with gold. The old puncher growled: "How far they from us now?"

"Eight or nine miles," Charley told him. "I saw them moving scrapers and such stuff in on Soda Flats, last night, from the trail." Quill nodded forebodingly, and Charley added: "That about brings 'em over the county line."

"Well," and Hoskins smiled craftily; "then they'll come the rest of the way by dead reckonin'."

Passing a branch trail they found nearly a score of punchers turning in behind them, on the way down the hills under orders; Andy Stroud, easy in the saddle, at their head. One of them, a deep-eyed, gangling sloucher, with humorous mouth, was in time to hear the last. He chuckled:

"Yeah, I understand the survey-stakes 've all disappeared, across Soda. Wonder how that could have happened?"

The pines were suddenly full of the rustling echoes of hoof and saddle gear. Charley May said to Stroud: "Lance puttin' your boys above the old wash?"

Stroud answered: "That's right."

"Nice interesting spot."

"I hear our sheriff," Quill Hoskins announced for the benefit of all, "is out now, cuttin' sign on the buggers that did that stake-pullin'."

There were one or two knowing laughs. Andy Stroud told them collectively: "You birds are a smart bunch."

They rode silently then along the rock-tusked stream, bound by a solidarity that needed no words. The one life these men knew, or wanted to know, surrounded them here with a completeness flawed only by their thoughts.

The pines thinned out, opening to sleepy pools of sunlight; they closed in again, thick; and then fell away for good. The river flattened and slowed, and across it the swelling, surging earth tossed a sea of grass.

They crossed a logged bridge, rolling long to eighty hoofs, and climbed the beaten trail. A glimpse of distance opened out. They turned now toward the ranch boundary, heads lifting, alert. And now the sense of trouble on this range deepened their taciturn silence.

A mile from fence they drew in to scan a knot of horsemen moving this way along the foot of the ridge. Six in that bunch. Dallas Waidler, sheriff of Santa Bonita, stout, and ponderous with dignity at any distance, was recognizable. Three deputies were with him.

"And two strangers," Charley May summed up, shoving his horse forward. A large question drove them all down there.

Waidler pulled his horse broadside and said heavily, "All right, now, boys," as though he expected interference. Trace Pickett and Buck Ewing would give no recognition to this quick barrier. Ewing was strong with self-possession, and with something else that came out of him to make it real. Trace raked the semicircle once, sharply, and said, "Well, Waidler!"

The sheriff waved a hand in a commanding gesture. Andy Stroud murmured, "You know what you're doin', Dal." The barrier melted reluctantly.

Charley May looked after the departing half-dozen. "I'd exchange my pass for the hot place," he said, "for the privilege of watchin' Old Rusty's face for the next half-hour."

Maxwell called up admirable control. When Buck Ewing walked smartly in with Trace Pickett, and Dallas Waidler at their heels, Rusty glanced across the desk at Kincaid and then lifted opaque eyes.

"To what am I indebted for this attention?" he inquired dryly, a fine shading of scorn on this last word. He spoke directly to Pickett, rejecting the cold authority of Buck Ewing. Buck fastened a freezing glance on Kincaid, who wasn't aware of it at all, if his manner meant anything.

"Maxwell, explain for me the disappearance of my survey-stakes across Soda," Trace fired out, obviously loaded for bear, and inclined to crowd the quarry. "Damn it, man! You've gone too far. The flats are not inside your boundary——"

"And I'm not sure my men know anything about it," Rusty finished for him, chipping the words off like granite, with full control. "It happens that I heard about them stakes," he went on strictly. "I've asked the sheriff here, to do something about it."

If he disposed of it thus, Buck Ewing, speaking for the first time, was ahead of him. Ewing dropped flat words into the pooled quiet of the office:

"Never mind. Those stakes will be back there today. My advice to you, Maxwell, is to see that your sheriff is on the ground to prevent our men from being fired on. If you don't," Buck ended, with a softness that deluded no one, "those shots will be returned."

Rusty, getting up, stood more like a weathered pine than a man under fire. His head-shake was minute, but definite. "Waidler will be busy elsewhere."

Trace Pickett interjected violently: "If you can't maintain law and order in this county, maybe the government can do something about it!"

There was evident here a trip-hammer drumming on one aim that angered by its insistence. It left a sullenness behind it that was more than a promise of strife—it was a certainty. And Buck Ewing, standing firm and dark and unpredictable behind Trace Pickett's bursting fire of words, confirmed that certainty.

Kincaid, warned by Rusty's wrathy snort, lifted his voice without haste. "The sheriff of Santa Bonita is responsible only to the county commissioners, Pickett. You know that."

"They'll come to time too, if the Governor deems it advisable to declare a state of insurrection!" Trace flared angrily. He slammed his fist on the desk. "You've got a sheriff, and you refuse us his protection." It sounded now as though he hoped this refusal would hold; as though, defiantly, he invited it to hold.

Quiet flowed back, if not peace, or the hope of peace. The faces of these men were coldly reserved. Except for Trace Pickett, they looked as though they could not see the grappling forces surrounding them, and knew it. But Rusty Maxwell could have picked his way blindfolded in this hostile maze. He said bluntly:

"Hell, we ain't got any sheriff. Henceforth, from this minute on, I declare the office of sheriff vacant." He swung toward Waidler. "Write out your resignation, Dal. Right now. I'm acceptin' it in the presence of witnesses."

Waidler laboriously complied. Kincaid used this moment to watch Rusty Maxwell. He was great, standing there over Dallas Waidler's bent head at the desk. With that thick silvered jaw and those craggy brows, it was incredible that any fight of his should overreach the lengths of a skirmish. His big fingers, toying with the unclasped badge, looked inexorable, and symbolic.

Trace Pickett flushed with resentment. Bitter impatience jerked out of him: "You're plainly trying to obstruct justice! I won't have it, do you hear——?"

Ewing stopped him, an iron formality riding his impressive mien. "Let it go," he said, and his words had less of advice in them than cold command. "We've smoked them out. We'll handle this from now on in our own way." It was as though he and Trace were absolutely alone; the stiffness of pointed silence affected him not at all. Lips flat, he turned to the door and strode across the stone gallery toward the horses.

Trace accompanied him, fuming inwardly. They swung away with their escort. Kincaid stood in the door and watched them grow small, and then he turned and caught Rusty Maxwell's metallic eye.

"This Pickett," Rusty growled, his voice disgusted, "was never introduced to a game called poker."

Kincaid delayed. "I'm not so sure," he said finally; and Rusty's head lifted. His response was exploratory:

"You mean survey-stakes wasn't their main concern?" He groped at the possibilities beyond, faintly bristling.

Kincaid waved a disposing hand. "Buck Ewing," he declared, "can put a face on anything." He regarded Rusty thoughtfully, and continued: "He's welcome to any seeing he got in, here or at the fence. But it's a good idea." He started for the door.

"Where you goin'?"

"I'm taking a little ride," Kincaid told him, and sauntered on toward his pony.

2 M was a welter of stone and adobe, and big pine barns, on a high level. The house was low and sprawling and galleried: a man's habitation, windowless in summer, because here glass attracted accidents. Maxwell's corrals

looked like a stock yard. Bunkhouses and odd structures sided the barns; the cottages of the straw-bosses, many of them married, stood under oaks on the bank of a feeder deflected from the Standing Stone.

In blinding mid-day haze Kincaid turned down the bench and jogged over range dotted here and there with cattle. Ten minutes later a rider topped a grassy swell and angled forward; Kincaid fastened on him a bright attention.

"Well, Charley?"

Charley May smiled. "I was wonderin'," was his answer. "Then I saw Their Highnesses pull out toward the flats, and I figured you had things in hand at this end."

"How about you?"

"I did all you said." May gave an account of his activities. To this Kincaid added a summary of what had happened at Maxwell's office, and Charley looked sober.

"You took cartridges out to the Spring camp?"

"Yeah," said Charley.

Kincaid nodded, saying: "And see to it that the boys pack their rifles. I don't want any wild shooting, and I don't want anyone caught short. Make that plain."

May assented. With further instructions from Kincaid, he racked off jauntily.

Kincaid pushed on. He did not strike the range fence at the expected point of dispute, but several miles to the north of it. In the last half-mile three 2 M cruisers rode forward from various vantages and then, seeing who it was, flicked hands and turned back. He passed the wire and rode on alone.

A fingered ridge ran here, east and west, spaced with scrub-oak and pine seedlings, and Kincaid followed it.

He was off 2 M now, but still in Santa Bonita. In the north-west Comanche Mountain loomed higher and darker as he got farther away from it. But Kincaid's gaze probed the flat-lands, returning and returning. He couldn't see much, in the broken land, until the long sweep fell away to Soda Flats.

Over there on its far side, a stippling of miniature objects marred the undulating heat glare, and above them a smudge darkened the golden illusion of the horizon. Heightened attention ran into Kincaid's lean face as he looked that way. He rode on. Later he made out the midget scrapers and teams; the dwarfed work-cars and smoke-vomiting locomotives; the dots of swarming men, like navvies; and the far-gleaming rails running away toward White Oaks. The railroad was coming on. There was something inevitable about it, even in Kincaid's non-committal measuring. He sat long, watching it.

Later still, on a rash but well-considered impulse, he rode down toward a point which those rails would pass. The survey-stakes were back, and Kincaid looked at them sharply. He shook his head, well knowing them to be stakes driven through the body of any possible peace in Santa Bonita.

He rode back toward 2 M slowly, fully aware of what might lay in wait for him, but keeping to the open. Half-way to the range boundary a swinging hummock disclosed to him an advancing party of mounted men. These were undoubtedly the survey party; transits and axes rode on an extra horse; they were excitedly interested in them-selves, subtly triumphant, and looking repeatedly back the way they had come. Kincaid pulled his pony aside, but held on.

They fell silent of a sudden, seeing him. Alertness sat on them. They rode past slowly, and Kincaid, looking across, saw Buck Ewing and two other men he had no taste to have behind him. No word was spoken. Nothing could add to those glowering looks, touched with sneering. Buck Ewing looked at Kincaid once, hard, and turned his attention definitely away; and it was this man on whom Kincaid found his definite response fastening itself. In a moment the clink of curb-chains and the soft thud of hoofs was gone.

So uneventful a meeting belied its own innocence, and Kincaid, canvassing the possibilities and finding them great, could not understand it. Those men had looked as though a triumph rode with them which he could not touch and with which he had nothing to do, and his unrest grew with the minutes.

A mile farther on the answer was plain, when Kincaid saw a still heap sprawled in the prospective right-of-way, between the rows of stakes, as though the South Western Pacific, reaching ahead, had already run down a victim. He reined in the moment he saw it and stared. He rode forward slowly then, slipped out of the saddle, took three steps and knelt. But it was no shock to him now, and the sightless up-turned face of Ike Dages, a 2 M puncher, was no surprise.

Dages had been shot twice through the chest, the sand under him puddled with blood; his heart was still.

Kincaid turned on the ball of his foot, without rising, and stared under his horse up the long tangent of survey-stakes in the direction the survey party had gone, Buck Ewing with them. His movement was abrupt, his lips curt; his thinking was inscrutable, but all his calm was gone.

"So that's how it is," he said; and now the thing that boiled up in him was near the surface. Buck Ewing had set a savage pace for the game that had begun with the act. And it was Ewing's choice. But 2 M would remember.

V

ANOTHER morning, Kincaid swung away from the ranch and followed the trail into the hills. An early sun flashed slanting rays deep into the woods, touching to life a deep-red fire in the pine trunks. In this fresh coolness the river chuckled secretly and brief glimpses showed the timbered masses of Comanche to be dark and proud.

Over the first ridge Kincaid emerged from the pines, crossed a long, narrow and grassy valley, thick with white-face cattle, and re-entered the trees; and now he had left the trail and was picking his way at will. But it was not an aimless way for all his unhurried ease.

A handful of riders remained in these hills, mostly beyond the Gap to the west; but the greater part of Rusty Maxwell's six-score men were lower down and were not working cattle. Kincaid held in the background of his mind the careful map of their stations and all their movements. He would meet none of them on the land covered on this ride, nor, he was thinking in his deliberate way, would anyone else be faced with that likelihood.

He threaded a series of sleeping gray parks and climbed the back of steadily rising ground through thick woods, and then he was in the high meadows. A warm sun-burst seemed to have exploded up here and the closed-in feeling of the slopes was gone. Kincaid, for all that, advanced with increasing deliberation, and vigilance was with him. He was looking for something which, it came to him after a while, he was not going to find, at least not here and not now. He gave that up presently and struck out in a new direction, with full intent written in the action; but there was no permanency in the relaxation which returned to his restrained, efficient movements.

A few minutes later he pulled in with a shortness that fetched a grunt from the dun under his legs. Up this open hollow, to one side, a similarly poised rider looked this way. It was no puncher, The clothes were not blue cotton or blue duck, bright with many washings; and there was an un-masculine flair about that soft-crowned, roll-brim hat. . . .

Surprise drove Kincaid up the hollow with level gaze; but his face was quiet as he said, "Good mornin', Miss Pickett," and removed his Stetson.

Valerie Pickett smiled, holding her restless horse to its position. "I thought it was you," she observed.

She had dressed in well-worn riding boots, gray breeches and pearl gray waist. Her collar was closed and plain, touching the round neck with the look of smooth strength, and that erect head with pride. Her blue eyes laid friendly frankness on him, and warmed him.

"You wanted to see me?"

Valerie assented, occupied with this simplicity in him that had no lack of depth in it. "You won't mind what I have to say?"

"No," he said, and meant it.

"Then I won't apologize for bringing the railroad here to you. Mr. Kincaid, you must see with me how foolish this fight is!"

There was a womanliness and a reasonable vehemence in her that played insidiously on the fiber of his convictions. Here was one woman who was fitted to talk man talk, and he would not disregard her words. But neither would he be hurried through this hour.

"This is a strange thing," he said slowly, and looked at her again.

She said quickly: "I know what you are thinking. I will be quite honest with you. I felt that you would listen to me—that Mr. Maxwell will listen to you. It isn't as though this were persuasion: the railroad is bound to come." Urgency got into the timber of her voice. "I can see purpose in you," she began afresh, with an uprush of confidence. "It seems a shame to throw it away."

"Is that why you speak now?" he asked, and strength lay in his own eyes, and a deep steadiness.

"Of course." Practicality lent her a small surprise. She matched his directness in an untroubled way. A pause fell.

He was thinking about the freedom and richness in her small, square shoulders and in her proud face. She was a person who was not bound by the loyalty and the hard laws of his life as he saw it; yet she was no stranger to these things. There seemed rather a fidelity to something within herself, which she had brought here, and which she was trying to explain.

But there was more: a favor and a faith hard for a man to turn his back on. The man who turned her aside would be giving up so much more than his own dreams that the answer was something which only years of regretting emptiness could compute.

"If it were a personal contest I could find nothing to

say," Valerie went on. "But we all know the bloodshed that will be caused, the lives which may be snuffed out; all without gain, in the end. Isn't that asking too much?"

He saw no pointless meddling in these words charged with a high intent. She was sincere; she was earnest. Bloodshed would and did dismay her, and lives which might be forfeit were her profound and real concern. In this girl, all this was sane and responsible and surely right.

Kincaid looked away because, when he looked at her, he could see nothing else. She filled his eyes and his mind alike. He said: "We ask only to be let alone."

Her voice turned soft, but it allowed of no evasion: "How did it happen that Mr. Maxwell's men were sent against the last survey party?"

He was armed for this, if his outward poise was a true reading. He delayed, and his sobriety somehow drove past her for the first time. "So that's the story you got," was what he said. He looked over with unhid appraisal, and his gray eyes seemed asking for comprehension.

"Is it untrue?"

Before he answered, Valerie felt suddenly that in his hard, resilient body and his indestructible quiet there lay an accusation against the South Western Pacific which had never before been put to her in any light. Lance Kincaid was neither hasty nor lacking in judgment. In his firm tanned skin, grained by the sunlight, those clear eyes carried a knowledge which no argument could have dislodged.

"It is if I can believe my boys."

Valerie tested that thoughtfully. "Was your man badly hurt?" she said.

"He was killed."

Her distressed silence said all that she could have wished it to do. But from the way she withdrew from all this, he saw there was no hopelessness in her. "I know how concerned you must be. It would be unwise to approach Mr. Maxwell just now." That was her constrained apology. "But I still have hopes of a peaceful settlement. You must not deny me that."

Kincaid's waiting denied it in spite of all he could do. But it was kinder than words, unmeaning words; and he wanted to be kind to this girl. She said:

"You and I have made a splendid start, haven't we? Aren't we friends?" Her fine-drawn brows were anxious.

And he answered: "Yes." It did not matter that she was thinking of the railroad, and he of something else. This was the measure of her courage. She could fight without heat and without giving up anything of what she was; and he knew that here was something he would have missed, were she to stand helpless and untouched in the sweep of the strong currents which claimed them both.

Her hands were at rest on her pommel, one of them ungloved and flexible and brown. Kincaid looked at it and listened to her proposal, robbed by its simplicity of any obscure meaning.

"Perhaps you will stop to visit at our car when you are near us, Mr. Kincaid."

He thanked her. And now a frank and honest wistfulness got into his talk: "I'm afraid I might not be entirely welcome, however."

"The consequences of that would not keep you away, would it?" Without archness, her blue eyes waited.

He said carefully, "Not if I wanted to come."

A small, fleeting cloud shadow passed over them and swept beyond. Kincaid thought, sadly: "That's how it will be with us;" and he looked at her closely. She seemed never to have known a blight. In her small, compact body she owned a grace and personified a reward that shook him and that he could never claim. Never until now had these things come to him with their full impact; and now it seemed that the meanings he had affixed to them were trivial. She was everything he thought to value, ever. She was the loyalty to which some man would fasten; for him there would be no other law and no other triumph. But she had come too late, and Kincaid knew it.

She had no such thoughts as these, he was forced to see. Pleasure returned to her, the freedom of spirit in which she had ridden this far; and she spoke with a deft touch of things amidst which he would have floundered.

"I am learning to forget everything but the sun and the hills," she said; "and now I have come near to forgetting them." Her smile was a softness and an indulgence, and she turned her pony. "I'm going to remember hard."

She was away while he was getting a grasp of that. The force of it was so accurate, as she swept out of the hollow and along its rim toward the next drop, an erectness clinging to her posture, that it spoke to his inner core and kept his hat in his hand long after he was alone.

He swung his horse and passed on. And heavy thoughts rode with him which had been far away half-an-hour ago. Their thrust and sway, the amazing power this girl's remembered presence had over him, were locked deep, even now; and his riding was as direct as ever.

He tipped down the bulging shoulders of Comanche and

threaded the trees. A golden mid-morning glow suffused the aisles and penetrating warmth re-awakened the aroma of pine gum; it hung on the motionless, lucid air. Kincaid listened to the dreaming silence and knew himself as alone as a man can be, and then he did a strange thing: reining in, he drew his Colt and twirled its cylinder and saw that it was right. Then he went on.

A steep pitch dropped him down into the canyon of the Standing Stone, disputatious among the ledges and rapids here. Kincaid struck a beaten trail into which he turned. The musing was gone from his strong face as he drew near to Mescalero Crossing.

This was a ford where the hill-trail crossed the river above the chasm of Slide Canyon. Choked with willow and aspen and marching evergreens except for this crouched clearing, it was a wild and remote spot. Down trail Kincaid glimpsed a corner of Frenchy Lesant's tumbledown, weathered saloon. He held on.

The saloon, a relic of harder days, but hard enough still, stood across beaten dust from the river in this gloomy glen, and appeared entirely deserted. He swung down at the tie rack and leisurely mounted the steps.

The interior was dark; it was dirty; it held murmurs of restless memory. In one corner a man with an ugly face straightened up involuntarily and then slumped again. At a table a sodden derelict slept, his beard buried in his arm, and yet held in his awkward pose an indefinable air of waiting. Lesant, heavy, impassive, stood timeless and observant at his bar. There was something inscrutable and hovering behind those faintly shining eyes and in the thick round jowls.

"Kincaid," he murmured.

They were old acquaintances, a little less than warm; and Kincaid returned that greeting with a look. "Rye, Frenchy," he said, and turned his back to the bar.

Lesant's sleeping eyes, safe from observation, flamed up. Wickedness was in this man, deep and devious; and struggling with it, while he hesitated, was caution. He shrugged then and set out glass and bottle, with a wondering look for Kincaid's high and sinewy shoulders.

Kincaid looked thoughtfully at the other men in this place. He knew there were still more, somewhere; and the feel of more men and of alertness was strong here. He satisfied himself idly about the rear door and the speaking shadows and turned back to the bar.

"Warm," Lesant offered stolidly, wiping the bar. He had a certain suavity.

Kincaid gazed at him long, drinking, and out of his abstraction drew abrupt words: "Frenchy, there's been a dozen 2 M steers shot."

Lesant's black eyes fixed. The silence ran on. "Bad," was his ponderous decision, when he had thought about it. "Where?"

"Far apart," said Kincaid. "Anywhere."

Trouble hung over this isolated saloon, over its dusty tables and the battered, unused piano in its corner; trouble, thick and turbulent, stood at the shoulders of these men. The breed knew it, and Kincaid knew it. If the others did, they waited in absolute silence.

"And so," Lesant's obdurate tone roughened, "you come here?"

Words awakened the place. A chunky man idled out of the back room, stabbed Kincaid once, and ignored him;

hooking his thumb in his belt and presenting his broad back at the front-door jamb.

Kincaid let his neglect answer, while Frenchy Lesant's cumbersome poise held. "It looks," Kincaid said, imperturbably, "like a railroad scheme to keep my boys spread out, and busy." He met the breed's arrested regard levelly.

Lesant's perceptible brightening was not unstudied. "That's so," he discovered, and then lapsed into disinterest. "I wouldn't put it past 'em."

Kincaid's measuring, probing look was a sharper thing. He opened his lips, and his dry words lay on this quiet with the firmness of sheathed steel. He said: "Forget it, Frenchy. It won't get you anywhere."

Dismay electrified these immobile listeners. The stillness tightened with a thin, keen warning no longer obscure and no longer impalpable. But cold confirmation of his stand, from which there would be no appeal, lay in Kincaid's unwavering gaze. He turned then, his spurs loud, and walked to the door. No one else moved. Kincaid had to brush this swarthy man's out-thrust elbow aside to pass, and he did so. In hanging deliberation, he stepped up and kneed his horse away.

Lesant stood frozen at the bar by nothing he could see. The man Kincaid had dislodged whirled on him angrily. Frenchy's pendulous face remained unmoved; but as these hardened, knowing eyes met in significant delay, one of the breed's fat lids drooped in an iron command. "Go get him," he murmured.

The other pushed through the saloon toward the back in accelerating purpose. His horse dozed in the sagging shed back there.

Kincaid left the place the same way he had come. Finally the climbing trail allowed him to turn into woods riding the canyon's rim. He had ridden slowly this far; but now he pushed ahead, until thought of the things which had passed today got in his fingers and his horse read it there, through the reins. A slowing plod carried him past windfalls and down timber.

That Frenchy Lesant should find his interest in the South Western Pacific did not surprise him. Lesant was a man of multifarious ways and few of those ways would stand the full light of day. But Lesant knew Kincaid too. Kincaid's hand had never been light at Mescalero; it would be heavy now, and Frenchy would be warned. He felt secure in that knowledge, and was asking himself what Valerie Pickett would find to say of it, when the rending smash of a rifle shot sent his horse wildly around. Kincaid's rolling duck carried him off balance and he went on, falling out of the saddle and to the ground.

He would have clung prone there, reasonably hid by close brush near the feet of his backing pony; but a second shot, searching the spot, sent him thumping over and over to the protection of a dead log. Crash, crash, crash! This savage and deadly firing raked the log and scattered a chaff of punk in his face.

Kincaid lay, gun in hand, fighting down his leaping pulse. He had had no chance to run, and he looked for none now. This was no stern test, meeting him under these remote and stirless trees; it was stark death; and if he was to walk past it he must thank his nerves and not his wits.

A bee buzzed along the log and there was no other sound whatever. The assassin had struck from the north, but as the waiting stretched out, Kincaid looked a piercing question to the south; and it was from the south that, hunching cautiously forward, he protected himself with the foot of a stocky pine. Now the delay was endless. These woods returned to their own; the hanging stroke of death did not seem cruel here, but a condition of nature. Nor did Kincaid's tenseness wear any of the drag of patience.

Twenty minutes passed, a half-hour. This drew out toward the third quarter when, fifty yards away in the direction Kincaid watched, the brush twitched. Another five minutes passed before a cautious head came into view. The eyes probed, beady, lethal; that look was ferret-like. It was quite apparent that this man was unsatisfied. After a mindless wait, his hands rose and the rifle was trained on the brush-obscured log. He fired once, ruthless, the echo crashing up; and it was in that split second of time that Kincaid replied.

The head withdrew abruptly, and Kincaid, on his knees, sprang for another pine. He reached it and nothing happened. Judging sharply, pitted against time now, he picked another pine and slammed into it from that charging run. Still no defiant admonishment came. Pushing rashly on, Kincaid presently relaxed at sight of a huddle under the screening fir. He walked forward then, wary, and stopped at the man's out-stretched feet.

A glance was enough, but he took more. He seemed trying to grasp beyond what had happened here; and his finding was not good.

"You missed this time, Frenchy," he mused, although this man was not Lesant, but that other who had disputed the door with him at Mescalero Crossing. But Kincaid saw no reason to alter the form of his thought.

He found the dead man's horse, shouldered him up and lashed him across the saddle, curiously methodical. The rein of the laden horse he hung over the pommel. A ringing slap on its haunch sent the animal crashing down through the trees at a startled trot which would soon slow, but would carry this grisly ultimatum without fail back where it was meant to go, and where it would be grimly understood.

VI

DAWN was a taut line drawn out across the eastern sky. It ravelled and broke; the curtain of night tore open. Pale yellow light, brightening and climbing, stole over the land to foreshadow the marching line of 2 M range fence. On a little rise directly behind it, their statuesque horses carved from dusk, all of a hundred men sat their saddles, Rusty Maxwell and Kincaid at their head.

They were here for but one purpose, and the attention of all of them swung in one direction. Now and again a lifted hoof thudded, a head-shaking horse jingled its curb-chains softly. But even the mutter of feeling words drew none of the hard, insistent eyes from the sight slowly assuming ominous reality out on the gray, sage-tufted flat.

The South Western Pacific had crawled across nearly all of that segment of Santa Bonita County which lay outside of Maxwell's boundary. Three miles separated those twin bands of steel from the doubled and trippled strands of prohibiting wire. But because the railroad right-of-way bisected the line at a long angle, all the preparatory bustle and activity of approach lay close under the unforgiving regard of 2 M.

Five miles away in strengthening light a welter of shanty cars, tie cars—engineers', and tool, and steel cars

—made dark disturbance in the center of embracing empty space. Nearer, work engines puffed briskly back and forth with a muffled coughing; tie gangs trotted through their work, emitting short, yelping cries; steel echoed as it dropped in place, and the clang of sledge on spike was harsh and clear.

Ahead of that clot of constructive fury, the wheel scrapers were piling up the road-bed. And here, spread out and stolidly alert, thirty rifle-armed men had their stand, sitting their horses without much movement. Occasionally one or another of them turned to stare toward 2 M, but Buck Ewing, riding indolently among them, did not so much as look up.

Rusty Maxwell surveyed all this with hooded, hawk-like gaze. His face was living granite, marked with deep, inexorable lines. He had had his say, the octopus still extended its slow, remorseless tentacle, and there was nothing to add now but the seal of his decisive action. Kincaid, at his side, matched his deep impassiveness. The others, rolling a cigaret or leaning down to yank straight a saddle shirt with curt movements, emulated this grim control. They were waiting.

The sun flashed over the flat-lands and painted the dun sweep with soaking gold. Already the stocky bays and sorrels of the wheel scrapers' teams were sweating; clean light glistened on their bulging muscles. But none of the easy, unthinking freedom of morning in the hills touched these things with cheer. There was a sullenness in the hour like a savage undercurrent; all the unrest of imminent storm clouded and thickened the atmosphere, and these watching men breathed hard.

Now the first scraper clattered by, its blade rasping the

up-turned rocks. With it came a trio of Ewing's guns. The teamster was clearly apprehensive. A gaunt, bearded man, he divided his acute scrutiny between the survey-stakes and 2 M's bitterly dissenting ranks, his eyes flaring white. But the nearest guard, a burly, brazen fellow, heavy with careless indifference, drew up with his blunt back presented to the waiting cowmen in narrowly calculated contempt.

It stung Quill Hoskins to restrained ferocity. "Yo're headed in the right direction, Garber," he called softly to the man. "You better start travellin'!"

Kincaid silenced him with a smooth gesture. "Wait till they touch the fence," his iron order lay across Hoskins' impetuosity.

Other scrapers came up. Under a battery of steady stares, they worked methodically as the morning wore on. Gradually the road-bed took shape up to the very fence. It was plain then that these teamsters did not know what to do. Buck Ewing's men, drifting boldly forward to cover the operations, offered no suggestion. Leaving his scraper, a teamster plodded away up the right-of-way. He was gone twenty minutes, and returned with muttered instructions. The scrapers were drawn aside and the teams unhitched and tethered in the sage. Andy Stroud, on 2 M's flank, observed the maneuver with a noncommittal grunt. He caught Charley May's deceptively untroubled glance, studied it momentarily, and turned his angry cheeks once more toward the open.

Down the road-bed the tie wagons came rumbling. Tobacco-chewing individuals dumped off the ties, which clunked hollowly as they struck together. A crew came after, aligning and seating the oak sticks; and no great distance behind, swarming paddies laid the steel and spiked it, and the steel cars shunted forward another length to the belch of smoke and cinders from the locomotive's squat stack.

Trace Pickett was overseeing the construction, his occasional snapped-out order lifting sharply above the guttural chaff of the paddies and the general uproar. Kincaid grew more alert on seeing that Ben Sharp and a score of his Jingle-bob hands, all mounted and all armed, were watching operations. A rumble commenced somewhere deep in Rusty Maxwell's solid chest at that sight, but did not break the surface.

A murmur ran through the gathered punchers flanking him, and then the cause of it was plain. Jube Pickett appeared and rode slowly forward along the right-of-way with Ben Sharp. But it was back toward the last camp siding that Kincaid's keen gaze laid. He could see the dwarfed Pickett car, standing with the engineers' cars on the quickly-laid spur a mile away; and from it, in this direction, rode a slight figure on a horse he had no trouble in identifying. Valerie jogged along until he could see the outline of her face. This would shortly be no place for a woman. Kincaid's gray eyes darkened and hardened.

Jube Pickett reined in on the road-bed across from Rusty Maxwell and a hundred yards away. He looked up, and his face was stern and set.

"Maxwell, the responsibility for whatever happens here rests with you," he called, his words grating through the gathering midday heat. "You're exceeding your rights— making a mock of State authority. But it won't work. The railroad is coming through here!"

Around him in studied disposition were gathered

Ewing's armed guards. Ben Sharp's riders were idling forward too, obviously keyed for the whip of sudden-breaking trouble. Old Rusty, behind his fence, was no more moved by these things than he was by the outspread panoply of the threatening Juggernaut itself.

His voice was solid, it was controlled; but it was adequate to carry across the chasm of convictions that lay between. He said, and his ultimatum was iron:

"Don't touch that fence."

A long moment passed, sluggish with resentment, and Jube muttered into his brush of a mustache. He appealed to Ben Sharp, turning in his saddle; his words too low to be heard. They conferred soberly.

Kincaid, his manner suddenly uneasy, noted that Valerie Pickett had drawn nearer. Presently she would be on the spot, for she had seen her father. Near enough so that their grunts and curses were audible, the steel paddies were laboring forward under the lash of Trace Pickett's tongue. Trace's eye was casting forward now, and he was burning with some inward flame; he appeared about to cruise up with his own say.

Jube and Ben Sharp reached some conclusion. They stopped talking and pushed toward the fence at a walk, their eyes steadily measuring Maxwell. Sharp wet his thin lips in a crafty way. He began: "Now, Rusty——"

Rusty, for all his crushing grip on himself, saw his old enemy's position clearly now. For a moment the old man relaxed his bitter guard, leaning forward with congested, brick-red face. He cut off Ben Sharp's patronizingly patient opening and bore against the man with the full force of his raging intent. His stubby hand flew up, pointing at Sharp:

"Not a word out of you!"

The quivering command struck Sharp with an almost physical impact, and he involuntarily drew back. Jube Pickett stopped too, plainly puzzled. He exclaimed: "Maxwell, this is all damned nonsense, and you know it!" He went on, and his words washed around Rusty without appreciable effect now. But 2 M was murmuring angrily and bunching.

Trace Pickett jumped off the steel car, pushed through his burly, shirtless paddies and came on. The intolerance in his imperious and slightly cruel mien was no new thing. Kincaid watched his sharp glance reach out to touch his sister, and he expected Trace to direct her brusquely to leave; but Trace Pickett saw nothing but his objective, and the barrier that stood across his path, barring him from it. The tilt of his lean jaw cried a warning.

Jube, with a dogged indignation, stepped out of the saddle to meet him. Buck Ewing moved close at the same time. There was an increase of carelessness in the way Ewing handled his body, with the growth of tension around him; but it was plain that he had a grasp, and a firm one, on every element present. A turn of his head, and he felt accurately the positions of his men and of Ben Sharp's. Then he faced the Picketts.

"What's your verdict?" Trace flung against his father, loudly and pointedly.

"We haven't any right to be lenient," Jube argued with himself in a troubled way. "Sure as fate it will only make matters worse . . ." He gnawed his mustache, at odds with his own stern prudence.

"Say the word," put in Ewing, with a dark flash of

inescapable meaning; "then you can go back to work." This was the crisis for which he had been hired, and his cold authority reached beyond these men and put them aside. The expression that crossed his strong features was like naked flame, but it was utterly emotionless.

2 M churned to a fierce restlessness. Quill Hoskins swore monotonously under his breath; Jake Kernan nursed his Winchester in a hungry way. All of them had ridden here, primed to explode at a word; and Ike Dages, their slain companion, had ridden with them. He stood at their shoulders now and they felt his blame.

The steel gang advanced until the maddening clang of their sledges and pry-bars assaulted the ears, and their unabated exertions laid a hectic frieze across the reddening vision of 2 M. Arrogant and muscle-bound paddies with a red stubble of beard, wickedly humorous eyes and the gall of Mephistopheles, winked together, and guffawed, and stared, and flourished sledges and fists like sledges. Conflict had no terrors for them.

The sight was a red rag to Maxwell's punchers. Charley May sat his saddle sidewise to this leashed violence, and Kincaid surveyed the crew narrowly. Rusty Maxwell, however, was the rock behind which the flood surged in momentary check.

Jube Pickett began: "I want to be sure——"

"Make sure, then!" Trace ejaculated sharply. His turbulent drive flamed up. "We'll go through here! What are we waiting for?" His father leaned on this, half-persuaded, and Trace added curtly: "Ewing, direct your men to do whatever they have to——"

"Father, stop!"

The words cut a clean path through the electric tension.

Valerie Pickett kneed her pony toward the knot, and Ben Sharp's darting glance blazed up and then softened.

"Miss Pickett, maybe you and me'd better leave this to the others," he suggested smoothly, barring her way. But Valerie, her pale cheekbones plain, avoided his move and drawing in close, looked down at the Major.

"Can't you see what this will mean?" she urged. "These men are ready for anything. They'll throw lives away, and the blood will be on your hands."

The clear timber of her voice laid a new note here. Rusty's men looked admonished but doubly determined. Valerie's father gazed up at her as though he didn't see her. He was trying to weight justly the problem in his hands, knowing that this moment, with its nice decision, could never be repeated.

"You can't let this go on," she told him, in a steady tone. "There must be some other way." Her plain dislike struck Buck Ewing without softening, and Kincaid was keenly aware of her definite womanliness. She looked at none of them, however. Trace alone seemed unconscious of the sharp cleavage her presence marked.

"This isn't your affair, Val," he rasped, and to Jube, quickly: "Send her away! If we're going to settle this——"

"No!" said Valerie. "Not in this way. Father, you must listen to me!"

Jube shook his angular shoulders without speech, and his hectored glance found Ben Sharp and then Buck Ewing. Ewing's saturnine disgust gave the effect of a scowl.

"I tell you, we'll defeat ourselves here!" Trace barked,

stirred to a deep, intractable anger. "By God, you'll let Ewing and me handle this, in the end!"

The paddies forgot their steel. They leaned on picks, or straightened up, tense; tobacco-filled jaws were stilled; eyes were fixed, in the anxiety to catch the response. The grimy engineer leaned out of his cab, his hand on the whistle-cord.

Jube Pickett had swallowed the spur in the army, and in him its philosophy lay deep-rooted. In his world superiors ruled, and his son was his subordinate.

"Not another word!" he thundered. He spoke, then, with an ingrained courtesy, to Valerie: "Leave us, my dear."

Valerie's regard was earnest, but she did not hesitate long. This was finality, and she read it for what it was. "All right, Father," she murmured. For an instant her exploring glance strayed toward 2 M. It brushed Kincaid and knew him. Then she turned her pony, its deliberate plod etching the silence as she moved apart.

Trace Pickett swung violently away, outraged impotence shaking him. He turned back, inarticulate—extended a hand toward Jube.

"You'll tell your men to hold up," Jube directed him authoritatively. "We'll let this ride as it stands for now . . . Do as I tell you."

The waiting whistle did not scream. As though a taut bow-string had been relaxed, something quick and deadly went out of the moment. Something that could wait.

Rusty Maxwell grunted, watching with slitted eyes as Trace strode back toward his waiting gangs, and Jube and Ben Sharp slowly followed him. Kincaid carefully read Buck Ewing's expressive shrug, and then he was following Valerie Pickett with more than his gaze. It was a brave thing that she had done. For the first time he regretted her vital concern. She had read accurately the fact that her influence alone could tip the scales away from sharply impending violence; and this time her course had been effective. It was more than Kincaid would have been sure of. His indignation against her father and brother was for this moment a vivid thing.

Talk flowed through 2 M, curiously divided. Like the rumor of night wind through the trees, it found Old Rusty remote and wordless. He sat foursquare and immovable, a monumental fortitude in him.

With Trace Pickett, the steel gang trundled back up the halted rails in empty cars, raucous and taunting. Buck Ewing's men coldly remained where they were. This, it appeared, was not without its particular significance; for although the oak ties had been dumped all the way to the fence, tie wagons continued to lumber forward with their jolting loads. Long piles were laid out next the fence, on either side of the right-of-way, and these began to grow.

"What the hell, Kin!" Andy Stroud blurted. "We're lettin' 'em fort up right in under our noses, if this goes on!"

Kincaid quieted him: "I know. What would you do? That fence is the dead-line."

"It'll be that fer some of us," Old Hoskins muttered, expectorating for emphasis. "We'll be stretched out with our toes to it, that's what."

"All right, boys." Kincaid's big shoulders moved with inward disquiet, but he was firm.

All afternoon they grimly watched the tie piles rise.

Buck Ewing's force watched too, tight-lipped; and now they were reinforced by most of Ben Sharp's men. The oak barricades, higher than two men, put them in a strong position.

The sun dropped behind a shoulder of Comanche Mountain, and shadows ran like water across the flatlands. Later, pale rose and mauve tinctured the eastern sky, and climbing upward, drew a curtain of soft gray after them. Dusk sifted down over sage and soil and men.

The last load of ties rattled forward and was dumped. Buck Ewing turned in behind the wagon and followed it back. The engine had moments since chuffed away. Fires far out dotted the obscurity where the camp was, and the tiny figures of the paddies, awaiting their supper, crossed and recrossed them. Ewing held on toward that busy scene after the tie wagon turned off for a made corral and the oat bags of the boss teamster. In ten minutes Buck passed into the edge of the far-flung camp. That he knew where he was going was plain from his actions as he threaded the piles of supplies and construction materials bordering the track, where the sage was crushed and the ground was rutted deep. He was looking for Trace Pickett.

2 M watched the far flickering fires across the level as they would have done the bivouac of raiding Kiowas. Some were dismounted; some, on the edges, drifted a bit. But there was no weary patience here, only the harassment of taut waiting.

"Hey, Lance! Rusty!"

Charley May pushed through in a hurry, and Kincaid

snapped away the cupped match with which he had lit his smoke, aware of alertness in the men surrounding him.

"Look just over the second ridge—there—maybe a mile west from the Gap!" Charley's low, exasperated words turned all heads.

That way a dull glow, lifting, fluctuating, vaguely silhouetted a distant bulge of the mountain. Kincaid drew smoke deep into his chest, and then breathed a white fog. He said: "Well, what of it?" in a tone of aggravated resignation.

"My hell, that's the high meadows!" Dallas Waidler exploded heavily. "They'll burn over if we don't stop it— the best grass we got, too!" He thrust toward Maxwell, and hoarse pleading got into his voice. "Send a few of us, anyway. I can't watch that!"

Rusty was faced with a decision that tore him silently. With the nose of an old wolf, he scented danger in whatever he did now. He listened to this dry rustle of cursing, surcharged with fury, and he put his broad chest against the inevitable answer to what he must say. He growled: "We're stickin' here," and looked deaf and stubborn.

Far light curled luridly up on the mountain's flank and angry smoke billowed and then whipped into high darkness. Kincaid pondered, in a regretting way, the course he had taken with Frenchy Lesant. It had failed of its effect, and he realized now that he had known it would. This thing had been on the way ever since he had warned the breed that if any more 2 M beef went over the old trail to White Oaks butcher-shops, he would burn him out. It had taken Lesant months to find his feet; but now, with the shrewdness of his kind, he was pitting himself against 2 M, adding his undercover strength to that of the South Western Pacific—this band of stealthy hard-cases more dangerous than Buck Ewing's gunmen.

"I'll have to clean out that rat's nest someday."

Kincaid knew it, and then forgot it, meeting the urgent words of Maxwell's fiercely resenting men. They had to be convinced that Rusty, for all his impetuous judgment, was in this matter right. Somehow he did it. The men returned to wrathy silence, their faces tilted and keen; but now there was in them a brittleness that could not last, that would soon burst into jagged fragments of violence.

VII

TRACE PICKETT leaned in the door of the warm and smoky car, and his lean face was heavy with his thinking. The telegraph key on the table chattered to a staccato halt and the operator's chair scraped as he turned. He pushed the paper eye-shade up on his forehead.

"Plenty of steel on the siding in White Oaks, Mr. Pickett," he said. "There ain't nothing we're even near to short of now, unless it's ground." He laid his cigaret carefully down, and shot a sidelong glance at Bill Wiles, the camp boss.

Wiles turned his cigar around in the waiting silence and leaned back in his chair. Ashes scattered down over his stout stomach, at which he made an ineffectual slap; then his calculating gaze came up. He fired what he plainly expected to be a telling shot.

"Murfree's saloon is with us tonight, Trace. Got in this afternoon. With Ewing's boys tied up out there, I couldn't stave Keno off. He ain't opened yet," he explained hurriedly. "I got him to wait till he seen you——"

Trace straightened irritably. "Tell him to open up," slipped out of him carelessly, in a reckless tone.

Wiles' fat-lipped mouth popped open. For weeks Murfree's tent saloon had earned Trace Pickett's irate attention, and Keno Murfree had hung on tenaciously, fattening on railroad dollars. This sudden switch in the superintendent of construction dragged Bill Wiles out of his chair with a look of concern, but without immediate words.

"Tell him now," Trace added, a flick to his voice.

Bugs circled and buzzed around the hooded tin hanging-lamp over the table and the operator looked at his key-calloused fingers. Bill Wiles intoned: "Nigh onto three hundred men idle, Trace! Nine-tenths of 'em drunk . . . That'll be clever!" His sarcasm was rich.

"Do as I say!" Trace whipped across to him, rasped raw in an instant. He resumed sourly: "If Buck Ewing doesn't smash a gate for us in that fence, we'll see what a hair of the dog will do to the micks." His lips snapped shut over that.

"All right." Bill Wiles' manner, as he stumped down the car shaking his head, said that it wasn't all right. But he had argued with Trace before. He pushed past and dropped off the car. Trace leveled brief instructions at the telegrapher and turned away also. As his foot struck the packed clay ballast alongside the car, reaching dry words came out of the dark:

"You, Trace?"

Trace stopped to look that way. "All right, Buck."

Ewing stepped into the faint glow of the car windows. His eyes shone darkly but his cold, composed expression told nothing. He grunted: "Well?"

The word revived, with brief completeness, all that lay in the mind of either. Ewing might have been grimly amused. Trace still burned with festering impotence.

"I'll do something!" he burst out, like a threat. Deep-ground impatience jerked his head up. "If you can't see your way," he went on, bitterly argumentative, "I suppose it's up to me——"

"Never mind," Ewing's solid words cut that off. He wiped his mustache, once each way, and a little silence fell while he read the temper of this man. Then: "Where's your father?"

"He's out at the car."

Ewing considered. He brought his thoughts to a conclusion, and said conversationally: "Well, let's bust that fence."

Trace stiffened. "What?" he said. "How?"

A taciturn smile touched Ewing's hard mouth. "Easy . . . You'll square yourself with Jube?" At Trace Pickett's abrupt gesture, he said: "Load a flat-car, heavy. Ties. Run it down there fast, and uncouple the last minute. You've got steel within fifty feet of that wire. The car will carry through, and my boys will mop up." It sounded simple, like that.

"Come on." Trace's nerve-strung grip closed over his arm, but Buck Ewing stopped rock-still until it was removed, his eyes inscrutable but not indifferent. Trace stepped back then, said shortly: "What's the matter with you?"

Ewing, dryly silent, moved away at his side. They found Bob Nelson wiping his engine on the Y spur which served as a turn-table. A five minute conference evolved a pattern of action which all approved. Paddies were amazed at the crisp order to load a flat-car; a rumor rippled through them, and they fell to with a will. A hairy fireman stoked the engine, roaring a ribald song, and the camp simmered with expectancy. Two miles away, in his private car, Jube Pickett wiped his hands on a towel and ducked his gray combed head to glance out toward the camp. He saw nothing unusual in the spread of glimmering cook-fires and turned away. . . .

Buck Ewing, watch in hand, surveyed the heavy-laden projectile standing on the track with a cold exactness and then turned to Trace Pickett. His watch-case snapped. "Nine-thirty, on the dot. My boys will be ready," he said, and swung into the saddle. "Tell Nelson to give that car a good stiff shove, and never mind the mess," he concluded; and waited long enough to hear Trace's assenting mutter. With no particular hurry, then, Buck rode out of the camp and down the line, and when he came abreast of the Pickett car, his glance was merely reflective.

Limpy Smail, easing his aching leg in the shadow of the car with a furtive rubbing, caught the whisper of Buck's passing. The glow of fire high on Comanche Mountain had told him that this would be a night full of alarms and dark sorties, and long after the faint sounds of Ewing's horse died out he tested the darkness like an old beagle.

2 M heard low calls through the smooth gloom and harkened carefully. A horse sneezed beyond the fence and murmurs ran on. Something was astir. Rusty grunted: "Soon now," as though he had word of what was to come. Kincaid, quietly efficient, saw that the punchers were thinned out along the wire; silence and vigilance were the rule.

But time stretched out, passive. There was death in this dragging, ugly quiet. Then Andy Stroud found Kincaid and murmured tensely: "There's a train startin', down there. It ain't goin' toward White Oaks either."

The far off rumble of exhaust came to them, like faint thunder in this vast emptiness, and presently the shredded clangor of a bell. Moments later Kincaid isolated the glint of a partially-obstructed locomotive headlight. It glided steadily forward with increasing acceleration.

Gruff words stirred like a forest breeze through Maxwell's men. They craned and dodged about to see. The locomotive swept on around a curve, spark showers starring the night, and now its exhaust was a swelling blended roar. Flanges screeled on the unsettled track, clanked rapidly over rail-joints.

Kincaid, peering sharply, made out the swaying form of a car in front of the locomotive. Loaded. Not with men either. His cheeks flattened. He didn't get this.

Too near the end of track, it seemed, to stop, the engine whistle emitted a hoarse scream. A hiss of escaping steam knifed through the snarl of grinding brake-shoes. The glaring headlight swung loose from its obstruction, boring a white swath through the night. It silhouetted the tie piles—outlined the rushing shadow of that detached flat-car, thunderous with momentum. The rocking missile came on wth a resistless flow.

"What the hell—!" Old Rusty roared, on a sharply rising note. Unguarded yells slipped out of the punchers; terrified horses scrambled back.

With a ripping, splintering crash the massive car jumped the rail-head and lunged over the close-laid ties. Nothing could stop it. On it charged, careening wildly, a note of terror in its destructive abandon. There was a series of twanging, jangling snaps, sullenly singing, as the range fence gave away like twine. A full length beyond the barrier, the flat-car nosed into the soil with a mighty ground tremor. Ties sloughed off and piled up with the hollow, snapping grind and roar of a breaking log-jam. A horse screamed, going down before that lethal avalanche—flinging its rider twenty feet. The man broke his shoulder and scrambled up, cursing madly.

The broadcast engine light showed his face, a wan mask of rage—showed the gaping triple fence, with stout posts sheared off, the ground ripped up—showed the canted car, the jackstraw debris of ties, a score and more of outraged men boiling around the spot.

Before the crash and clatter of this maneuver had sunk into the hills, a burst of gunfire succeeded it. Buck Ewing's men and Ben Sharp's opened up with deadly intent. Rusty Maxwell bellowed like a bull.

"Let 'em have it!" he yelled. His own gun licked out at a vermilion flash from between the dark tie piles.

On 2 M range, horses were wheeling under iron hands; men were jockeying for a clear field past their own kind. Lead spattered against the ranked ties, flame pricking the velvet dark from every point. A man screeched and a ways away a horse melted down with a curdling gurgle. Many punchers slid out of the leather to return Ewing's withering fire from the protection of their mounts, but Rusty and Kincaid kept their seats.

"Crawl behind that car!" Kincaid called to an unhorsed man who ran toward him. "Never mind your pony. Watch that hole in the wire!"

Old Rusty bawled defiance in deep-reaching gusts, careless of death sweeping the open with its invisible scythe. Herding the left flank of his defense, he would have thrust these men into the furnace blast. Kincaid, on the right, was as determined; but disaster cut at him, keen and close. A slug snarled away with some of his hat-brim, leaving a wrenching headache. The man he directed to cover behind the capsized car never got there. A bullet took him off balance and shook him like a sack, to toss him down empty.

Jake Kernan yelled: "Lance!" and Kincaid found him half-sprawled, dazed, clutching his bridle; blood streaming down his face. But he was more shaken up than seriously injured. With help, he clambered to his feet, submitted to rude and hasty care, silent and enraged.

The firing, if anything, grew hotter. Ewing appeared determined to sweep 2 M into tangled, inanimate windrows, blasting a way through. More than one puncher crouched behind the carcass of his pony, jerking the lever of a rifle with stinging barrel. On the edge of the headlight's glow, Gil Burr's saddle dropped from under him. Somehow he found his feet, staggering. A bullet in the shoulder hurled him around, and then he went wild. Howling curses, he ran senselessly toward the fence, throwing shots. A smashing blow halted that rush, but only for a moment. Lunging afresh, Gil hurled his empty gun and reeled down, a vague and moveless blot, twitching to the pitiless slugs that slapped into him.

Charley May's groan was anguished. With a gritted ejaculation he swung up. Kincaid, near at hand, pushed into his horse, hampering him; laid a grip on his hard shoulder.

"No, Charley!" he called. "Not you too. Gil's gone. Do you hear me?"

Charley May stared at him strangely; gave a tense double nod, lips melted together.

Kincaid let him go, and a moment later jerked around to the blow that burned across his shoulders. The odor of this place was bitter on his tongue. He knew, suddenly, that something was vitally wrong here; something that had to be changed. His probing scrutiny picked out Rusty, still up; and his pony took him that way. Maxwell met him with a fierce regard.

"Those tie piles are too much for us," Kincaid got out swiftly. "We'll be wiped out. Two of the boys are down aready."

"Three," the old man flashed.

"Rusty——"

"No!" Rusty knew what Kincaid wanted; he was adamant, his eyes hot. "Not a foot back! Not an inch!" Fire possessed his hard-bitten soul and he was savage.

"Rusty, some of these boys have got wives, kids—you don't own their lives!"

"By God, I own this land!" Maxwell plunged away.

Buck Ewing could be heard directing his warriors in a strident voice. That man was absolutely ruthless. Fire freckled the tie breastworks in a methodical way. Kincaid wrenched his eyes from that sight to follow Rusty. The old man was bitterly fixed; he would yield no more than he had said—not a foot, not an inch. Something that was not dread, but a rueful knowledge, seared Kincaid's mind. Pinched knees took him jumping after Maxwell.

Not in time, however. While he was yet five yards away, Rusty jerked and then crumpled, and sliding to the ground, Kincaid submitted to the twist of momentary fury. Rusty had fallen on one shoulder; he lay slack, and Kincaid's hand, lifting his head, felt soaking blood.

Andy Stroud hunkered near, his eyes shining hard. He voiced no word, breathing laboriously, until hasty examination revealed nothing but this nasty graze. "Ain't much," he grunted then. "Enough to put the old hellion out of it."

Kincaid and he lugged Rusty back. "Frank!" Kincaid's call crackled. Frank Luger wheeled his big horse—leaned, peering.

"Who is it?" Luger's voice was harsh and cracked with strain.

"The old man."

Without bicker, Frank helped them hoist Rusty across his saddle. He tipped a stirrup, swung a thigh behind the cantle.

"Get him home." Kincaid's rashness spilled in that snapped direction; he heeled away, grabbed a bridle. Andy Stroud yelped: "What, Lance?"

"Get these boys back. Now." Kincaid's pony circled, breaking. He jumped it forward. "Tell Charley May, and Jake," his voice came back out of obscurity, with a smooth decision.

Stroud stared sightless at the sky, cursed once, bitterly, and uttered sober wisdom in a strangely altered voice: "We can't fight him too."

Laban Gurley, round-up foreman for 2 M, took Kincaid's order to fall back stolidly. Dallas Waidler, a moment later, growled assent. The word spread quickly. Many of these men uncinched and dragged away saddles, firing as they came. Others cared for the dead, and seven or eight wounded men. Kincaid was over on the other flank now.

"Lance, what'll you do?" Jake Kernan flung out. There was a deep reluctance in this man, more than a dash of old Rusty's violent fiber.

Kincaid's brisk tone was constructive: "Jake, take three of the boys. You'll run the horses down here out of the lower pasture. All of them. Make it the Spring cabin—we'll work from there." Nowhere in these swift instructions was there an awareness of anything but necessity, balanced with cool judgment. Kernan opened his mouth, and shut it. Kincaid moved on: "Dallas, you can have a half-dozen. Strike for the high meadows, and back-fire that blaze. Challenge any man you meet up there—then shoot. Right?"

Waidler was gone.

Quill Hoskins jumped at Kincaid's mount, caught his saddle-horn. His voice shook with throat-filling wrath and desperation: "Kin! Goddle mighty, man—this is layin' down!"

"No." Kincaid's tone was solid, unswayed. "They've got a long ways to come, Quill. Our time will come."

Old Hoskins' unwilling groan was no concession. But Kincaid had his will. Gradually the gunfire across the range fence died down. The locomotive headlight was out now, and gloom cloaked this spot with unbroken, blood-stained mystery.

VIII

A GOOD mile from the breach in the range fence, in a wooded patch on the first ridge, the old line camp known as Spring cabin crouched under the stars. It was a high spot; below, the lower range lay all but invisible under mild dark space. Here a dozen men waited at the edge of the pines, their saddles at their feet.

"Old Rusty wouldn't of done it," young Rankin declared vindictively. "Ewing's pushin' through that hole right now, and the micks and hunks after him. You all know what that means, I guess. Old Rusty would've fought 'em to a standstill if it took a week!" Edgy resentment flattened his talk, made it quick and petulant.

"Shut up, kid." Quill Hoskins turned the dark shape of his face toward Rankin. "Kincaid's doin' what he sees best, and we'll all like it. You'll git the dose of lead colic you're hankerin' for, don't you fret."

"A swell way for you to talk!" the kid blurted. "I heard you bellerin' down below; don't try to hush me!"

Hard and pointed as the words were, they breathed stealthy life into more than anger and violent dissent. Pete Rankin's belligerent assurance stained the night with the hateful and burr-like conviction of betrayal; and an absent man was its object.

Hoskins spat copiously and moved toward Pete, and Rankin flung away, muttering choked words. Someone said "Hey, listen!" and they all stilled. The intermingling *whang* of shots racketed up from below, but the flashes were too far away to spot.

2 M was still in the saddle down there, being pushed back slowly and stubbornly; disputing the ground inch by inch and not always losing. Buck Ewing was finding the night a bristling wolves' den of wickedly fighting men. But now the firing which rose with a dreamy detachment to the men waiting for horses was spread across a wide area. They discussed Kincaid's course in quick, terse words, speculating apprehensively.

"What's this?"

A ground-murmur of hoofs froze them to still shapes. It was not many horses, only one, and it came up the slope from below. A low call identified Kincaid; he loomed high and near, and they collected, hat-brims eagerly tilted.

"They've sure spilled through down there, eh?" Old Quill opened up gruffly.

"Yes. They've lost men themselves, but they hang on." Kincaid spoke quietly. "Ewing's marking out roughly the ground the railroad will build over tomorrow."

A mutter met this plain statement of inevitability. Rankin rapped out fiercely: "The old man'll give somebody hell for this!" and Kincaid put his attention on him.

"Then you can let it go for now, Pete," was his uninvolved answer, touched with coolness. He added immediately: "You'll all save time if you get extra shells in your saddle-pockets before Kernan comes with the horses. Take plenty." Briefly he outlined what he expected of them: namely, that with the others, they were to hedge Buck Ewing's invasion of 2 M closely, hampering it without let-up at any point, and falling back only to save themselves. Except Rankin, they wanted only mounts to fulfill his asking, running with flapping chaps to the cabin, where boxes of cartridges burst open in hurried hands.

Kincaid, awaiting Kernan, shoved his pony restlessly along the shoulder of ridge. To every isolated clap of gunfire echoing up, he listened questioningly; needing to be down there, troubled by this deep and turbulent instinct; knowing that shortly he would.

A muffled rumble and reaching low cowboy calls along the ridge presaged the horses. Jake Kernan called: "Open that gate," and with an impetuous rush, a score of half-broken ponies swept into the round corral. Kernan said: "That you, Lance?" and almost with the clatter of the gate, ropes began to swish and tangle in the dark.

"Dab a rope on that triflin' roan," a puncher grunted from the fence. "Be damned if he approves of me—but he will."

"Hell with you! I got a bay pair."

"Gimme three cards," a murmur answered, and someone laughed grimly, not for an instant forgetting the gamble in this night. Then saddles swung and settled, and a cinched horse groaned gustily.

"Jake, I want you to cross the hollow," said Kincaid, "and circle down. Take your own boys and comb the *bosque.* You'll have to smell the ground out. When you draw fire, hold hard." He might have been giving directions for a stock movement.

Kernan asked no questions. With his reckless half-dozen he spilled down the bench. He was back at once, jamming his horse close. "Kin, look!" he shot out, and swept an arm.

Bonfires of splintered ties pricked out the distant gap in the range fence—eight, ten, a dozen blazes, big even from here. These high flaring torches illumined busy clots of ant-like forms. Trace Pickett's paddies were cleaning up the wrecked flat-car, the tangled maze of fence wire; and now wheel scrapers were breaking 2 M soil.

Punchers lined up on this ridge to stare, murder hot in their hearts. Rankin made a queer cracked sound in his throat and began to yell ungoverned imprecations into the absorbent night. "Let 'em come!" he blazed. "To hell with it all! I'm sick of it——"

He got no further. Kincaid yanked him half out of the saddle and grated: "None of that! Get hold of yourself, Pete. We'll fight them every foot of the way, and we'll lick them!"

Rankin shrank and stared, a brash glint lurking in his eyes. His shoulder hurt under that hard hand. Kincaid satisfied himself and let go, and Pete muttered something, kneeing apart. Kincaid said:

"Get started—all of you."

A thunder of hoofs rolled downward as they got away. The men separated and rode on, given distance and warning by persistent searching gunshots. The fight down here was in baffling dark, 2 M and railroad gunmen at large in a giant windowless room; but long ground swells banking the old wash marked the outline of natural defense. Kincaid, cruising alone, found the sage-tethered ponies of punchers who pushed rifles ahead of them as they crawled somewhere near. Often and often, in sinister spaced deliberation, shots roared in the gloom unanswered. Others drew biting, testy response.

Circling west, Kincaid found sharply unruly punchers,

suspicious even of a familiar voice, and finally located Charley May.

"We've held 'em right here for twenty minutes," Charley announced. "Ewing won't come any deeper to-night. Tomorrow—" His shoulders lifted against the night sky.

"Fine," said Kincaid calmly. He rode on, quiet and firm, dropping concise instructions and thinking his own bleak thoughts. A lifting backward glance showed the fire on Comanche Mountain burning more fiercely than ever, laying a sullen, trembling light for miles over the dark wooded folds. Dallas Waidler had his hands full up there, but here men scarcely gave the lurid beacon a second look.

Kincaid had to think of it, and of everything else. It was small wonder that, with all this, the one thing he found it possible to neglect should be his personal safety. Riding blind as all of them did, he had to take chances to save time. The man who called "Kin!" lowly, over on his left, aroused none of his keener caution, and he answered in like tone as he hauled up. It was the signal for an almost instantaneous flare and crash which seared the night directly in front of him.

Kincaid's gun was in his hand before his pony's hoofs left the ground. Reining bitterly down, he sent four blazing shots into the shadows. There was no answer, but there was a flurry and a rush, buried in the dashing arrival of the man whose call had betrayed Kincaid's presence and his identity. It was Ote Burnett.

"Kin, did you get it?" Burnett's hand reached him, inquiring, steadying. Kincaid said hardily. "No," and Ote ejaculated: " 'Fore God, what was that? We ain't in fifty yards of Ewing's guns!" There was a note of perplexed indignation here. "I'll keep my dang trap shut after this——"

"All right, Ote." Kincaid pushed forward beside the other, a dull undertow of anger tugging at him. There was no scent of Frenchy Lesant's assassins here, but of something far worse. As he expected, the spot from which that futile, treacherous shot had come was empty.

"Forget it," he told Burnett, and pushed off. West was the way that rush of fleeing hoofs had gone, and that way lay the faint smell of stirred-up dust. Then the odor of burned powder returned, like the pervading odor of trouble, and his nose was useless. He didn't move fast, and it was several minutes before Andy Stroud grunted, "You, Lance?" and lowered his gun.

Kincaid said nothing immediately, his hard thoughts grinding, and Stroud told him grumblingly: "Better do somethin' about it if you don't want a sieve called Pete Rankin."

"What?"

"Pete bulled through here just now and damn near got it," Andy admitted. "What was he in a rush about?" The shooting of five minutes before had no particular significance for him. With a fantastic notion bursting through him, Kincaid answered quietly:

"Maybe he was going somewhere."

Stroud grunted: "Rate he took, he'll get there yet!"

"Yes," said Kincaid. "He will."

He was suddenly dog tired, weary in some part of him that rest couldn't touch, and he wondered if Andy wasn't tired too. Andy was always so staunch and laconic that you couldn't tell. But there wasn't time to think of that and Kincaid turned his back on all of it, returning to his endless concerns. Nobody would consider rest yet, but food had to be prepared for these men. Kincaid saw to this.

Much later, he noted that the fire on the mountain was flickering out. It was almost midnight, and he was on his way to the Spring cabin. There were a number of cruising riders he hadn't got in touch with and he was bothered about them. The bandages and the bucket of coffee and the jerky at the camp might have drawn some of their number.

The place was dark as he drew near, but that meant nothing. Drifting along the pines with all his senses biting into the silence, Kincaid got help from an unexpected direction. It might have been his sense of touch that reacted to the impact of a presence here.

Easing out of the saddle, he hung the reins down and pushed his feet ahead. The reason for all this noncommittal quiet that met him was a mystery he didn't like and didn't trust. Gun in hand, he tiptoed toward the cabin's dark shape. Pine needles gave out no whisper of sound, but pine twigs were something he hadn't thought about. One snapped under his foot and he stopped, mouth ajar to hear better, staring, ready.

"Is that you, Lance?"

Kincaid straightened, and sobriety settled his features as he put his gun away. He moved forward, and his voice was brusque:

"You oughtn't to be here."

Donita Sharp's low laugh was without self-consciousness; it made light of his mood. "Why not?" she returned calmly. She met him and put a hand on his arm, a small hand and a confident one. "Why can't we see things as they are? You know I love you."

The disrupting ingenuousness of this Kincaid ignored for the moment, turning. "Come inside the cabin. You found no one here?"

"No. But there's the feel here of men—of men's anger, I think. I'm glad you came, Lance." She moved in beside him without hesitation, stood quiescent while he lit a candle in a bottle. When he turned, her eyes were liquid and shining and they clung to him in a quiet expectancy. She wore no hat and her honey-colored hair filled with warm glints.

He gazed at her, pondering what to do with her. Alone, his guard down, he had been heavy with care; he still was, and more than that, Donita had no relation to his roots. It took an effort of will to put his mind on her. This laid a hard abstraction on him which, as she saw it, smoothed the smile from her cheeks. Her gloves were off, held in one hand; standing there, she made a picture of self-reliance touched with a close concern.

"You are tired," she said sensitively, and came nearer.

"I suppose I am. But I've got work to do."

Donita found no admonishment in the statement. She gazed into his high, lined face, aware of his broad shoulder-spread and the solidness of him, quick with strength. The solicitude in her hazel eyes was meant to be plain to him; it hurt when he took his notice away. She reached out to touch his brown throat because the simple act wrapped them closer together.

She said: "You don't want me here, do you . . . Lance, why evade the truth? Things have gone pretty bad with you tonight."

"I won't say that."

She was not to be put off. "If you're going to win your fight," she told him composedly, "I'm your only hope. What else do you think has brought me here?"

His tanned cheeks broke into quizzical lines running toward the eyes. More than words suddenly lay between them, and with an acute perception he knew what it was. His reply was grimly amused: "You're as ruthless, in your way, as old Ben."

"Perhaps. But honest." Although she turned her clear-skinned face to glance momentarily toward the door, he felt her attention strike back toward himself.

Kincaid, silent, thought the question of honesty irrelevant to this strange proposal of hers. That it was a proposal he never doubted, any more than she had bothered to deny. Finally he said: "You want my word for something."

"No," she said. "No, Lance. No ultimatums," and he knew then that she wanted the thing his word could only promise. Bargaining wasn't in her head; it was in her heart. He told her, disturbed:

"Ben Sharp couldn't stop this if he wanted to."

"You're sure, are you?"

Anxiety wasn't in the words, and he did not test her again. It was after all not her influence with Ben Sharp that was in question, but her power over him, Lance Kincaid. It washed against him, that power, with a steady beat he presently found to be that of his own pulse. Donita's firm round face, partially shadowed by yellow candle-light, the parted lips, the full, rounded chest; these dragged at him as they always did when he allowed himself a full awareness of her.

A faint perfume of femininity emanated from her to drum on his senses with soft insistence and have its deep way with his thinking. It thrust back all the crowding facts of this night, and they were alone together. Donita's subtly flowing emotions were attuned to it and counted on it.

She broke out: "Lance, I want to help! You stand so— alone." It was a slip, that flashing revelation of her deep feeling about his position and his chances. She felt it in the wakeful steadiness of his regard, the slow shake of his head. His wise gray eyes were so near, so far away. "I'll not let you oppose me," she resolved in a droll way, but her searching hazel irises were not humorous.

"Is that what you call it?" he asked. This was an idle conversation—here and now. The dusky cabin with its broken benches and sagging table, and its air of timeless patience, was waiting for something behind all this. Out there in darkness men were fighting. He knew sharply, from that corroding remembrance, that Donita would never mean to him what she so strongly desired to. Her effect on him simply wasn't that strong. His shoulders went up—an almost imperceptible movement, but she caught it. She was prepared for his next words, for the drastic meaning in back of and coloring his next words.

He said: "I'm afraid all this is just . . ." and then it came to him how rotten that would sound.

"Time wasted?" Donita's acute feeling of days ago about Valerie Pickett had rung a thin small chime of warning in her. Her mettle showed through now, clear and flawless, and she was suddenly straighter. Her small shoulders looked set. "Lance, I knew there was someone else. Is it Valerie Pickett?"

"How could it be?" he said simply.

She weighed her answer. Her words were soft: "You're very young, Lance. Younger than your years, I sometimes think."

And now he was impatient. So much so that there wasn't any sense in his flat reply: "That should make me safe, then."

Donita studied him wistfully. "You don't look at me when you say that," she said thoughtfully, with a knowledge of her own.

He continued to stare taciturnly at the candle, and asked abruptly: "How did you get here?"

She started for the door as though awakened, and, surprised and discomfited that she should follow his thought so promptly to its end, he moved with her. In the doorway she stopped, a small shadowy form without particular defense. Only her eyes and a part of her white forehead caught the light.

"Be sure to ride far around," he told her quietly.

She did not want to go at all, her waiting was so plain. He made an obdurate shape above her, with no capitulation in him. Suddenly her small arms flung out and bound his neck. "At least you'll kiss me good-night, Lance." Her words got tremulous with a wanting deeper than guile.

Kincaid drew her close, a lithe figure, pliant rather than soft. There was still unaccustomed fire in her deep eagerness, a fire that heated his smoky mind and all the rest of him. He pulled her tight against him, drinking from those lips—then roughly broke away.

"Good-night!"

Her answer to this quick growl was a happy laugh.

Her light form disappeared from the faint outline of the door. A moment later, standing there, Kincaid heard the soft stamp of her turning pony. It drew near and then swung off. A strong glow crawling his veins, Kincaid was wildly and irrationally tempted to call her back. But the word that he spoke, low voiced and scarcely audible, was a forceful "Damn!"

IX

KINCAID turned back, bemused, into the musty cabin. The truth was that he was impatient with himself, and at the same time the thought of Donita Sharp's insouciant directness of method sent a chuckle through him. He didn't particularly think any less of her; but clearly he could never think more. For a moment the puzzle of her destiny claimed him; and then he was striving as carefully to take his thoughts away from her as he had tried before to give her the full benefit of them.

It was no sound that chained him for a long moment in his position, but again an intangible rolling up of menace that never ceased to follow his movements to-night, and now swirled close. He was conscious of the hanging ball of his thumb touching the bone grip of his gun; alive to his position in relation to the candle and to the whole room; keenly aware of strung muscles that, in the next painful instant, might have no time for the wrong move or even the wrong twitch. Taking his eyes off the tallow-daubed bottle holding the candle, he drove them to the blackness of the door. The face he saw there, cold and cynical and somberly alert, sent a thrill shocking over him. Buck Ewing stepped in quietly, his high frame taking form in the light.

They looked at each other meticulously, and silence thundered in this dusky log room. Kincaid dropped shut the trap over a crashing riot of thoughts and poured all his faculties into a bright attention. He said softly: "I didn't think you were so foolish, Buck. Your life isn't worth a nickel on this range tonight. Why did you come?"

An obscure satisfaction slackened Ewing's habitual mask-like taciturnity. His reasonable talk was a concession.

"A woman's curiosity, Kincaid—or shall we say interest?" Buck savored that in the recesses of his saturnine nature, and the rest was dropped negligently: "You seem to have come through without a scratch. Shall I tell her that?"

Some of the sternness went out of Kincaid's bronzed face at the unmistakable inference of Valerie Pickett's concern. He didn't believe it was a trick, and a strong sobriety got into his words.

"Much obliged, Ewing."

Buck made a disclaiming gesture. His dry lips parted for speech and then stayed that way, and it was his eyes that cried a quick vigilance. Sure that he heard the rapid strike of ponies' hoofs, he took one long step that carried his back away from the door; and now he raked Kincaid's waiting face with a black warning.

Kincaid jerked his head aside slightly. His words were a hidden murmur. "Go in the back room for a minute."

Ewing's unwinking regard read him and withdrew on a note of reservation. With a rustle of boots the man faded beyond the weak circle of the candle's light. Kincaid looked at this briefly and decided to leave it burning.

Feet slapped the dust near the corral through quick, low words, and skittered forward. A voice beyond the door said, "You, Kin?" and Frank Luger walked in, followed by a dusty companion. Luger didn't wait for anything; he broke out: "Kincaid, be hanged if Buck Ewing ain't loose around here. I seen him!" There was headlong meaning in his talk, savage with a desiring threat.

"You sure it was him, Frank?"

Luger was profanely sure. "You ain't seen nothin'— ain't heard a thing?' he demanded. His stare, and that of his companion, was keen with an excitement that wouldn't rest.

Kincaid said "Use your head," easily, and before it went any further, he queried: "Rusty, Frank? How did you leave him?"

"He's all right," Luger grunted; and then, unable to escape the conviction that rode him: "If Ewing *is* on the prowl, Lord knows where he'll hit first! You better keep your eyes open." He gulped down a dipper of cold coffee and stuffed his cheek with jerky. Chewing vigorously, he ran his eyes over the walls of this place in a restless questing, and rash talk still bubbled in him. Kincaid stalled off any more questions, and Luger, throwing him a sidelong glance, said "I'm goin' now," and turned out of the cabin with long strides. His saddle partner hustled after. Kincaid listened to them pound away.

"So Maxwell ran into lead," said Buck Ewing, from the door of the rear cubby. Slow amusement was in him, and an impelling curiosity to know more. With his advance, Kincaid hugged the candle, so that its light played on Ewing's face and on all of him, but not on Kincaid himself.

He said: "Just a graze, Buck," and Ewing dropped it. But he didn't go. There was a quietly smiling confidence in him, and besides that there seemed to be something he had left unsaid. Kincaid let this arbitrary delay run out, and then murmured: "Yes?"

Ewing took a short breath and suspended it. Afterward he said deliberately: "Kincaid, would you like to see me out of this fight?"

Kincaid, weighing the hard, smooth temper of this man, was careful with his words. "What's your proposition, Buck?"

"Donita."

Ewing was standing there squarely before him, his rawhide body straight and his level eyes opaque, and he dropped the name between them without any softening. It was more like a challenge than a proposal, and Kincaid found admiration threading his alertness. He murmured, "So it's like that, eh?"

He knew now that he had not seen this coming in its full force. "If you're going to win your fight," Donita's words came back to him, "I am your only hope." Something of her shrewdness got to him and awakened his amazement. Had she meant to offer her influence with Ben Sharp, or with Buck Ewing; or what had she meant? At all events she had set a price he could not afford; and now he saw the chance of a queerly twisted recompense which Donita had not counted on.

Ewing's searching pause spanned the wait before Kincaid's following, gauged speech. "You can rest easy on that score, Buck," he said. "Donita is a closed account as far as I'm concerned. Is that what you want?"

Covert pleasure turned Ewing's veiled glance aside and tilted his strong face slightly down toward the floor. Watching it with new hope, Kincaid saw an earnestness of thought give way to flashing intent. Then Buck leaned swiftly to pick up something lying half in the dark beneath the table, which both of them recognized.

It was a glove belonging to Donita Sharp. It lay there, under the light of the candle, in Buck Ewing's rock-like hand; and neither said anything. A whisper of sound on the roof like the stirring of a squirrel etched this silence and a cat's-paw of cool air, flowing down the high slopes, rustled the pines outside and bent the candle flame over lazily. Ewing's eyes, when they came up at last, seemed of burnished onyx.

"I almost believed you," was what he said, his diction painfully colorless. His skin, under the tan, was bleached gray, and there set up in him a violent flux it wasn't in his power to cope with.

Kincaid, breathing evenly with an effort, felt something cold brush by him. Menace pushed against these flimsy walls and flowed back, and the impulse that lit Buck Ewing's stare with malevolent flame was so dynamic that it was like a fatal knowledge, instantly registering. Quiet stretched its aching tautness out until Ewing's brushing movement cracked it. He folded the small, full-molded glove in a forbidding way and pocketed it, his small nod summing things up.

And still Kincaid stood silent. There was nothing he could say that would convey the meaning he must convey if he opened his lips. A deep and biting irony embittered this moment, turgid and stained with violence. Kincaid's feeling about Donita Sharp was one thing; but Donita's glove, here, said something else that Buck Ewing was certain he understood; that his jealousy would not have denied.

Ewing's gun hung on a hair-trigger, sensitive to a jar. He measured his man with a somber foreboding behind that frozen mask, and what he found was an iron rashness matching his own. Kincaid saw no hope of walking out of this without a fight. Anger at the mad whim of a sportive chance made him as cruelly ready as Ewing was. Buck misinterpreted it. In Kincaid's hard blankness of expression he read confirmation of his worst suspicions, his worst fears. Donita had been here—there had been a rendezvous. And Kincaid had lied; he had lied for a purpose of his own, with no other consideration in his mind.

Time piled up. Ewing's dark rage churned like lava in his veins, and Kincaid said quietly: "I suppose that changes your ideas."

Ewing's intolerant head caught the full light, his eyes deep and flashing and dangerous. "It changes them like this, Kincaid: when I go out of this fight, we go out of it together!"

The resonant words sank into an embracing silence and hung there, the echo of a hate and a defiance strong with impetuosity.

Kincaid told him, in a gentle voice that softened none of its meaning: "Deal yourself a hand, Buck. We might as well get it over with."

Ewing was a coldly calculating man. He had climbed a ladder of guns to his position, and he knew the game thoroughly, allowed himself illusions no more often than he gave himself the luxury of a headlong rage. In the midst of this one, so strong was his habit, there yet ran a thread of reason. The violence of his hatred warned him. His immobility held, and he bore down on his raking answer.

"There'll be another time," he said.

"So you'll wait for it. Is that it?"

"That's it."

Ewing cut off this strong talk by moving without haste toward the door. He was not there yet when the rumor of a fast horse drifted along the ridge. Buck Ewing froze. He and Kincaid eyed each other sternly and waited for what the succeeding moment was bringing them. A second, soundless rider rode with the man out there and looked this way with a fleshless grin. Then, while they held hard and fast, death swung by, continuing along the ridge. Both men imperceptibly relaxed. When the pony hoofs faded into emptiness, Kincaid jerked his chin toward the open.

"You better go."

Ewing stepped out at the door and disappeared from the impressionable surface of the night as smoothly as he had arrived there. What he did was to follow the cabin wall, move noiselessly into the dark trees and steal on through black obscurity until he came to the pale opening in which he had left his mount. Toe in stirrup, he paused here for a long listening interval. The profound silence seemed to displease him, for he changed his mind, disengaging his foot; bridle in hand, he led his pony quietly off through the trees in a direction opposite to that from which he had come.

The ridge flattened for a ways and then dipped downward, and the pines thinned. At the edge of the pooled space beyond, Ewing listened and watched for some minutes. The down-flowing current of air was edged with the faint, charred odor of dead fire. Comanche bulked above this grassy hollow, vast with secret stirrings. Ewing decided, from a dull, rhythmic plucking, that the vaguely moving object on his left was a grazing steer.

Turning to the right, he threaded the fringe of pines. Later he stepped into the dust of a trail carved through the trees, and here he mounted and drifted on, but not far. A rush of hoofs coming this way swung him sharply into cover, and his pony crashed through brush with a brittle display of noise. Horsemen yanked in back there; Ewing, thinking fast, emitted a breathy, choking snort.

"Cow," discovered an alert voice from the trail.

"Cow, hell! You heard Kin. Spread through here, quick!"

Ewing pushed into a sleeping pitch-black aisle and curved rapidly away from the trail and then back toward it. Finding it empty, he kneed into a rack that carried him a half-mile before he allowed his pony to single-foot. Presently a whispering rumble stole back to him from somewhere ahead; and when the main trail at last swung off, he followed a lesser track until the mutter of a falls in Slide Canyon came to him no longer from ahead, but from below. The trail wound along a pine-laced rocky brink and then dropped down, clinging to humps and to one long and bare switchback where hoofs scraped the rock in a ragged gash of sparks. Twenty minutes later Ewing turned into an old and wide trail deep in the gorge, where the scent of his own dust was touched with dampness.

Frenchy Lesant's saloon put out a reaching finger of yellow light in the crushing gloom. On one end of that moted beam Buck Ewing drew in and sat thoughtful for a time before he went on. His arrival appeared to evoke no notice. Racking his pony, he went up the steps of this shadowy place whistling a soft tune.

The single smudged lamp burning within cast little more light than a match. These dark walls absorbed all trust and all safety. They seemed deserted too, till Ewing's glance fell on Lesant's severely attentive, round face down the bar. Lesant said gruffly, "Oh—you, Ewing?" and replaced something under the bar, a laxness running back to fill his bulk. The inner door moved slightly and a long glint like that of a rifle barrel lowered and then withdrew. Ewing moved to the bar with a heavy indifference.

"Me," he said. "Were you expecting someone else?"

Lesant flared: "By God, you know who I'm expectin'! He won't get away from me again."

Buck studied the breed's wrathy visage. "So," breathed out of him; "he was here, was he?"

"And left his card," Frenchy averred forcibly. "I dunno how in hell he done it." In jagged spurts of talk he told of Kincaid's visit, and of how, two hours after his departure, the man who took his trail had come back tied across his own saddle, a corpse. Ewing listened, unstirring, to the end.

"When was this?" he said, narrowly attentive.

"Yesterday."

Something dark and sinister, more sinister than the genius of this room, flowed into Buck's lean-cheeked face, tipped slightly down as he stood at the bar. He was so tall that Lesant had to look up while his small and beady eyes read this superior force of evil he felt. And it was genuine. Ewing was thinking, not of a dead man tied across a saddle, but of Lance Kincaid and Donita Sharp: these figures which had twisted in and out of his smoky thoughts since he had left Kincaid. Remembrance of the glove in his pocket stiffened his flat muscles and drew his lips out in a thin line. Lesant, knowing hot metal when he saw it, struck without further hesitation. He growled:

"I figured the grass fire would bring Kincaid to me with his tail high—thought you was him. If it don't fetch him——" He paused expressively, then whipped out: "I'll build a fire plumb under that hombre!"

Ewing flashed him a sultry glance. "Never mind Kincaid," he directed conclusively. "I'll take care of him. You take your orders and forget it."

Frenchy barked: "Hell, Buck——!" and Ewing reminded him almost fiercely:

"I'm telling you what to do."

Lesant shrugged to conceal the savage leap of satisfaction in him, and turned toward the back bar. "*Tequilla,* ain't it?" he grunted.

Ewing caught his eye in the mirror and nodded heavily. "I can do with a drink." He poured a slug into him quickly and waited for it to take hold. Later he had a second; and with his third before him, leaning toward it, he let his head sink into the hollow of his shoulders; and the evil of this place thickened and held these men in a brooding silence.

Dal Waidler and his men found Kincaid sitting his saddle quietly in the night's blackness, on the edge of the bench near Spring cabin. They swirled close, and Waidler, peering, said urgently: "Lance, we run into a man a half-mile back over the ridge. He got away."

Kincaid said, "All right, Dal. What about the fire?"

"It's out."

Without asking further details, Kincaid gave Waidler instructions, and added: "There's jerky and something to drink in the shack. I'm riding for headquarters." He turned his pony out. Down the ridge and across widely sweeping range.

Since a boy Kincaid had memorized every lift and depression of this land with the particularity of love; he knew its tyranny and its wild and sweet loneliness so well that at times it seemed his own property. His heaviest sense of responsibility came with the remembrance that it belonged to another man—and he was remembering that now. It would be the hardest task in his book to tell Old Rusty what had been done in his absence. Rusty would rant and rave; he would jump Kincaid, but that was nothing. What was hard was the hurt Kincaid would deal the old man far back in the recesses where his stoic soul lived, and whose cry no one would hear.

A long ways off, 2 M headquarters was a cluster of waiting lights. Women were still up, there in the houses along the feeder ditch. The ranch house was dark, and crossing the yard later at a foot pace, Kincaid only accidentally picked up the glowing end of a cigar in the blackness of the gallery. That Rusty should be sitting up still, in his condition, did not rank Kincaid's riding reflections; he got out of the saddle slowly, girding for a stormy session.

Rusty, sunk in a rawhided chair, a rag around his head, let him come up the gallery to stop a few feet away, a tall and angular shape. Then, lowering his cigar, he grunted: "I know what you done. I reckon it was the right thing."

Kincaid, surprised, breathed twice and amended: "It was the only thing, Rusty."

The cigar twitched impatiently, but Maxwell passed it over. "What's done 's done," he qualified dogmatically. "Where's the railroad crowd now? Are they workin'?"

"Yes. They're building up the old wash." Kincaid gave an exact account of the South Western Pacific's activities since the successful breaching of the range fence. It was bitter hearing for Old Rusty; yet, curiously, something about it seemed to please him too. This got into his roll as he pulled himself out of his chair. He walked to the end of the gallery and stood there, staring out into star-shot darkness for a minute before he tossed his cigar away and came back. It got into his talk too, smooth and congratulatory and yet somehow uncompromising. He said, heavily and implacably: "Well, tomorrow will be another day."

X

THE day would be hot. Fingers of pale rose, and then bright orange, flaming up through the early morning purple, found Kincaid quartering a wooded bench bulking far across the range. Where it broke downward, he drew up in the edge of the trees and there waited.

Golden lights spread across the east and forced back the lid of night, and gloom flowed out of the old wash with slow reluctance. Down there a boisterous activity was in progress: had been in progress all night. For more than a mile the South Western Pacific had penetrated 2 M like the malignant inroad of a cancer. Clanking engines chuffed and tooted, and steel rumbled in the cars; the cries of men and all the noisy disturbance of bustling industry rose to Kincaid on the still, echoing air.

Construction was being pushed across this forbidden ground; the paddies yelled a ribald challenge to the hills, thrusting the rails forward with an incorrigible zest. Buck Ewing's guards were spread out thin along the right-of-way, bunched fanwise at the spear-head of the advance; they were still strengthened by Ben Sharp's Jingle-bob men. Below Kincaid's position, 2 M drew a net around this invasion; a net which expanded stubbornly but surely, yet did not break.

With this picture riding his wide shoulders, Kincaid

turned away, a strong preoccupation on him as he jogged the five miles to the ranch house.

Smoke Givens, Maxwell's cook, came to the dining-room door and put his head out. "Doan' you even eat?" he inquired accusatively, across the yard.

Kincaid dropped the rein over his pony's head, and swinging off, looked at that black and worried face. "Right now," he said.

Old Rusty was wolfing an early breakfast: a habit he'd learned on roundup. He set down his coffee cup and looked up, but Kincaid, sinking on a bench, only shook his head. The sound of frying came from the kitchen in waves, and this room was more bleak than silence would have left it.

Food had no relish for Kincaid. He walked out again before Maxwell was done; and when the old man emerged, fresh mounts for them both were standing saddled. Kincaid gave Rusty a single straight glance of appraisal. Maxwell's eyes were calm; his ruddy cheeks bore a stolid serenity they had not known for several days. He pulled himself aboard, his lips set with the effort.

Between saddle shed and blacksmith shop, a lane gave off the beaten yard, running toward the feeder and following it past the oak clustered houses there. Around its curve, on the *acequia* bank before the first house, stood a group of women. Their talk dropped to a murmur at the appearance of Rusty Maxwell, and their strained faces turned this way. They stared with a fixedness plain to read. This man was the law to them; his word was terrible and final to some, but Mame Waidler spoke up to him.

"Rusty, what are you sending our men into?" she demanded severely. "I gave you credit for more sense, if I have got to say it." She was a firm-faced woman with iron gray hair and an ample bosom.

"Mame, we've got a job to do," said Maxwell heavily. "There ain't no help for it." But he looked at her with a furrow knitting his brow.

"You're a hard old man," she told him. "You don't spare a thought for the mothers of all those boys who look to you—not to mention us wives. It's your place to do somethin' about this; but if you don't, I'm warning you, we will!"

Rusty moved uncomfortably and his eye strayed. He said gruffly: "Sho, Miz Stroud! Don't you cry, now."

Andy's young wife daubed the tears from her pale cheeks, blinking faster, a deep sorrow in her helplessness, and the other women gathered closer with twitters of sympathy. But it was Mame Waidler who answered.

"A fine way to talk!" she retorted shortly; "with Gil Burr layin' dead, and him her cousin." Her lips tightened. She spoke out with the authority of familiar contempt: "You get out of here and do what you're s'posed to, before these kids hear me tell you off like you deserve!"

Rusty looked at the half-dozen young ones who didn't try to climb his stirrups today, but stood at gaze with their hands behind them. A sigh escaped him. He mumbled, "I'm sure sorry, Miz Stroud," and kneed ahead, his eyes humble.

At the next to the last house, Jake Kernan's strapping bride hurried off the porch. "Mr. Maxwell," she exclaimed. "Kize Hubbard is laying in there and he wants to speak to you."

Hubbard was the man whose horse had thrown him when the tie-laden flat-car had plunged through the range fence. Kincaid and Old Rusty exchanged a glance, and Rusty nodded. They got down.

Kize lay on a cot in the front room. His broken shoulder was trussed up and his face was drawn. He lifted his head, but it dropped back with the sweat of pain starting out on his brow. He said: "Rusty, you ain't givin' up, are you?"

Rusty grunted: "No, Kize. I ain't."

"These women make a man crazy," Hubbard complained, his mouth twisting; "all but Sue, here. *I* know Ike and Gil and Burt Long are gone, and some of the other boys got it pretty bad. But that ain't no reason for doggin' it!"

"Don't you fret any," said Rusty solidly.

Sue Kernan stood quiescent behind Maxwell. A sturdy ranch product from toe to heel, apple-cheeked, with club-like ropes of straw-colored hair, she was little more than a girl. Kincaid said to her quietly: "You're not worried?"

"No," she replied, on a sustained note; but in her cornflower blue eyes he read the ever-present thought of her husband's safety, like a secret hurt.

Maxwell and Kincaid walked out without further words. Riding away, they felt a wave of accusation roll up behind them more eloquent than Mame Waidler's barbed thrusts. But Rusty knew his mind. The younger man broke his reflections more than once to glance at him.

The early sun lifted above the tawny billows eastward, splashing with strong light the little *rincon* up which the railroad advanced. Rusty rode to a knoll overlooking that scene and sat with clamped jaws, taking it in.

Below him his men hugged the draws and grassy depressions, watching Buck Ewing's advanced gun-guards, their rifles at their sides; at long intervals a warning shot punctured the jangled medley of construction. Farther back, small bands of punchers roamed in search of the weak spots.

It was from one such cruising group that old Quill Hoskins pushed ahead, wearing a wrathy scowl. "Damn it, Rusty; this is a hell of a note!" he burst out. "We can bunch up and ride in there, if you'll say the word. They may down a few of us, but we'll sure scatter them micks aplenty. I'll warrant them rails won't go no farther, anyway!" The urgency in his talk made a strong appeal.

The others came up with flashing eyes and hawklike mien. One of them growled, "That's what I say, Hoskins," and dropped curses in the direction of the enemy. Muttered argument broke out in the group like fire in old grass, and at high words Kincaid faced that way. "What's that?" his tone overrode all this talk.

A puncher said, "Rankin, here, says if we'd busted down there half-an-hour ago, we'd be tellin' Rusty about it now, and not askin' him."

Hoskins jumped his pony that way, glaring at Rankin. He bit off: "Damn you, kid——!"

Kincaid looked at Pete Rankin with an alert care. This boy had the stamp of insurgency upon him: a wildness and an intolerance without direction. Watching the way he shoved up to meet Hoskins in front of Maxwell, like a mature man without fear; and remembering the episode of last night, Kincaid predicted a stormy career for him. Old Quill was bent on supplying an instalment of it.

"Drop it," Old Rusty rumbled. Quill whirled and came charging back. He dared to face Maxwell, and he did it now. His voice rose.

"What are you goin' to do, Rusty—that's what we want to know!"

The grizzled old puncher was on edge, cocked for trouble; but Rusty, a man of granite with blind faith in his own power and judgment, seemed not to see it. He sent Hoskins a glance that didn't quite reach across, and without a word swung away along his line of defense. Then, before anyone could speak, he was returning.

"Pull those boys back," he directed in his abrupt way, jerking his chin down the slope. "I want 'em in the timber here, along the edge of the *barranca*," and he waved a hand behind them.

Kincaid was in charge on the spot and it was to him that Rusty spoke. Quill Hoskins snorted angrily and another man grumbled, "Hell, that's just that much farther back!" But Kincaid said levelly: "You heard Rusty, boys. Pass the word along."

Within half-an-hour 2 M knew Old Rusty's will. There was vehement protest all along the line, and faces darkened at having to give ground without ostensible reason. At one point a man sent spaced, ringing shots down the slope in bitter resentment. Rusty shoved his horse over there and tongue-lashed the man. "You'll begin shootin' when I tell you to!" he roared. "Until then you keep your pants on!"

As the men fell back, lining the converging trough of the *rincon*, they began to realize that Maxwell had studied the ground like a general. In the timber they found excellent cover; and, where the slopes pinched in at the bend of the river, they would be fighting downhill. Theirs was now the advantage which the railroad had had at the range fence, and range-bred eyes were quick to note this.

Meanwhile the game was a waiting one. As morning dragged on and became midday there was no halt in the forward push of the track layers. Cries and the anvil-ring of sledges floated up; the hot piny scent of this high country air was masked by the sooty odor of soft coal smoke. The South Western Pacific had penetrated a good three miles into Maxwell's land. A stout fence was going up along either side of the right-of-way. The surveyors worked only a short distance ahead of construction; ahead of them, Ewing's guns spread in a semicircle, eating steadily into the hostile territory.

Jube Pickett's organization was a unique and efficient battering-ram. The sight of this steel-jacketed invasion acted powerfully on the watching men, and on none was its effect more corrosive than on Old Rusty. 2 M represented his hold on life and on the world; it was the only reality he had or desired, and to see his empire cut in two at the virtual direction of an enemy, and with the help of that enemy's crew of riders, embittered his soul and encased him in stone.

Charley May found Kincaid and ranged up beside him in sober silence. At length, lowering his voice and throwing his chin toward Maxwell, he murmured: "I don't like the old man's look. He could chew nails, but he just sits there and stares, kind of gray."

Kincaid looked at Rusty, inscrutably reflective. "It cuts

him to the bone," he agreed. "But this thing is just started. Rusty's got cards in his sleeve."

"Seen 'em?"

After a pause, Kincaid said, "No."

"They want to be high ones."

Kincaid mentally assented, and then he fell again to asking himself how high those cards were.

Early in the afternoon Trace Pickett started a gang of men to work weakening a parallel *barranca* between the rails and the river, preparatory to reinforcing it against the hazards of the rainy season. Old Rusty watched this in a brooding way, his lower lip thrust out, and seemed scarcely to see it. But an hour later he said abruptly to Kincaid, in his unmoved rumble, "I'm goin';" and he wheeled away.

Later the sun was a low flash of level light, raying through the dust which billowed above the *rincon*. Down there, soft gray was already creeping out, wiping the glisten from steel and from perspiring faces and arms; and now Kincaid saw sidings being laid along the old wash, where it widened out for half-a-mile in a sandy arm. There were extra gangs for this work, and while the main line continued to bore onward, the camp began to move up on the sidings; first the engineers' cars and the Pickett coach, and then the shanty cars, and gondolas and flat-cars piled with the materials of construction.

2 M followed these proceedings with wrathy indignation. Andy Stroud looked across at Kincaid with a dogged fury written in his long-jawed face.

"They're takin' root," he called. "Rusty wants to be damn sure what he's doin'!"

Supper was ready in the Pickett car. Jube patted his daughter on the shoulder and seated himself opposite her. He was methodical in his movements and he remained thoughtfully silent, but Valerie read the strain and the responsibility in his angular shoulders. Trace came in late after a hasty wash-up, and threw his hat on a padded bench. The gesture expressed him. He drew up to the table briskly.

"Is Murphy getting the steel up any faster?" his father queried.

Trace gave an impatient wave. "It isn't that. Things just haven't gone smoothly here. But I'll keep them moving for all that." He was breezy and self-assured; smugly satisfied with his work. Glancing at Valerie, he winked almost jovially.

Valerie maintained the reserve she had worn all day; her answering gaze was a light and impersonal thing. Trace, watching her curiously, finally said: "You're as sober as a judge, Val. I suspect I have your hearty disapproval."

"I disapprove of violence, certainly," she told him quietly. "Mr. Ewing deliberately invites it, and you, Trace, allow it and abet it. That is plainly as wrong as it can be for these ranch people to resist."

Trace barked a laugh. "That's just it! They haven't a leg to stand on," he scoffed, "and Buck Ewing was hired to call their bluff. You can see for yourself how well he did it." He leaned back, confident that he had demolished her argument. Devils of ruthless good nature danced in his dark eyes.

"He wasn't hired to leave a trail of slain men behind

us," she came back at him, her cheeks warming. "It is shameful and unjust, and I deplore it."

"Just like a woman!" he snorted, swiftly frowning. "I've said a dozen times, this isn't the place for you. Just because you haven't the stomach for the methods a man must use sometimes to get his work done——"

"Father is in charge of the work, Trace," she reminded him steadily. "You didn't tell him you were going to smash a car through Mr. Maxwell's fence, because you were capable of not telling him. He has let you know what he thought of that, but it is too late now. If he had known in time there would have been no fight and no fatalities."

Trace impetuously opened his mouth to shout her down.

"We'll have no more of this," Jube intervened quietly. "Something had to be done, that's clear. We are in the right," he strove, as always, to take a sensible view; "and we'll be as fair as we're allowed to be. This is a delicate situation at best . . . I don't know," he broke off thoughtfully, "but what I ought to make an attempt to see Maxwell about these cattle-guard crossings. We've got so many to put in across his range, and if we try to satisfy him on their placing it may go far to mitigate circumstances."

They talked it over. Trace was indulgent, and then brusque; but his dissuasion was without effect. Jube had decided. Finally Trace said dogmatically: "I won't trust you among those men. They'll kill you. I'll go instead."

Jube smiled slightly, getting up from the table. "I'll be safer than you will, Trace." He left them with that, and his son sat looking out of the window with a scowl.

Valerie caught up with Jube at the car steps. "Father, I'd rather you didn't go," she said impulsively.

Jube attempted to reassure her. "I'll be quite all right, Valerie. Don't you worry."

"At least take someone with you.," she urged, seeing that he was fixed on going. A step crunched below them, and they turned to look down at Limpy Smail. Limpy stood a little awkwardly, smiling an old man's smile.

"Major, if you're headin' some'eres, I'll just poke along kind of handy like," he proposed diffidently.

Valerie's quick smile warmed him, but his face fell as Jube said: "Not this time, Limpy." Jube stepped down and moved off toward the camp corral. A few minutes later he passed the wire on a pony and angled up the slope alone. Valerie's troubled gaze followed him until he disappeared from view in an onward-running gully.

Eyes from above accompanied his advance. A dozen men awaited him a few yards below the pines. He rode on, his hands in the air. "That's far enough," a grim call reached him, and he stopped. Three men stepped out, their faces intent in this indirect evening light.

"Hell, it's old Pickett himself!" Quill Hoskins discovered harshly. He swore black oaths in his beard and his stare cut wickedly into Jube.

"Never mind, now," Jake Kernan droned. He pushed aside the old puncher's hovering rifle and confronted Jube, to growl: "What you want?"

"The hell with what he wants!" Ote Burnett burst out truculently, from the growing group to the rear. "How about what we want?"

Jake had his hands full, undertaking to quell this gush of violent impulse. A few minutes later Kincaid arrived to find his men boiling around Pickett's horse. He said sharply, "Hold it," and pushed through to Jube. "Yes?" he said. There wasn't any cordiality in that terse word.

Jube said, his voice uneven: "I want to see Rusty Maxwell. Will you give me a safe conduct to the ranch?"

Kincaid studied him so long and coolly that Jube thought he meant to refuse. He dropped a nod, however, and turned. "Break away, boys." He had a hand on Jube's curb-chain, leading his pony. One man ejaculated gruffly: "Hold on, Kin———!" and then a hostile silence fell. Kincaid pushed through these men unseeing. Later he and Jube Pickett jogged along toward 2 M headquarters.

Old Rusty came plodding across the ranch yard, his hat off and his white hair fluffing in the run of breeze. He saw Jube and stopped, and his ruddy face went set and blank.

Kincaid drew up and sat his horse in silence. Rusty's metallic eye drew words out of Jube.

"Maxwell," he began, "I've come to see you about these cattle-guard crossings." Rusty had not asked him to get down, nor so much as opened his inflexible-looking lips, a wary and contemptuous menace in his bearing; but Jube proceeded with all the suavity and assurance at his command. "We insist on being fair about this. I want to please you on these crossings." He made it sound more like a business amenity than a favor.

A mockingbird trilled in the pause that ensued, sweetening the evening and giving it depth. Then Rusty opened his lips, and dry words came:

"It don't make no difference where you put your cross-in's. They won't be there long."

Jube tried to dissemble his stiffness at this obdurate

stand. "Come, come, Maxwell; we both know better than that," he cajoled. "I'll do everything I can for you—maybe grade the banks down to the crossings where it's necessary." He had more to say, doggedly explanatory. Rusty heard him to the bitter end; but Jube's ingratiating smile didn't get across. Rusty's barren eye skidded away, and his bleak manner precluded argument.

"You do what you're a mind to," he said, and half-turned to leave, plainly disinterested. His glance struck Kincaid; his head jerked. "Come up to the office."

Kincaid called to a man hovering in the offing. "Get up a horse, Al, and ride back with Pickett." He got down himself, and strode after Maxwell.

If the wind had swerved suddenly to another quarter, Jube Pickett could not have felt the change more pronouncedly. There was no place for him here, no one to hear his words. He looked about him, and in a moment of inner vision he saw what he was doing to Old Rusty. Then Al walked a pony toward him, and before those implacable eyes Jube's chin came up. He and the puncher rode out of the yard.

In the office, Rusty turned away from the safe with an envelope in his hand. There was a calculating squint in his gaze as he held it out but his words were off-handed. "That's a draft on my bank for ninety odd thousand dollars. I want you to go into the White Oaks Exchange and sell short, all the South Western Pacific stock you can swing." His hard eye lifted and steadied. "Do you get me? I want you to hammer that stock until you run the railroad's credit plumb into the ground."

Kincaid's face didn't change, but he stared. There were, he was reflecting, still a few surprises left in this indomitable old man. Rusty spoke as if he were arranging for the delivery of half-a-dozen dressed beeves to a butcher.

"Of course you know you may lose every cent of this." Kincaid tapped the draft with his finger-nail.

That appeared to strike Maxwell as immaterial. "All you got to do is what I tell you. Keep under cover as much as you can; but don't let anything scare you off. And start tonight." He jerked his chin downward and his leather lips folded inexorably.

Kincaid nodded slowly and turned outside. Saddling a fresh mount under the flaming sunset sky for the long ride to White Oaks, he glanced back at the house more than once, and finally shook his head. His admiration was tinctured with a sense of lack. This, then, was what the old man had had in his war bag, and on which he counted heavily. What if it wasn't enough? Kincaid knew only too well that he might not be allowed to do what he proposed; that someone might divine his object and spike his guns. If it was Rusty's object to pound down South Western Pacific, he would undoubtedly meet with some success; but would it not take more than this to bring those crawling steel rails to a halt?

XI

A HERD of prime beef steers clattered bawling down Cherry Street in the direction of the loading pens and people moved along the walks. White Oaks bustled cheerfully about its business under the bright morning sun.

"This," Kincaid murmured to himself, "is like lighting a powder keg with a match."

But it didn't bother him. He looked both ways along the street and then stepped into the Cattlemen's Exchange.

A score of men stood around in here, studying the boards or arguing in knots. Most of them were booted stockmen. Already the air was layered with smoke; and the heavy voices were a steady murmur, except when a clerk rose to note some new quotation on the board. Kincaid nodded to acquaintances and talked for a minute with an old acquaintance of Rusty Maxwell. Then he went over and let his eye run down the general listing.

South Western Pacific stood at 40.

Kincaid had already spent a half-hour at the bank; his credit was arranged for. Now, after some minutes' computation with pencil and envelope, he gave a clerk an order to sell four thousand shares of South Western Pacific, short.

"Ten percent margin on that," the clerk grunted.

"That's all right."

The transaction went through. Kincaid left the Exchange and walked back to the stable. Some time must elapse before he could expect any evidence of instability in the railroad stock. It was dull waiting, but he managed somehow.

An hour passed. Kincaid returned to the floor of the Exchange. He was about to proceed with his activities when Ben Sharp strode in. Ben was feeling genial and expansive today. His eye sharpened as it fell on Kincaid, but he nodded. Kincaid returned the nod without hurry, and turned to glance at the board. Ben put his own construction on that action. He believed Kincaid was here because Rusty Maxwell was interested in beef quotations, and his mind returned to his own affairs.

Gail Childress, the post-master, spied Sharp and called across the room: "I see South Western Pacific is off a couple of points this mornin', Ben. You ain't unloadin', are you?" Childress was a big man and his drawling voice carried. Kincaid heard the words. Other men glanced around.

Sharp smiled feebly. "I ain't carryin' enough of it to juggle with, Gail. Somebody in El Paso must be makin' a turn-over."

He fingered his chin and studied the board uncertainly for a while; but five minutes later Kincaid saw him walk out with another man, the affairs of the railroad forgotten.

Satisfied that his original maneuver would bring the stock down no more for the present, Kincaid made a second and more determined raid. This time it was fourteen thousand shares that he sold short. The order clerk's glance flickered with the knowledge of what this meant. The sale went through, and Kincaid walked out once more. But this time it was not long before he was back, standing in a position from which he could follow the market reading.

In less than an hour, South Western Pacific took a dip of 3¾ points, and after that crawled down by half and quarter points until the reaction was absorbed. It was apparent that activity in the El Paso market was influencing the situation. Kincaid observed all this with an alert attention, and he saw that other men were beginning to take note of the slump in the railroad issue. It wouldn't be long, he judged, before wind of this got around and an attempt was made to do something about it.

He had been selling on ten percent margin. Consultation of the figures apprised him that he would be able to make a final turn-over of seventy-five hundred shares, and, satisfied with his management, he was completing the transaction when Ben Sharp stormed into the Exchange.

Ben had got word of what was afoot. He shot a look at the last quotation, saw that South Western Pacific stood at 32 and a fraction, and whirled on Kincaid.

"What in hell does this mean?" he roared furiously.

Kincaid faced him coolly. He had nothing to say, stowing his notations in a pocket and holding Sharp off with his eyes. Ben croaked:

"I can see Rusty Maxwell's hand in this! He won't get away with it—and if I was ten years younger, by God you wouldn't either!" He waved a trembling hand and his face was a knot of rage, veins pounding in his throat and forehead.

Kincaid scanned this spectacle inscrutably, his high shoulders unmoving; and Sharp came to himself with a choking snarl. He knew that all the ranting he did now would help matters none at all. Whirling, he flung the clerk an order to buy in South Western Pacific for a rising market. He meant to try desperately to stabilize the issue.

Kincaid waited a moment, then moved apart. His bolt was shot. Before Ben Sharp's purchases took hold the railroad stock sagged another half point; but this, if Sharp meant business, would shortly be another story, and Kincaid meant to tell Rusty what that story was.

Ben had to plunge heavily to bring the stock out of its stagger. He was in for seventy-five thousand dollars before it began to rise at all. Thereafter it came up slowly. By the time Ben finally pegged it at three points below the opening price, he had invested a sum which Kincaid computed as better than one hundred and seventy-five thousand. Contemplating this result, Kincaid began to con Rusty Maxwell's motives afresh. Had Rusty hoped to involve his old enemy deeply in the affairs of the railroad he could not have managed better. It was a revealing flash of the deep guile in Old Rusty's mind.

But entangling Ben Sharp in itself was of small consequence, and Rusty would see that. For the first time Kincaid sensed an object and a complication in this affair which had not been apparent before. It laid a sharp restlessness on him, and a need to be back on 2 M. Under that compulsion he moved toward the door. Ben Sharp stopped him.

"You ain't done with me yet!" he bellowed. "And you can tell Old Rusty just that! It'll cost him plenty to play this game; and where I'm concerned there ain't any limit and there won't be any end, till he folds!"

"I'll tell him."

Tall and collected, Kincaid looked down and read the virulence of this man, the savage desire to hurt and then destroy. That mad hatred was Ben Sharp's mainspring, and each succeeding blow Rusty Maxwell took at his enemy only wound it tighter. When it snapped, if it ever did, it would smash Ben and it would annihilate any part of 2 M within his reach.

Men were grinning at Sharp's vehemence. Ben didn't see it, and didn't care. He began again, words boiling out of him wickedly; Kincaid cut off that tirade by turning his back on it and walking out of the place. Sharp yelled after him from the door: "A way will be found to break you! Don't you think it won't!"

Kincaid wheeled sharply; not at this last bilious bomb from Ben, but because feet slapped the dust of the street in a savage burst.

"What is it?" the words rifled across the murmur of this town.

Trace Pickett charged through the thick sunshine, coming from the depot. His imperious black eyes raked Kincaid and leaped to Ben Sharp; he slowed to a position midway between them, dynamite in his impelling mien.

Sharp walked over to him and whispered a word in his ear.

"So that's why he's in town!"

Sharp's meaning seared across Trace's determination, and welding with it, hurled him toward Kincaid. He grated, "I've been waiting for this!" and his proud brows were prominent. Caution wasn't in him. His shoulder up, a fist flailing, he lunged violently.

Kincaid, frozen in his stand in the way a roper knows, might have been rooted there. Trace slammed into him and staggered aside as if he had struck an oak tree. Ben Sharp shrieked imprecations and wild advice, and Trace recovered himself with a blazing rage, silent, taut, and now wary.

Anger licked a bright flame up through Kincaid's ice. He heard none of these shouts, none of the running as men gathered at this spot, a high expectancy on them. His stare fastened on Trace Pickett's lean and corded countenance, carved with a sovereign arrogance. Something near to murder flooded those fierce eyes. Trace had never been defeated by life or by other men; mastery was the only lesson he knew; he was the dominant victor turned beast. He would blast Kincaid by storm or by treachery, his glare cried, and with this Kincaid knew he had a fight on his hands.

Trace threw himself forward again, this time with acute precision. There was no solid impact. Pickett's rugged, whip-hard frame flickered about Kincaid with an incredible agility; his fists chopped and sledged Kincaid's head and his body in a way that darkened the aching sunlight of this street; turned him around; bewildered and banished his somber thoughts. Kincaid lashed out blindly, a steam-hammer stroke, and the blow caught Trace on the shoulder and flung him back. That agile shape danced in again, and Kincaid repeated the thing. His head cleared; he was aware now that he had a boxer, a trained man, to contend with. His lips snapped tight and a doggedness flattened his look.

If Trace read it at all he thought he had his man rattled. He leaped forward, ripped in a feint and a solid punch that bent Kincaid's ribs with an inner agony, and followed with a kick which gouged skin from Kincaid's thigh.

"That's it, Pickett! Stomp him down!" Ben Sharp cried mercilessly.

Trace hurled at Kincaid's middle. He was fighting at a killing pace. Kincaid swept a powerful blow sidewise; it brushed Trace's arms aside and crashed into his head, scraping him off his legs. His body piled into his adversary's and went down with it, and then they were groveling and striking in the dust, grunting their violent wrath in heaving gusts. Kincaid felt a knee sink into his stomach with stabbing pain. With an up-rush of fury he tore Trace loose and flung him a dozen feet.

Trace lunged up, a madness on him. He dived. But now Kincaid threw off the last restraint, a wicked will driving him. He was without thought, he had no consciousness of feeling. The blows Pickett shoveled into him were less than nothing. Deliberate and cold, he hit that white, enflamed face with everything he had. The wrench heeled him back and the face disappeared.

A shout beat across his senses with a far away surge. Dimly he sensed what it meant; but he had to finish this thing in his own absolute way. An arm met his grappling hands, and then a lax and heaving torso, laying along the dust. He tore the rest of that shirt away getting this boneless bulk to stand upright. Trace tottered, he caught himself and raised his arms with a vile oath, his fists balled.

Kincaid didn't slug him again. With the flat of his big hand he laid a blistering outline across Trace's bloody and livid and vacant face. Trace buckled and melted down with a groan like the wheeze of a folding bellows. He was done.

Kincaid stared across that inert form at Ben Sharp, and for an instant a hush touched the crowd with menace. There was more than blows and the brute impact of bodies in this reckless appraisal. Sharp blazed: "You'll pay for this!"

The crowd's unnerved stirring had nothing to do with Kincaid's contemptuous grunt. He was paying now, he knew ruefully, with the awakened cry and sting and ache of all his punished muscles; he expected to pay no more. Shouldering away from the spot, he left half-a-dozen men hustling Trace Pickett down to the hotel.

Two hours later, on the trail home, Kincaid's eye followed the smudge of a train moving afar across the flatlands. "There goes Pickett," he thought with grim amusement; "crawling back to his job." But what claimed his sober anticipation was the situation that awaited him at 2 M.

He pushed on in his unsparing way.

Mame Waidler accosted him as he came up the feeder lane. She stood marked with a telling curiosity, under a gnarled oak, and Kincaid drew in beside her, pulling off his hat.

"Lance, what is this about your goin' out to wire the Governor—is there any truth in it? What was the message?" she demanded keenly.

"What?" he said, startled into surprise.

"Old Rusty told us this morning that the railroad would be pullin' out of here, to the last spike and sliver!" Mame asserted. She was already on the defensive, as though she expected subterfuge. "He wouldn't say no more, but the men had it around that he was puttin' pressure on the Governor and it wouldn't be long."

"I know nothing about it," Kincaid told her. He had heard enough, and his eye quested hungrily toward the ranch house. Mame would have held him, her spite and her mistrust interminable; but he broke away.

He had not been wrong: Old Rusty was involved in some plan he would entrust in detail to no one, and it was far more than the aimless feint Kincaid had read in it. The strong necessity to know all of it pulled him forward.

Smoke Givens was likely to poke his curly poll out of the door if a spiral of dust twirled across the ranch yard. He appeared now, and Kincaid hailed him.

"Where's Rusty?"

"Ah dunno." Smoke stuck out his lower lip as much as to say that Maxwell didn't trust him any more, but it didn't bother him. "He ain't been around heah since mawnin'." He mumbled on, but Kincaid, not listening, swung out of the yard and down the range, a gathering haste in him.

Somewhere on the bluffs overlooking the old wash was where Maxwell would be. Smoke boiled above the dark pines down there, deeper than ever in 2 M, and Kincaid's bruise-stained face grew lean. He broke through trees along the Standing Stone's rocky course and pulled up as a cruising puncher racked forward.

"Where's Rusty?"

Frank Luger's craggy glance searched Kincaid's cheeks and his hard mouth with attention. "Kin, that's a damned queer thing! Dal Waidler saw him ridin' toward the hills four hours ago, and nobody's spotted him since . . . What's the matter with you?" he broke off, noting an angry abrasion under Kincaid's ear. "What happened?"

"I ran into Trace Pickett in town," Kincaid disposed of the marks he bore. "Rusty's been gone for some time, eh?" His eye climbed the bulging shoulder of Comanche through a gap in the trees, then swung back to rest thoughtfully on the river. "What's going on down in the wash?"

"They been pushin' steel steady," Luger said, and his face darkened. "They're workin' in gangs and never stopped last night at all. It ain't in reason! . . . Kin, the boys got it that you rode to White Oaks with what'll stop all this in your saddle-pocket. Is that straight?"

"No," said Kincaid shortly; and then he was sitting up, stiff with attention. It had seemed to him that the river changed while he looked at it. He had his look upstream, eyes narrowed; while Luger tried to get something out of him, he pushed his pony down to the water's edge. He was right. The rocks were noiselessly but surely submerging; within the few minutes he had been here the water had risen four or five inches.

The truth knifed through all the uncertainties of this day. Old Rusty in the hills—the water rising! It could only add up to one thing: Rusty had knocked out the head-gate of the dam built up there by 2 M to regulate the flow in the dry season.

"Good God!"

Frank Luger was seriously startled. "What, Kin? What's eatin' you?" he burst out.

Kincaid called his answer in the midst of a wheeling plunge. "Rusty's pulled the plug on the high pond! With the whole railroad camped in the wash, they'll be drowned like rats!"

Luger yelled something that was lost in the rush of wind as the spurs roweled Kincaid's pony into a leap and then a mad run. Kincaid took the ford at a slant, the water lashing up in sheets which prisoned rainbows for an instant. The pony took the far bank with a surge of bulging haunches, and now Luger's cry carried:

"The hell with 'em, Kin! Come back here!"

But Kincaid would not explain that he was thinking, not of several hundred laborers alone, caught in a trap of devilish certainty, but of a girl with chestnut hair and a direct and faultless pride.

He knew how fast that drowsy river could rise. When the crest of the tumbling flood Old Rusty had unleashed came thundering out of the hills, nothing could stay its terrible destruction; all that would avail would be the reaching of a place of safety. Kincaid knew too what would happen to that weakened *barranca* giving into the old wash. It would go out like a rotten levee. Anything in the path of the rioting waters would be swept into oblivion and deposited on the shores of eternity.

"I've got to warn them!" the groan issued from the depths of Kincaid's agony of decision; for there was one part of him which said that Rusty Maxwell was hand in hand with God in this; while the rest of him swore that Rusty didn't know, he couldn't dream that in the path of his retribution were women and all the noncombatants of a big railroad camp.

Kincaid's horse burst through pines at an utterly reckless gallop and then charged slantwise down the slope of the *rincon*. He had flanked 2 M, and his first check came at a warning yell and a bullet which flicked by him with a wicked backdraw. He hauled in, a hand up. But it was the flash of his magnetic face, with its strong message of imminence, that brought Buck Ewing and his man jogging forward in a keen inquiry. The eye of a rifle looked at Kincaid with a steady waiting.

Buck's heavy tone, as his wheeling horse blocked the way, was disinclined to recognize any extenuation of this appearance. "Kincaid——"

"Drop it, Ewing!" Kincaid slashed through tension and enmity; his words came like the wind before storm: "The dam's out in the hills—those people in the wash have got to be warned!"

Ewing's somber eyes leaped; he began to swear in thick, ropy anger. He spat out: "If I thought you were running your brand on me——!"

Kincaid didn't pull around him. He jammed his pony straight through; for a long second he and Buck Ewing were thigh to thigh. Lightning played on this sunny slope, and two wills locked in the mindless combat of bulls tearing up the soil. Ewing's strong and dark face thundered his doubt; there was a deep desire in the hatred of this man. Kincaid flung at him: "I tell you there isn't a second to spare!"

His trenchant boldness lashed Buck Ewing's pony aside. Buck growled out his charged fury; but he didn't break loose. Kincaid jerked his heels in a gash of the spurs and plunged on toward the railroad camp. A gun banged behind him, but his horse never faltered and no slug cut past him with its fierce flutter. He heard no pound of hoofs, nor did he look around. Foam slapping on him and by him from the pony's mouth was a greater trouble, getting in his eyes.

XII

DROPPING into the old wash with a gouging slide, Kincaid pulled out of the dust opposite a broken line of weathered shanty cars. A man or two wandered about, and some peered out of the little windows. There were several lines of track here; the Pickett coach wasn't in sight. Nearing the fence which hemmed in the right-of-way Kincaid lifted his pony into a sharp run. A guard farther along yelled at him; but Kincaid swept over the fence and sided the cars until he came to the first break in their coupling. He pushed through there.

A locomotive was trundling several tie-freighted cars up the main line. Kincaid's pony reared and pawed in fright. Throwing his weight forward, he jumped it across the rails ahead of the first car.

His sudden appearance created a stir. Men dropped what they were doing to look; some cried out and began to start forward. An alertness ran across the cinder ballast of this camp. The work engine tooted a series of short, alarmed blasts and someone hurled a chunk of coal which curved past Kincaid's shoulder.

"Get out of here, all of you!" he yelled. "The river's on a tear—you'll be washed away! Get out; get up the *barranca,* anywhere!"

His driving will sheared through this hard belligerence and gave them pause. They gazed with screwed-up faces, and Kincaid made an expressive sweep with his arm. "Get out, if you want to save your lives!"

Leaving it there, he pounded up the right-of-way. Beyond the strung cars ahead, a welter of paddies and tie wagons and another engine marked the end of steel. Then Kincaid saw the engineers' cars, and past it, Jube Pickett's private car. He headed for that. As he drew close, Limpy Smail came hurrying down the near side of the car. There was a forced intentness in the watchman's lined old face and faded eyes and he had a gun in his hand.

"You git away!" he shrilled, stumbling back as Kincaid yanked in. "You can't come here!" He wanted to shoot, and all that stopped him was the fact that he knew this competent breed of men of unreadable face and flashing action.

Kincaid spilled out of the saddle to tower above him. "Sorry, oldtimer," he dropped smoothly, twisting Smail's .45 out of his grasp. "No time to talk." He slithered the gun under the wheeltruck and sprang for the car steps.

Valerie Pickett stood at their top. A strange expression came over her clear features as she looked at him. She said: "Mr. Kincaid! Why—— I invited you, but I didn't expect——"

"This isn't a visit," he cut her off swiftly. "A river dam in the hills is out; this wash will be flooded. You must leave here immediately!"

"But Mr. Kincaid—are you sure?" She stared, genuinely startled; and even in the midst of his unceremonious haste, he found time to note that she did not question his sincerity. The look on his keen, sun-darkened face answered her question. "We must do something!" she exclaimed. "I must gather my—— Where's Father, and Trace?" She fastened on Limpy, who hovered here, agog now. "They must be told! Limpy, go—find them at once!"

"They're up on the job," Limpy burst out. He started that way at his fast hobble.

"Come with me!" Kincaid told Valerie urgently. "Never mind your things; you haven't a moment!"

But standing in the car vestibule, Valerie cast a flashing look at the walls of the wash, and then after Limpy's bent and hurrying shape. "He'll never make it!" she was apprehensively certain. It was not of herself that she was thinking at all in this moment of crisis.

Kincaid's hard glance swept the wash. A stand of cars prevented him from seeing the weakened *barranca* at which the danger threatened. His hand flung backward for the pony's bridle; he seemed to rise in one swift step to the saddle. Half-a-dozen jumps showed him the *barranca's* brink, taut as a bow-string, over which a foot of water gushed, running like quicksilver. The men were boiling back away from there, already warned, their yells echoing; the hoarse wail of the work engine added to the rising mêlée.

Kincaid cried to Valerie: "Don't go back in that car for anything! I'll try to find your father—then I'll come back!"

Valerie nodded a wordless assent. Kincaid slashed his pony. Water spanned the floor of the wash and ran swiftly forward; the crumbling *barranca* was a torrent; and yet this was only the fore-runner of what was to come. It was difficult to identify faces in the mad wave of men charging this way, but Trace Pickett was beating up the team of a wagon heavy with scared laborers.

Through a gap in some freight cars, almost in front of Kincaid, Jube Pickett pushed out on a horse he used to jog up and down the line. His quick stare made a sweep of the wash and pinned on Kincaid.

"My God, Kincaid——!" his horrified ejaculation whipped out.

"Come out of here!" Kincaid's yell galvanized him. "This wash will be bank-full in two minutes!" He almost lifted his pony around. Swift-surging water washed the hocks of both animals and raced down the tracks; mud and dirty spray splashed up as Kincaid threw his mount toward the Pickett car again. Valerie stood on the steps, her pale face a picture of stoicism.

Jube Pickett was just behind Kincaid as the latter wheeled close to reach for Valerie. "Will you take care of her?" he called. "I must do what I can for our men!"

"Yes, Father!" Valerie's light voice lifted. Her eyes clung to him. "And please see that Limpy gets to a place of safety!" Kincaid swept her into his hard arms and she relaxed in them without stiffness, one of her own reaching around his shoulders.

"Hurry!" she breathed fervently; but it was not Kincaid's haste she invoked. Her fear-torn gaze was on the scores of men dashing through rising brown water. The whole camp was a scene of furious activity, of turmoil. In a foot of muddy slush Kincaid broke for the lowest point in the bank of the wash, where a draw came down from above.

Down the line of cars, men who had been sleeping poured out on the tracks, a wild mob in red underwear.

There was no order and no hope of order. Jube Pickett bawled after the engineer of the work locomotive; but that individual, his string and his engine clustered with men, was steaming down track with the throttle pulled wide open. It left two-thirds of the camp to its own devices. These men washed outward on either side in the mad will to get out of there. And now the railroad crews were trapped by their own wire. Horses from the smashed corral plunged against the fence and tripped; the barbs of snarled strands caught at men's clothes, to hamper their escape.

Trace Pickett strove to do something definite. At his order men attacked the fence-posts as rapidly as possible with axes. Another group used floating ties as battering-rams to snap off the posts. But there were few who were not thinking exclusively of themselves. Some foolishly attempted to find refuge on the car hoofs; Kincaid saw Trace slug one man and try to drive him away as he started to climb.

At a point where the top strand of the wire was down, Kincaid got his tired pony to take it. Valerie did not weigh much, but the double weight was a terrific strain. Somehow the animal made the jump. Kincaid rammed it toward the haven of that yawning draw.

He was not there yet when an earth-shaking rumble made Valerie gasp and clutch Kincaid tightly. He knew what it was, but he flashed a look that way in time to see the *barranca* melt before a tremendous wall of water. The flood tossed a lashing brown wave thirty feet in the air. It smashed over and down with a shock like the crumbling of a granite cliff; the only sound that pierced the succeeding roar of destruction was the fear-maddened screams of the horses.

The deluge flushed down the wash at a terrific speed. Witless men fought and trampled one another; Kincaid forgot all knowledge and memory, alone cleaving to the preservation of life. He could not have thrown his horse toward the saving draw at a wilder pace. Valerie's head was down, her face flattened against his chest; she sensed rather than felt the great pound of his heart, and the snap and flow of his straining muscles.

Snarling thick water curled up the pony's threshing legs; its progress was a splashing plunge with a lurch in it. Kincaid's mask-like face jerked aside. They hung suspended on destiny's cord. They were under the brink of that trembling deluge, they were on the treadmill of a dream, they were in the draw! A sharp-swelling spate of flood-water, impelling them bodily from behind, only lifted them irresistibly toward safety.

The pony clawed gravel and lunged dripping out upon safe ground.

The strong scorch of menace alone penetrated to Kincaid's senses before he knew that he had won. As he leaned to put Valerie Pickett down, the scent of her hair, the aroma of her whole lithe and flexible person, keen and improbable, clung to his nostrils like a remote madness. When her feet touched ground and her soft and yet vigorous arm released its hold on his hard neck, she slanted upward a look of mute gratitude. Low, late afternoon sun transformed the azure of her eyes with hidden shining gold and brought a bright auburn glint into her chestnut hair, and she was incarnate fire in his blood.

All this got to him for that one instant, like a flash

of secret knowledge across a sea of oblivion. Then both fixed their whole awareness on the roaring cauldron that was the wash.

A tidal wave was not more headlong than the terror which boomed through the railroad camp like a broken log-jam. Devastation rode the advancing wall of the flood. Tracks, box-cars, shanty cars, wagons and tool-boxes and equipment were smashed and twisted with rending crashes which blended into one mighty, snarling roar. Hundreds of ties chewed and snapped, tossed up on the swirling brown current; far below, the buckling, ripped-up track thrust shuddering black arms skyward, which crashed down amid the grinding and tumbling of railroad cars.

More than one man barely skirted his violent end in that convulsion of brute nature. By scores and dozens they won to the high gravel pitch of the *barranca,* scrambling in the fierce struggle to defeat the sucking sweep of these insatiate waters. A dead horse floated by, its feet jutting. Others, swimming, were struck by debris and carried under. As the thunder of the flood swiftly subsided to an oily menace, the yells of the men could be heard once more.

Those who reached firm soil ran along the water's edge in a kind of fury, leaning down or throwing themselves flat to haul out others. Both banks of the wash were lined with a feverish activity which sprang up magically. Valerie Pickett, as soon as her freezing horror relaxed its grip on her limbs, ran down the bank tugging large men aside to get through them, staring into their faces, calling her father's name. Bedraggled Limpy Smail, when she ran into him, waved his hands and protested something vehemently; obviously explaining to himself, as well as to her, why he had not kept track of Jube. She hurried on.

Trace Pickett, with his usual hard competence, had come out on top. He broke out of a group of excited men and stopped in front of them, and he stared across the dozen yards that separated him from Kincaid. The mud on his clothes and the bitter memory of the morning's fight written in his features took nothing from his taut .poise. There was all about him a darkness and a crowding hate.

"Come over here, Kincaid!" spurted out of him in a swirling rage.

Kincaid looked over there with a tight control riding his will. He said: "Here I am, Pickett," and his coolness reached out like the leaping lash of a stock-whip.

Trace crouched in the stress of hurling his authority forward. "Come here!" he thundered. His holster was empty; he spread his hands as if for a rush, but it was in the air and in Kincaid's flat stare that Trace would not plunge. The paddies stirred and muttered at his back. One man pushed a gun into his outspread fingers, and Trace shoved it back; the man thrust it in Trace's empty holster.

"Kincaid," Trace droned his rifling accusation, and his arm swept the wash; "you did this to me!"

Kincaid, in a sudden heat with this man, and the mean intolerance of him, flung out, "It's done," and waited for that to sink in. "Why don't you go for it, Pickett?" he threw in contemptuously.

Trace's high shoulders froze in a set position with the down-clamp of his hanging impulse. The total destruction of his work had brought full night to his soul, a blackness of violence for which the sun-glinting flood and these clamoring men were a background unreal and immaterial. He flamed: "You think you can't be reached. By God, that's your mistake!"

Kincaid waited.

"I'll reach you!" Trace hurled down, the impetuosity of this man a violent thing. "This railroad will be built if it has to be across your dead body!" Plainly he whipped himself to the point of mad action. His brow glistened with the starting sweat; his stare fixed in a basilisk intensity.

"Pickett, someday I'll have to finish you," Kincaid threw across the tautness between them. He knew it was true and knew that he would have to.

"Not now," said an almost composed voice. Jube Pickett stepped from behind the group surrounding his son and walked between Trace and Kincaid, like a soldier into the line of fire. His firmness alone controlled the moment. He told Trace: "This man rode down to warn us. I won't have what you propose, do you hear?"

Trace stormed, "You don't know what you're doing."

About to retort sharply, Jube passed it over. Valerie, having searched elsewhere without success and then turned back, hurried forward, a luminous glow beneath her steady regard.

"Father! You are all right?" she exclaimed, at once disbelieving and content. Her hands rested on his arm. Jube enfolded her with simple dignity for a moment. His sober thoughts were unfathomable but his glance lifted briefly to Kincaid.

Valerie disengaged herself and turned toward Kincaid.

She started forward, a hand lifted, and said clearly: "I must thank——"

Trace was before her, his movement fierce. "No!" he declared solidly. His stubborn high face took on a granite look it had not known before. "You won't touch that wolf, and you won't speak to him. And that's final." He put himself in front of Valerie, and he did not see the urgency and the regret which sprang to her face as he turned to Kincaid. His words were a rasping jar:

"Go your way, before it's too late."

Kincaid's anger with Trace was still bright and bitter on his tongue. He saw the dominance of this man standing across his path as Rusty Maxwell saw it: an arrogance that defied resistance. He ripped out: "Pickett ——!" ungovernably, like a threat; and there stopped, overtaken by the uselessness of words. He was aware of Jube Pickett's frowning dissent, of gathering restless railroad men at this spot, and even of the mute, begging supplication on Valerie Pickett's clear features, without looking at them. Abruptly he turned to his pony, prepared to ride out of there.

Jube Pickett broke from his chained fixedness. He started forward, arresting others with a gesture, and called after Kincaid: "Wait. I want to know how this thing happened."

Kincaid, settling into the leather, looked down as Jube neared. There was the darkness of secret thoughts on Kincaid's cheeks; his eyes were sharp. He answered nothing.

"You can't go like that, man!" Jube urged seriously. "You knew that flood was coming—you knew more about it! What was the cause of it? I demand to know."

Kincaid eyed him levelly, then looked away at the brown roily flood in the wash, silent still. But there was no evasion in him. He said, and there wasn't any emotion in his words: "You've got your own idea of the cause of it. If you haven't, you'll never have it explained." He lifted his rein.

Jube turned the color of old leather at this bluntness. He watched Kincaid move deliberately away, and he didn't offer to interfere and didn't speak again.

Kincaid was not surprised that he was able to ride up to join 2 M without so much as seeing the glint of Buck Ewing's guns. Those men were busy along the wash. Half-a-dozen punchers met him below the pines. Quill Hoskins told him, in a curiously triumphant growl: "Wal, Kin—you could've stayed right up here and seen as much as anybody. But I reckon in a day or two we can all jog down to view the remains."

They thought the railroad was done for good. All of them reflected Quill's simple and direct confidence, meeting Kincaid's glance with half-apologetic and wholly gratified grins. To Charley May, Kincaid said: "Charley, hasn't the old man drifted back yet?"

"No."

Kincaid's eyes clouded. "He rode into the hills alone. Wasn't anything done to cover him?" There was a picture in his mind at this moment of French Lesant's sallow and pendulous face, blank with hidden evil.

Charley said uncomfortably, "Well, you know———"

Kincaid turned his pony without delay. "Come on with me," he rapped out. He and Charley passed into the trees at a rapid lope and broke across the open toward the lifting hills.

It was a long ride, a hard ride. Kincaid spared his horse none at all, his lean face drawn to tight alertness. Charley May stuck at his side. The rising trails drew them on and up into heavy growth, where the sun reached only the spiked tips of the pines. They passed along Slide Canyon, smoky and still, and were not far above Mescalero Crossing when Kincaid hauled in and lifted a warning hand. The reaching, hollow echo of a rifle-shot reverberated across this silence and sank deep into the lonely hills.

"I was afraid of this!"

Kincaid raked his pony ahead, straight into the trees toward the high dam a mile or more above, Charley May in his wake.

XIII

CLIMBING the silent hills in mid-afternoon, Rusty
Maxwell found ample and engrossing company in
the thoughts which rode with him. A man used to grappling with the obdurate forces of nature, he had planned
long and coolly the destiny he was to bring crashing down
on the railroad; and with a full knowledge of his weapons,
it was to nature herself that he turned in this hour.

She appeared to rest a benign eye on his activities. The
sloping miles of alternate range and woodland which ran
upward toward frowning Comanche were as well known
to him as to any saddle man in his employ. Never had he
found the ridges quieter or more inviting than today, and
it came over him with a surge which ruddied his skin
that Ben Sharp's aim was treacherous, but that the railroad's ruthless design was piracy: was a strange kind of
civilized insurrection with which he would under no circumstances arbitrate.

And yet Ben Sharp remained his inveterate and deathless foe, and Rusty's mind quested hungrily toward White
Oaks as he jogged upward. There events not unconnected
with Ben Sharp's fortunes by this time had already taken
shape, whether in Rusty's favor or not, and it was too
late for him to hesitate or turn back. It was in his thinking that he could keep from no man what he had done
after it was over; but it had not occurred to him that he,

Rusty Maxwell, need have consulted anyone concerning his own actions.

He passed into and out of piny glens and threaded rock patches with the unhurried deliberation of certitude. Only when he came within hailing distance of the high pond did he alter his usual plodding methods, and this was merely to seek open ground so that the two men whom he had put on guard at the dam since the shooting of his stock had made him wary, might see him in time.

No call came and no welcoming stir broke the silence of this remote spot. Rusty rode on in his ponderous way until he was able to view the dam and the broken rocks round about. Here he sat while his pony switched and jerked its head, and the question he found here fed into and through the mill-stones of his mind. He had told Fred and Breezy what he expected of them. They were to stick in the face of anything—and they were gone. Where?

While Maxwell mused, there came to him the flat crack of a rifle-shot from afar, rolling across these rough hills and shuddering down through the pines. The white head raised and cocked, and the look of his glance turned inward with the earnestness of his listening.

"A mile away," he grunted; "maybe mile and a half." Wrath leaped through him at the thought that his men were hunting, then cooled to the assurance of what, unquestionably, they hunted. "Got jumped," he muttered, nodding; and he pushed his horse in the direction of the sound which by now had died away, yet echoed still in his head.

There was a physical stolidity in Rusty which had no relation to the keenness of his tried and trustworthy faculties. In this rough country he was as cautious as an old wolf. The feeling of heighth was here, but little open ground. Pines ran together in thick groves, rocky ledges and spires broke the swells; ever the land rode upward to attain Comanche's lofty eminence.

Three quarters of a mile north and west of the dam, Rusty drew in again to measure the vast emptiness which hemmed him in. A breeze flowed coolly in these narrow corridors, and down it struck the punctuation of a second shot, near now. Maxwell pushed on. Later he slipped out of the saddle and moved ahead with a vigilant attention.

A voice sang out on his left: "Ho-old on, there . . . Oh," it broke off in a recognizing grunt, and Fred Breen showed himself, rifle in hand. He was a big-chested, broad-browed, square-jawed man with sandy hair and quick, light eyes. Breezy Drake's rifle crashed beyond him, and this time was answered from above, the reverberation striking off the crags.

"Who is that up there?" Rusty grumbled, his hard eye thrusting the question home.

Breen said, "Frenchy Lesant and one of his lean coyotes, Rusty. They tackled us at the dam this mornin'. We run 'em up here and now we've got them cornered."

Rusty ruminated in his careful and thorough way. There rumbled out of him: "Lesant, eh?" Something flickered in his deep eyes, and he added: "Well, hold 'em." He turned back to his pony without further words and climbed laboriously to the saddle. While Fred Breen measured his inscrutable ways, he swung the bay and rode down the way he had come.

High Pond possessed a languid beauty in a wild way. The dam was old now and mossed; a deep, reaching sheet of still water flanked it; just beyond the crowding, gnarled pines, myriads of insects swarmed above the hard reflected shine.

Old Rusty saw none of this. Getting down, he put his attention on the strong, trickle-spouting head-gates. There was no question about it: a tremendous head of water lay packed behind that barrier. An old and rusty crowbar leaned against the stonework of the dam. With this Rusty attacked the buttress-work of the head-gates. The propped, water-logged beams dropped out, one by one. And now, well in the clear, Maxwell began to work out the head-gate sticks.

The first, often removed and replaced, was easy. The dark glossy surface of the water began to crawl forward toward liberty, splashing over the edge. A second beam prized out, that escape increased; with the third, it grew to a torrent which Rusty found more than difficult to deal with. He worked methodically on, his broad jaws clamped. Massed weight, the countless tons of accumulated water here, rushed to this one point. With a sudden splintering boom, as if something exploded under the earth, the head-gates went out completely; and with a savage snarl, High Pond began its wild career down the tortuous course of the Standing Stone, leaping and thundering through the rocky gorge, a white froth in its throat.

As though this burst dam released something of his own fierce passion of youth, Maxwell rode briskly back up toward his men. Fred Breen was gone, but he came sliding out of the trees. He saw the beaded perspiration on Rusty's broad red face and soaking through his shirt, and he said: "Where'd you go?"

Rusty's look was slow. It was Breezy Drake who came up, rifle in hand, to say, with a hard grin: "Knocked the dam plumb out, didn't you?"

Breen barked "What!" incredulously, and Breezy supplied: "I seen the floodwaters flashin' through the trees, from over there." He threw out an arm vaguely. As they stood, a dull and heavy booming rolled up to them, and Drake nodded. "Hittin' Slide Canyon full force now— all of them falls in there . . . Rusty, if you ain't the damnedest man!" There was reserved admiration in his tone, and a query as well.

Maxwell ignored it, pulling the rifle from his saddle-boot. He jerked his chin up the slope, his manner business-like. "They still up there?"

"Sure. What's the dope now, Rusty?"

"We'll get 'em," Rusty said unemotionally.

Breen snorted: "We can't get 'em! They're holed up there in the rocks and it's a stand-off." He scowled as he explained the situation. Lesant and his companion, one Durkin it was believed, were forted up in a position from which it appeared well nigh impossible to dislodge them.

"We'll try," Rusty decided, in a tone much like a mandate.

They drifted through the trees and Breen pointed out the breed's position—so well, in fact, that they drew shots from that quarter and Rusty swore under his breath, slapping at the shower of pine needles sifting down over him after the passage of a rifle slug.

"Ain't much use proddin' them up with lead," Breezy growled, trying for a shot and then shaking his head.

"They're tucked up in great shape, and they even been rollin' a·few rocks."

"Spread out," said Rusty abruptly. "Keep your gun up and your eyes open. I don't propose to fool with these birds. They tried to get you, didn't they?"

"Well, more or less," Breezy threw over his shoulder dryly, moving off.

They set to their task with stout intention. It was hard on Old Rusty, this skirmishing in the brush, coming on top of today's exertions. He pushed ahead with the tight-lipped vigor of a younger man. This was his day, and he rode it as he rode his hunches.

Without success, however. An hour dragged by, and a second lengthened. Maxwell was testy with impatience. The results of his water stratagem were decided by now, he knew; but before he could learn what they were, there was this affair to be settled. And it persistently would not be settled. All movement of the slightest kind within a sixty-yard radius of the nest of rocks sheltering Lesant brought a prompt and dangerous retaliation.

Rusty dropped back in a thunderous mood. It was without surprise that he rose out of the pine scrub and went to meet Kincaid and Charley May, advancing from below, their sharp eyes probing the enigmatic slope.

Kincaid rode on till they met, and then, swinging down, he bent a thoughtful look on Rusty.

"Well?" All Rusty's pent exasperation and suspense got into that explosive word.

Kincaid nodded. "You got your wish," he said. "That head of water swept the railroad out of the old wash to the last splinter."

An expression akin to grim content stole into Old

Rusty's iron visage. Seeing it, Kincaid shook his head. "You couldn't wait, could you?"

"What do you mean?" Maxwell bristled, his white brows lifting with suspicion. "Wait for what?"

Kincaid told him: "You've wasted the best weapon we had. Later on, you could have flooded the railroad right-of-way by three or four feet."

"I've ruined it now," Rusty got out bluntly. "Anyway, using the lower dam would call out the law sharks and run us into a nice tame lickin'." He shook his head intolerantly. He knew that Kincaid's thoughts had been fixed on the Low Lake dam, in the Basin. Never for a moment had Rusty considered letting the South Western Pacific reach that deep into his land.

"Perhaps the two-or-three-month delay in legal intervention might be just the required thing."

Rusty, looking up through lowering brows, was not going to admit himself in the wrong. Kincaid, seeing it, added quietly: "A little more of this, Rusty, and we'll all be explaining ourselves out of a blanket manslaughter charge."

"What?" Rusty snapped. He looked away, his eyes inscrutable, while Kincaid explained about the railroad camp which had been set up in the wash, and the struggles of all those people to escape the flood. Kincaid concluded: "It was a near thing. All their horses were lost as it was."

Rusty had anticipated none of this. He said gruffly: "Anybody drowned?"

"I don't think so. I got down there in a hurry when I saw it coming."

"You, eh?" Old Rusty's stare was fixed for a moment. Then it slid away. He said: "Well, we got work on our hands right here and now," and it was plain he didn't want to talk any more about the railroad or the flood-waters.

"What was all the shootin'?" Charley May asked.

"This Lesant." Kincaid's brows went up, and Rusty continued: "Him and another man. They jumped Fred and Breezy, and the boys run them up here in the rocks."

"What'll you do, boss?" Charley pressed him.

"Smoke 'em out," said Rusty simply.

"Wait." Kincaid eased himself in the saddle and considered. "The three of you," he said reasonably, "have been at them for some time, haven't you? . . . Go back and pound away. They haven't smelt Charley and me yet."

"And so?" Rusty grunted.

"We'll nail them." Kincaid was turning away along the pine slope as he made this calm promise. Maxwell's craggy stare followed him and Charley May for a while, but he did not call after.

Kincaid and Charley made a wide circuit, and in the rising rocks left their horses. Gun in hand, they clambered up where the world opened out below them in tumbled folds running down. They wasted no time, keeping to the crevices. Breath came short, and hands were raw from contact with the naked stone; neither particularly noticed it.

Old Rusty wisely refrained from advertising anything unusual by an increased display of gunfire. Kincaid had to delay for precious minutes, with the evening spreading and lowering over the dense pines below, before a shot from Frenchy Lesant discovered to him the man's exact position. A two-mile circle had been made to reach this point, and they were letting themselves down toward the breed's covert from almost directly overhead.

Shots clattered down there and granite chips showered from a spot near Charley May's head. He sprawled flat and turned wide eyes on Kincaid. "The devils 've spotted us," he murmured in a breath. "We're in a worse position than Old Rusty."

"Wait." Kincaid took his good time, and when he finished his investigations he gave a satisfied nod. "That was a ricochet from the boys." An odd expression crossed Charley May's eyes, and Kincaid said gently: "Better that than the other."

They pushed on. It was now a foot-by-foot advance, letting themselves down the rocks. Brilliant yellow swam up out of the sky, and the pines beyond gave off a kind of dark glow. Kincaid, crouching at the back of a rock slab, turned suddenly and put an arresting grip on Charley May's ankle. Charley stilled. They found themselves hearkening to a secret murmur of voices. Kincaid made a decisive gesture to Charley and inched out over the rock to its edge. A downward glance showed him Lesant and Durkin, crouched in a granite niche protected from every point except overhead. Kincaid thrust his gun over.

"Frenchy," he said, his voice level and low and clear, "I told you this would finally happen."

Lesant, mortally astonished, flung himself over at that voice—too hastily and too awkwardly. As he landed on his back, his elbow struck the rock, numbing itself so that the gun in his fingers clattered free. But the breed had fight in him for all his bulk and his treacherous nature. His other hand flashed across like a darting snake. Too

late! for a shot from Kincaid made the dropped gun leap
and clatter into a crevice beyond reach.

"Just make a move, Durkin," Charley May invited,
with deadly amiability. "It'll be your last, but you won't
know it."

Durkin took his hand off the lock of the rifle beside
him as though it were hot. "Thanks," he said dryly. "I'm
not havin' any."

"Not even to please me?" Charley urged, with well-
feigned incredulity. And at Durkin's quick scowl:
"You're bad-tempered, Brazos. I always suspected you of
it."

Lesant, rubbing his elbow, lifted a wicked stare, and
Kincaid called into the evening: "All right, Rusty. You
can come now."

Maxwell and Breen and Drake climbed up to find
Charley May fastening the wrists of the two captives
behind them with their belts.

"Trouble is," Charley complained lightly, "I can't bring
myself to agree to dump these two prize specimens down
a coyote hole, yet I don't feel obligated to do any better
for 'em." He brushed granite dust off the doeskin vest
and glanced inquiringly at Rusty.

But Maxwell eyed these two with short patience, and
it was Kincaid who said: "Where's your horses, Lesant?"

Frenchy was glad enough to tell, his rat-like eyes bright
in the glow of sunset as he watched every move, every
look. When Fred Breen brought the ponies, the breed
had to be bolstered into the saddle. Breezy Drake abused
him: "Hell! You needn't grunt, old terrapin. We're doin'
all the work."

"What are you going to do with us?" Durkin jerked

out nervously; but these men who represented 2 M could feel Lesant's will behind the query, and caught his alert waiting.

"Why take 'em anywhere?" Fred Breen growled.

Kincaid let that sink home, while Brazos Durkin's breath sucked in sharply; then he said: "Tie their legs under the saddles, Fred."

Breen burst out: "Kin, these rats don't deserve anything! They tried to kill us. They tried to rub you out— or Lesant did, anyway." Kincaid said nothing, and Fred, his square face obstinate, did as he was told. Old Rusty stood blocky and unmoved, waiting.

"You and Breezy," Kincaid told Fred, "are taking these two south to the border, and when you get there, shove them across. Don't let them go short of there, and don't make any mistakes. Have you got that?"

Breen kept his head down for a moment. When it came up his eyes were mild. "I got it."

A moment later the quartet, prisoners and guards, rode away together. Rusty Maxwell snorted and wheeled away. Kincaid, still watching, saw the jaunty set of Frenchy Lesant's shoulders even through the grossness of the man. His eyes narrowed briefly and then cleared. Whatever nefarious trail Lesant rode in the future, Santa Bonita would never lay eyes on him again.

Charley May returned with his and Kincaid's horses. With Old Rusty, they turned down the hills in the fading glow. Maxwell would not talk, and Kincaid was thinking. Charley dropped back, rolling a smoke. Rusty slanted a look at his range boss and said: "How'd it go in White Oaks?"

"I did what you wanted done. I rode the railroad stock

from forty down to thirty-two. Then it came back to thirty-eight——"

"How's that?" barked Rusty.

"But Ben Sharp," Kincaid continued, "threw a good hundred and seventy-five thousand in to save the market." His glance was acute. He saw Maxwell subside. "Of course you know I dropped better than fifty thousand of your money, on the rise," he added.

Rusty grunted, "That's all right." He had no more to say on the ride down into 2 M. Two miles from the ranch-house, Kincaid pulled out. He murmured: "I'll go down to the *rincon* now," and pushed off. Charley May went with him.

Kincaid was not surprised to find fires built in the pines overlooking the old wash. 2 M's crew watched down there desultorily, but it was largely a matter of form. Dal Waidler told Kincaid: "They're holdin' their ground, Lance; Ewing's men and all. The water's practically run off, and from what we could see, it left things in a complete mess . . . The construction gang's camped on the edge of the wash now, but I've got the boys persuaded they'll pull out by mornin'."

Kincaid reserved his opinion of this, making an inspection. To Gurley, Kernan, Andy Stroud and others he gave orders to tighten up their vigilance. "This isn't done yet," he warned them quietly. "We can't have Ewing springing a raid, much as he'd like to." They listened to him without dissent. The fires burned to coals, and as night thickened, the men were back at their posts.

Two hours later, Kincaid found Fred Breen and Breezy Drake at Spring Cabin. Apparently there was nothing unusual in their seeking something to eat here, but Kincaid said curtly: "You didn't take Lesant and Durkin very far."

Breezy glanced sidelong, and his cross-thrown look was a sharp thing. "They won't be back," was all he said.

Meanwhile, at the ranch, Rusty ate a prodigious supper and retired to his office, cigar in mouth. He had recovered his poise and was at peace with himself, and he had settled to an hour's casting up of accounts when a stir in the yard caused him to look up.

The house was lit up tonight, and broad yellow beams fell across the yard. Rusty gazed past the open door of the office without the power to move for that one moment, and his jaw dropped. Was this a ghost that he looked at? Out there in his yard was Ben Sharp getting off his horse.

XIV

OLD Rusty dropped the tally-book propped in one calloused hand and jumped to his feet, his cigar falling to the floor unnoticed. He moved at times like a rolling bear, but agility of a ponderous kind was in him as he got to the stone gallery in three strides.

A luminous glow filled all the yard, closed in by the dark sky; but Ben Sharp's angular form and his face were plain in the yellow bars of light flung across the dust. A turgid rage jerked his bony body this way and that.

Maxwell gave him no time to vent his imperious spleen. He rumbled: "Forty years ago I told you never to set foot in my yard. That still goes!" And he hurled his hate and his contempt against the other man with implacable energy.

Ben Sharp shambled forward a few feet, dragging up defiance from the core of his vitriolic being. Fury shook him like a terrier.

"Maxwell," he droned, in a kind of choking intensity; "you roped me into this railroad smash——"

"Caught in your own trap, eh?" Rusty flashed back.

There was a glaring, naked enmity between these two that set up an undercurrent across the night-enfolded ranch yard like the sullen rumble of thunder behind the horizon. Their heavy-toned, headlong words might have been forked lightning.

In the clear light from the office, Ben Sharp's eyes held a deathless flash and glow, red, baleful, like the glare in the eyes of a beast of prey. He could not see Old Rusty's face except as a pale blot; but Maxwell's big form made a clean-cut outline on the edge of the gallery.

Ben blurted: "When you turned that water loose it went down Grade Canyon and it washed away my barns and corrals. I'm here to do something about it!"

The mounting hatred of the years could not bear much more. The moment stretched between them with the tautness of strung wire; both men were caught in its fierce compulsion. Old Rusty's deliberate and quite mirthless chuckle rumbled up from his depths, and it touched a spring in his old foe. Sharp ejaculated unintelligibly and his thin arm jerked as he went for his gun. Rusty was not far behind him.

Orange flame leaped thunderously across the dust. It seemed to Maxwell that fire raked through and through him, and an insuperable lassitude that relaxed his muscles but not his hate fought its way through his brawny frame and pierced his vitals. A leg gave away. He had fired three shots, fixing on that white and blazing face opposite; on his wavering knee he fired his fourth and fifth, resisting now with grim intent the buck of the gun. Then something ripped loose in him unwarningly. He was in the dust on the edge of the gallery, an ungainly sprawl. He gasped, only to draw searing heat into his lungs. He struggled to rise, stared—to see Ben Sharp on his hands and knees, his head heavy; trying to lift that gun, and failing. Ben Sharp was ham-strung.

Rusty started a great laugh, a stentorian laugh, of mingled triumph and sharply rising indifference, in the midst of which, a long ways off, there came to him the flutter of hurrying feet and high-pitched voices; and then abruptly he knew no more.

Smoke Givens was the first to reach the scene. "Gawd's flamin' chariot!" he babbled fervently, in accents of awe and fright, as he surveyed the results of the gun-fight.

Rusty Maxwell, doughty and undefeated old warrior that he was, lay half on his back, his broad face and his sightless eyes plain in the golden splash of light from the office door. Light he would never behold again.

Twenty feet apart, Ben Sharp was a crumpled heap in the ranch yard. One twisted arm poked up, the sharp elbow jutting. But he too, was quite dead.

Women and two or three half-grown youths came at a run out of the gloom of this night. It was Mame Waidler who turned Ben Sharp over, stared briefly, and then grunted: "Humph! So this is what it all come to!" But she was not indifferent to what so violent a wrench would mean to her world. "Jimmy!" she commanded her eldest son, a freckled, thirteen-year-old replica of Dal Waidler, already stocky; "get you that Stocking pony of yours, right away! You've got to ride down and tell Lance Kincaid and Daddy and the rest what's happened. Tell them to come quick. Hurry, now!"

Half-an-hour later Jimmy Waidler was led to Kincaid in the darkness of the pines. Men gathered, silent and impressed, while the boy stammered out his story.

"Tell us everything plain, Jim," Dallas Waidler directed his son. "You're real sure, are you, that Rusty's gone—gone for good?"

"Ye-yes," Jimmy got out. "There wa'n't a twitch or flicker in him, Pa."

Kincaid was glad of this obscuring gloom. He felt his lean face drawn and pinched with the suddenness of the news. His hard eyes stung with a sorrow that could not flow. Old Rusty, with his pugnacity and his great endurance, a largeness of heart such as few of these men would ever know again—gone forever. It left him, Lance Kincaid, in a position of full responsibility; but that was the least of his heavy thoughts as, with half-a-dozen quiet and subdued men, he rode in the direction of 2 M headquarters.

Buck Ewing sat on the porch at the Jingle-bob ranch, smoking a contemplative cigaret. Donita had not come out to him yet, but with the thoughts he had to keep him company, Ewing was in no hurry.

He had been a daily visitor here since old Ben had been laid away. Donita now seemed a different person, quieter and more reflective. But it was not this change in her that held Ewing's circling thoughts, but the fact that Donita was now the mistress of a fifty thousand acre ranch.

She had always appealed to him in a way that was totally new to his experience, a way he could not fathom. And there was nothing in her new status that made her any less desirable. Fifty thousand acres; thousands of dollars invested in one thing and another. The thought kept intruding on Buck, even as did the thought that between them, Kincaid and Donita owned an empire beyond even the dreams of a range hog such as Rusty Maxwell.

It aroused Ewing's cupidity. Part of it might be his

except for Kincaid. The expression on his strong, carved face flattened as he mused on.

"The idea is bound to hit them," he reflected bleakly. "Things being what they are, who wouldn't want to throw together?" His long lips hardened. "But they'll never throw these ranches into one under my eyes," he promised himself dourly.

He was fixed on that, unshakeably. "Kincaid's got to go," he knew. And he must be removed while there was time.

It was just here that a hitch occurred in Ewing's cogitations. Schooled in a long experience of underground motives, he saw his situation clearly. Before, it had been a gun grudge, pure and simple, between himself and Kincaid; an enmity the measure of which had to be poured out in blood. But in his present frame of mind, Ewing's was no longer the insensate flame of hatred such as had carried Ben Sharp to his end along with old Maxwell. The traffic would not bear another slaying of a major figure, for all the violence of the railroad feud; and this time Ewing intended to remain on hand after the smoke had cleared away.

"No," he mused, his dark eyes somber with his thinking; "Kincaid will have to be taken care of another way. And that way's got to be found."

Donita broke in upon him at this point by stepping out on the porch. She had not gone riding for pleasure since her grandfather's death, and she still wore—Ewing suspected because it suited her so well—a close-fitting black frock with free and sweeping lines.

He got up as she joined him, and put all his attention on her. There never had been a time when her scintillant impulses were clearly predictable; and bereavement had taken nothing from her essential capriciousness. Buck was attentive to the point of punctilio in his earnestness; and this for the time appeased Donita and seemed to soften her toward him.

But Ewing felt under a definite strain when at last he left that afternoon late. Care to show Donita none of his sardonic edges was like work for him, and relaxing in all his stern fiber, he did not return at once to the old wash, where the work of rebuilding the railroad was going forward under the protection of his guards. Once more his mind returned to the problem of how to deal with Kincaid, this stumbling-block in his undeviating path, and he rode far. . . .

Dusk found him riding down the old trail toward the deserted buildings of Mescalero Crossing. Frenchy Lesant and his lean, range-hardened jackals had disappeared on the day of Ben Sharp's death. Ewing had never got any explanation, but he needed none; and it was of this circumstance that he was thinking as he neared the gloomy place.

A hundred feet from the old saloon, he drew in abruptly. His pony's hoofs had telegraphed no warning in deep dust, and for this he was thankful; for to his surprise, two ponies were tethered to the sagging rail by the steps. Ewing stared, unmoving, and it was something of a jar to recognize Valerie Pickett's horse there, siding the other.

Ewing backed away and slipped into the trees, prepared to get to the bottom of this. Time was nothing to him. He did not know how much later it was that two figures emerged from the tumbledown saloon to swing up and ride away together, but the sky had begun to thicken with dusk. Ewing did not move from his concealment until they were quite gone, but his features were dark and almost predatory, and the blood of a revived animosity pounded in his throat. The man who had been spending time at this remote spot with Valerie Pickett was Kincaid.

"Why, damn him!" Ewing grated. "How many women does he expect to play around with?"

For that moment his jealousy was a naked and a bitter thing. It gave away, in time, to crafty thought. His discovery was so much more than he had ever expected that it brought him back another day. For a second time he saw the pair meet here where no one, as they evidently thought, would ever know. More than an hour Ewing watched from a safe covert, turning this thing over in his mind. And now he saw something which he had not dared, before, to grasp too precipitately. He saw his way clear. Riding back to his job by a roundabout way, he perfected, as nearly as possible, the plan which he meant to carry out.

It was raining the following day, when Ewing rode up to the Jingle-bob house and got down—a steady drizzle, one of the first of the fall season, punctuated with occasional downpouring showers. The Jingle-bob outbuildings and corrals had been rebuilt since the floodwaters had carried them away; through the rain, their new pine wood was yellow.

Donita had got used to Ewing's quiet drawl and his following eyes. He found her in the big living-room, littered with bear rugs over hardwood flooring, and tastefully and expensively draped. He was careful about the dampness of his boots, but Donita only smiled, a quick light running across her face.

"Boot tracks mean a man in the house," she said. "You've no idea how used to it I've become, all unawares."

Unaccustomed warmth softened Ewing's habitually cold face. If she could only be got to mean these lightly-dropped remarks he felt he would be content. But today he did not grasp immediately the proffered opportunity to talk about themselves. His comments ran on the railroad work with a persistence that finally conveyed to her the suggestion he desired.

"The railroad will go on, I suppose," she revealed her essential indifference to what it might do. "And Lance has inherited Rusty Maxwell's stubbornness and his determination to preserve 2 M." She wove her slim fingers together, and looked up with those fatally vivacious eyes. "Sometimes I think Lance stood behind Rusty and supported him, he is so firm."

She was devilling Buck in her demure way, and he knew it. His darkening cheeks were a concession to sentiment which Donita could savor; but his words were calculated with the accuracy of an iron reserve. He said: "Kincaid? I think you over-rate him. I don't believe he's worrying about anything." Just the right inflection here, the proper amount of disinterest and conviction.

Donita's smile lessened. "You don't know him, Buck." It was, she felt, out of a profound and wistful knowledge that she herself spoke.

Ewing wisely held out the bait of obdurate silence, and she resumed in a quickening tone: "Why did you say that?"

Buck said evasively, "What?" and she pinned him down. He told her dryly: "Why, I'll admit to having seen Kincaid off the reservation a time or two. Apparently he's meeting someone at Lesant's old place on the Standing Stone. I didn't inquire into it, but what I saw was enough to convince me that our friend hasn't forgotten his fun."

Donita's face had shed all its superficiality of ease. "What do you mean; that he is meeting some—girl at this place?"

Ewing spread his hands, as much as to say, "What could you expect?" But his black gaze never left Donita's revealing features, and he found himself confronted by thoughts he had not expected. He felt that he knew what proof of the meetings between Kincaid and Valerie Pickett would mean to her; and, torn two ways, he hoped that she would verify it, and contrarily, that she would find a sufficient disinterest in the subject to keep her away from Mescalero Crossing.

Donita's next words were metallic. "After all, why shouldn't he?" Her tone jarred Ewing and it jarred herself. Each knew her attitude to be false. She strove to return to naturalness, and her flow of talk, about anything but what was on her mind, was quick and nervous.

She seemed anxious, of a sudden, to be rid of him; and Buck, hard in his own way, was darkly resigned to what it meant—knowing that if she persisted in her intent, the truth would only drive her apart from Kincaid, and, he was certain, toward himself. Yet his face was somber under the stress of this necessity when, half-an-hour later, he took his leave. Closing the door behind him, he heard the swift clatter of Donita's heels as she ran upstairs to don her riding clothes. Later still, with the afternoon closing in toward evening, regardless of the moisture which ran down his flat cheeks, Ewing watched from the screening pine-fringe of a neighboring ridge as Donita ordered up a pony, mounted it and set off at an urgent canter in the direction of Comanche, high but almost obscured in the gauzy veils of rain which thickened and grayed the air.

Kincaid slid out of the saddle before Lesant's old saloon and climbed to the porch. On its edge, shaking the heavy drops of rain from his slicker, he paused to scan his surroundings. It would soon be twilight. Scraping gray clouds and dripping, somber pines made this glen depressingly gloomy. The Standing Stone had fallen to a monotonous murmur over those black rocks, and every dusky covert looked drenched. Kincaid measured all this, and shook his head slightly. It was unlikely that Valerie would ride here on such a day.

The unplanned informality of these meetings had been preserved. The first had been purely accidental; they remained casual, so that Kincaid had not been moved to ask if he should expect her on any given day. They met here, if at all, at the same hour, however; and it was already hard upon that time.

A few minutes later, as Kincaid's thoughtful glance rested on his rain-soaked pony, the soggy splash of hoofs raised that glance in a deep anticipation. Valerie Pickett rode down to the ford on the other side. She did not wave and did not call out, but under the protecting brim of the Stetson her face unmistakably brightened.

As Kincaid helped her out of the saddle, she landed

with a lithe spring and then looked up with the glow of full confidence.

"Rather wet," he smiled.

"Isn't it! But good for the range, wouldn't you say?"

They spoke with ease, these two; almost with absence, and the thoughts of neither were on their words as they stepped inside.

It was dark here, until Kincaid lit a candle-end, and for others might have been repelling. Frenchy Lesant's fixtures had not been dismantled, but the liquors and a few portable remains of the saturnine breed had long since mysteriously vanished. Rain water penetrated more than a few spots in the dubious roof, and a steady dripping hollowly echoed and permeated this place with a deeper, melancholy silence and desertion.

Arranging her hair with deft fingers, Valerie said lightly: "My piano is receiving its baptism."

Kincaid chuckled and wrenched the instrument out from under the drip along the wall. He swept its top with an old rag, and dried its keys. Valerie struck a chord, and another, and sat down before the piano, her white fingers lingering on the time-stained keyboard. She swung softly into melody, quaintly off-tone.

Kincaid, watching her lighted profile, murmured: "That evokes ghosts for me. Ghosts that a good tuning would banish."

Her eyes answered him, understanding eyes. They dropped, and the stillness flowed to this gentle river of song, which spoke for them of age-old verities and sober circumstance; with which there was no need of words.

It would have been difficult otherwise to express what these stolen hours meant to them both. That they were, in a sense, conditional opponents, on opposite sides of the railroad struggle; that she represented the strongest principles of the South Western Pacific, he the head of the opposition, with real power behind him, only salted their mutual attraction with zest. But there was more than this. Kincaid found in Valerie something more penetrating, more elemental than charm. There was a potency about her that silence only served to increase, a clear and shining fitness that bade him claim her.

And he could not. There was another fitness that no desire could supersede; a fitness that said this thing was not to be; that soon or late, this trysting-place would be lost to them, and there could be no place for that erect head and those forthright and courageous shoulders in his life.

The depth of his quietness brought her gaze up at length, a warm and confiding message, for this instant charged with a melancholy and a dreaming that took nothing from the day. She said softly, "You seem sad, Lance," and the words released all his stoic will.

His hands were light, they didn't have to insist, as he leaned down and drew her up. The music echoed into dripping silence. Her fingers reached his broad chest and stole on, and when his arms closed about her slim, straight back, they were clamped together by a strength and a pure willingness that made them one. Her lips were firm and fresh and frankly his, and the aroma of her hair wrapped him about and set him outside a world of cares. This was the full measure of a man's wanting. For this long and forgetting moment he was—they were both—gloriously and rightly complete.

Donita Sharp clattered down the stony trail to Mescalero Crossing under a methodical compulsion. Fear rode her. She was wrong, she told herself, and Buck Ewing was wrong; but she had to know.

From the ford she heard the tinkle of the piano—saw these two ponies in the dim light; and her face was drawn and strangely hard. She slid out of the saddle stiffly and went up the steps, as the piano broke off. The hand she laid on the door-jamb was clenched. It did not remain there; she stepped in—stopped.

The dusk here, made golden by the candle, was not thick enough to conceal what she had come so far and so fast to see. Kincaid and Valerie Pickett were in each other's arms before the piano, a distance and an isolation in their faces. They turned, arms still entwined, and saw her standing there, white to the lips, and the moment was long.

"I'm sorry." Donita's voice sounded choked, small. Before either could speak, she was back through the door. When they reached the porch—for something drew them there, with sober expression—Donita was hurrying away through the rain and the descending night, kneeing her pony into a retreat which had become a flight.

XV

VALERIE and Kincaid were more than a little disturbed by this sudden visitation. Only their undoubting belief that no one could possibly know their whereabouts had carried them as far as they had gone. It was like a confirmation of the conviction that nothing enduring could exist between them, to have Donita Sharp break in on them at that precise moment.

The light was almost gone out of the sky and the rain had set in once more, descending heavily. Mescalero Crossing was bleak. But it was not lonely enough to thrust back the persistent thought of what it meant for them to be seen together here.

It was on Valerie that the brunt of any odium for such a discovered meeting must fall, and Kincaid forgot his own position in thinking of her. That she did not resent what had befallen them was plain: her hand lay still inside his arm as they gazed into the rain-drenched, lowering dusk. A little furrow divided her brows and her gaze was serious.

"I shouldn't have allowed this to happen," Kincaid muttered. Something of his regret for any adverse wind which could touch her got into his voice.

Valerie glanced up slowly, her lips parted. She replied quietly: "You were not alone in it," and for all her troubling thoughts her tone was temperate. She added: "I am not sorry."

He was admiring now, but he could not miss the note of finality in this. Something had happened; she was not sorry; yet for all that it was over. The fine balance of these meetings had been irreparably destroyed. The railroad, at first an octopus whose grip they had broken, now rose between them like a ghostly wall. They had barely spoken of it for days, this inhibition on them, but it was in their thoughts always; the feel of it got into their looks and actions and molded their lives.

"I must go," said Valerie, making a restless shift of position. Mistrust of this somber spot got to her at last; her glance at the impenetrable pines was suddenly strong with awareness.

Kincaid had known she would feel this way. Into his reluctance to release her crept honest solicitude. He urged: "Wait a little while. It's raining hard now. I don't want to put a thorough wetting on you too."

She glanced at him plaintively. There was the same all-pervading compulsion on her that he stood under, strong and clear; but emotion had taken another direction now, and the bond between them was wistful. They stood silent, thinking their thoughts.

The thoughts of youth are long, long thoughts; it was deep dark, and the rain still poured down with unhurried abundance, when they turned back to enter the old building; for the damp air in this enclosed canyon bore a raw edge.

A hundred yards away, enfolded in dense shadow, Buck Ewing sat his saddle. He was unprotected from that downpour among these slant-roofed pines except for inadequate slicker and Stetson, but he sat erect and nodded his head with cold satisfaction as he saw the forms of those two darken the faintly glowing door once more.

Ewing had got to this place ahead of Donita. He had watched her fevered approach with pity and with chagrin; and while he had no other way of telling what transpired within Lesant's old walls when Donita entered, the manner of her precipitate emergence told him all that he required to know. It meant much to him. Donita, it appeared plain, must have satisfied herself for good and all on the subject of Kincaid. Unadmirable as he found his own course, Ewing at least had the practical assurance that he had succeeded in extinguishing her infatuation for the man.

But he was not content with this. Besides the deep-coursing spite he bore Kincaid, there was a thin blade of amazed scorn for the Pickett girl. It came to him that if he could drive a wedge into her armor and perhaps send her fluttering back to her place with a good scare, then Kincaid's discomfiture would be complete. It was no more, Ewing reflected with grim logic, than making the most of the cards which had been dealt him.

Accordingly, he pushed out of the trees and rode forward. Rain rumbling on the roof of the saloon deadened the rumor of his coming, and he mounted to the porch and put himself in the door before Valerie and Kincaid became aware of him. The surprise on his face was vague as he gazed first of all at the lighted candle.

Seeing that high and saturnine face, Valerie made a sound that was neither a movement nor an attempt at speech. It was one of those signals of startlement which cannot be dissembled. She was standing in a dry area near the back of the room, Kincaid a little before her. Kincaid's flat muscles flexed in a tension that was deeply instinctive; his face froze the crowding thoughts that swept the room like a tornado, and for a long moment the murmurous quiet here was heavy and false.

Buck Ewing's mild voice was suave. He said, "Why, this is a surprise. I expected no one here, and the light puzzled me." He turned his features so that the yellow candle-gleam struck his long cheek blandly, and in this waiting pause he remarked further: "The storm's pretty bad—thought I'd get out of it. I suppose you are doing the same thing." And his dark eyes made bold to find humorous the assortment they made.

Valerie broke from that fixed poise, and she put her words between them with calm exactitude. "We were just going," she said, as the rain made a perceptibly lighter drumming on the roof.

Buck's brows lifted, and his gesture was off-hand. "Another minute or two—" he protested easily. His politeness was flawless, and so pointed that it brought a flush to Kincaid's lean cheeks.

"I'm going back myself," Ewing said to Valerie. "Perhaps you'd like me to see you to the car."

"I'll do it," Kincaid thrust the flat statement into their sparring. He was deeply distrustful of Ewing, knowing the man's enmity; reading his profound and exigent change since their last meeting. That Ewing's object here was not what it appeared could scarcely be doubted, and for Kincaid the odor of evil was stronger than ever. Only Valerie's presence prevented him from rolling his will against Buck Ewing to the full, for it did not escape him even now that Buck should be familiar with the old haunt of Frenchy Lesant.

Ewing's swinging, steady glance read all this and behind it the leap of his strong desire to reply in kind was plain. But Valerie interposed: "Thank you, Mr. Kincaid. But I think it would be wiser if I returned home with Mr. Ewing."

Kincaid inclined his head submissively. He had, it struck him, brought sufficient upon her without adding to it in this instance. He believed he was saying good-by to her; and that with that embrace and that kiss which Donita Sharp had interrupted, the best of all that lay between them had been attained and culminated. The rest—his desire now to talk, to cling for a little while to what he knew he must lose—was anticlimax.

None of them had any desire to prolong this stiff impossibility. Ewing mentioned quietly, "I believe the—ah, rain has slacked off," and Valerie, wordless and outwardly composed, slipped into the damp raincoat of which Kincaid had relieved her. It was her eyes which said goodnight to Kincaid as she moved to the door with Buck Ewing at her shoulder, but Ewing showed white, even teeth in a dry smile that said even more. It said: "Now I've got you where I want you, my fine friend," and there was no mistaking this. Kincaid threw up his head in dull anger as the two passed out into darkness.

He poured all his will into his listening as the bottom step out there complained and grew silent, and saddle-leather spoke. Ewing uttered a low word, and pony hoofs sloshed. They moved to the ford and there made a wading gurgle; after which silence returned, as weighty as if it were palpable, and rested on Kincaid's limbs and on his sober, down-tipped face.

And now the clamoring thoughts arose before him and all about him, and he was trying with a straining care to fathom what Buck Ewing would make out of that which he had discovered. That Buck was absolutely ruthless was a major premise. Kincaid was appalled to find that he could no longer afford to scorn Ewing's worst.

"If he lays a word against Valerie," was the burden of his grim conclusion, "there's only one thing left for me to do."

In the meantime, he was forced to face a thousand angry speculations. None of them brought an answer, and at last he extinguished the flickering candle and moved out to his patient horse. The night was thick and enigmatic around him as he rode away.

Trace Pickett seldom finished his paper-work in the engineer's car much before midnight. Tonight, driven in upon himself by the stormy weather, he was cleaned up and on his way back to the private car by nine-thirty.

The heavy sky was lowering and fog threw a reddish, diffused glow over the camp. Trace slipped and stumbled up the wet ties in a disgruntled mood. A muffled cry sounded from down the line, and the endless panting of an engine at rest, and at the car steps a hidden figure lurched down and out of his way. Limp Smail's face was an up-turned blot as he pulled his worn slicker closer about him.

Trace grunted: "Why don't you crawl in?" in a disposing tone, and Limpy snorted:

"Because right here's where I'm s'posed to be. And

if I wasn't, who in tarnation 'd know what was goin' on, anyway?" Limpy had been forced to fight off Trace in a testy way, and sting him to get more than a quarter of his attention, since they had known each other.

"What's going on?"

"Wal—maybe nothin'."

Trace paused on the step. He knew that tone of cagey reserve. "Tell it," he directed tersely. "Isn't the old man in yet?"

"The Major's in the hay," Limpy retorted austerely. And as Trace waited, he added a hesitant: "It's Miss Valerie."

"What about her?"

"Wal—she ain't come in yet." Anxiety fought with the reluctance to betray a confidence in the cracked old voice.

"What!" Trace's tone got large as he stepped down solidly; his quick hand caught Smail's thin arm. "Suppose you tell me the rest of this!"

Limpy now perceived the extent of his lapse. He would have drawn back, but there was no way to turn. Trace Pickett's mounting, imperious will bore in on him. He stammered: "She—she just ain't come back. You leggo of me!"

"Where did she go?" Trace grated compellingly.

"I dunno . . . Ow! I'll tell!" Smail's voice rose. "She's been meetin' somebody at that breed's old saloon above Slide Canyon. That's all I know about it!"

Trace flung him back with an oath, on the instant galvanizing into action. Seething indignation at his sister's folly flung him through the drizzle to the camp corral. His movements were violent, all his weariness forgotten, as he threw saddle on a pony and cinched it home. He was away before anyone observed him. Back at the Pickett car, Limpy Smail nursed his wrenched arm, muttering nervously under his breath and glaring into the darkness.

Trace knew better than to head up the *barranca*. He followed the right-of-way down to 2 M's range boundary and turned north along it. The pony jogged steadily, and he turned up his coat collar. It was even wetter amongst the trees. Here Trace slowed his pace briefly. He was perhaps halfway to Mescalero Crossing and now he began to range upward.

He was in a narrow trail amid scrub pine when he heard some muffled sound ahead which sent him noiselessly and abruptly off the trail. His pony was hidden a few feet from the trail, but he had to crouch over its neck to get behind the scrub growth himself. Here he waited, the greasy rain trickling down his back; but it was not the cold wetness that chilled his spine and set his edgy teeth together.

Two dark shapes took form and neared. Trace raked the obscurity with fierce eyes. It seemed his driving will alone that enabled him to identify Valerie's straight and taut figure—and then the other, Buck Ewing. Trace stiffened.

"Ewing!" What he believed to be the truth knifed through him with that soundless exclamation. The unmitigated gall of the other froze him. He had from the start chafed under Buck's coldly intolerant authority, and now he saw the man's boundless effrontery and that cynical and saturnine face through a curtain of sudden-born rage.

"This is what he believes he can get away with!" Trace whispered. It did not occur to him to question the supposition that Ewing was the man whom Valerie had been riding to meet at that remote and deserted building on the Standing Stone.

They passed by without words in the moment it took for his electric thoughts to shock through Trace. Their dusky forms merged with the night, and for a minute after they had gone Trace hung there, rummaging the darkness and the past with turbulent and smoky wrath.

He stole out, finally; put his pony forward with a leashed haste. Then he was riding the curb again, probing and alert. It was difficult to keep these two within view and within the purlieus of his knowledge, but for several miles he did it. They took the way he had come, down the range-fence; and more than half-a-mile from the railroad camp they came to a pause.

Trace could hear nothing of their words. These were brief, and Valerie rode on alone. Trace saw this and read its meaning, but he had awareness only for the immobile Ewing, sitting his saddle where she had left him. Trace thought, "I've got to let her get well away!" and clamped down on his surging, bitter impetuosity.

After a time, a match flared in cupped hands before Buck Ewing's face, and after that the red fleck of his cigaret brightened and lowered at intervals. When it made a glowing arc to one side and went out on the wet ground, Trace pushed forward, a tension and a fury riding him in this way he could not help.

He had no hope of drawing near to Ewing unobserved. "Ewing!" he called in a guarded and yet unbridled tone.

Ewing's rock-like pose did not alter in the slightest.

He turned toward that stabbing cry and waited. Trace came on swiftly; but something kept him from crowding close against this unpredictable and lawless man; something that was not fear, but had no relationship to confidence.

"Well?" Buck queried in his dry, forbidding tone, and the warning here was clear.

Trace burst out furiously: "Damn you, Ewing; what do you mean by taking my sister to that hole in the hills— meeting her there? You've taken too much on yourself this time!——"

"Never mind." Ewing's flat and hard defiance flowed across this interval of night with a physical impact. All his lethal vigilance was uppermost.

"By God, I will mind!" Trace's flaming hatred gushed in bright illumination. "You may be considerable of a man—but there's still some things you can't do! Right this very now is where I put you in your place, you hound!"

"Pickett!——" Ewing rolled out.

"The hell you say!" Trace raged. "I'm going to smash you!" And he rammed his pony madly forward.

Flame split the enfolding blanket of obscurity at Ewing's waist, and the flat crack of his gun racketed into the padding mist. Trace was caught totally by surprise in his blind ranting; he folded out of the leather with a sighing "Huh!" and his pony jumped sidewise a few steps and so stood.

Ewing waited in his impassive way. It had begun to rain again, the drops beating down with heedless, drumming regularity, but he wondered if the shot had been heard at the railroad camp. He knew what he had done, knew finally and completely, and had already moved beyond it in his thinking. But it was not his way to rush anything. And so with deliberate movements he got down and determined in a brief examination that Trace Pickett was dead.

"He is," he mused bleakly; "and—" he paused to stow the sack away as he rolled another smoke—"I didn't do it."

Ambiguous as this might be, it was clear to himself. Lighting his smoke inside his slicker, and holding it cupped, he proposed to know definitely whether his shot was to be investigated forthwith. It took iron nerve, but Ewing had plenty of it: he stuck it out. And when that second smoke was ground finally ino the soil, he knew what he meant to do.

No sound visited the smooth surface of the night, nor had any during that long five minutes. He was safe for this time at least. Methodically, he picked Trace up and flung him across the saddle of his horse. His belt caught over the pommel sufficed to hold him there. Ewing made sure that nothing was left lying on the ground, and then he swung into his own saddle, and leading the extra horse, turned away from there.

Riding back toward Mescalero Crossing, Ewing relaxed nothing of the vigilance which had made him what he was. Somewhere in this wide and enfolding night, Kincaid was riding; but this, for once, was right and proper. Buck would not have had it otherwise.

His approach to Lesant's old place was circumspect to a degree. The candle, he saw, was out; and when, five minutes later, he thrust his head silently in at the swinging back door, he judged from the thinning scent that no one had been here for an hour at least. He dropped caution for celerity.

Trace's horse he tied to the rack before the steps, where he meant to leave it; the rain would obliterate all tell-tale tracks, but this horse, here, told its own story. Trace himself, Ewing carried inside the building and arranged carefully on the floor, seeing that his gun, unfired, was in his holster and that all else was as it should be.

"If that doesn't look like murder," Ewing mused, stepping back to survey his handiwork, "I simply don't know my own business."

A moment later he was in the saddle and riding quietly and secretly away.

XVI

WHEN Valerie Pickett opened her eyes against the gray of morning it was not to put sleep behind her. She had rested little and poorly. Since she had left Buck Ewing to hurry back to the car the night before, her frame of mind had been no easy one. The face of Donita Sharp had not left her thoughts since the girl had burst in on herself and Kincaid; and Ewing, never a graceful figure in her sight, bulked larger and more ominous than ever.

What would they do? After a time Valerie changed the form of this reiterating question. What could they do? But she did not honestly want the full answer to this, and she strove to thrust it away from her.

She did not blame Kincaid for what had happened. She was only regretting that this thing should have overtaken them both; and as she made ready to meet this day with what serenity she might, she could not avoid asking herself what it held in store for each of them.

It was not long before she received an inkling. Her father found her in the dining compartment and said, "Good morning, daughter," with his usual good cheer. His eye sought Trace's empty chair, however; before he sat down to his coffee he walked back to knock at Trace's own compartment. There was no answer to his summons and he looked in. He was back in a moment, to say to

Valerie: "You didn't tell me that Trace had already gone out this morning."

"I didn't know that he had, Father."

Jube looked at her for a moment. Without more words, then, he turned toward the platform of the car. From there he hailed a stout man moving by: "Bill. Find my son, will you, and send him along for his breakfast."

Bill Wiles scratched his stubbled fat cheek. He didn't move. "Ain't seen Trace this mornin', Major. I don't believe he's crawled out yet, has he?"

Jube straightened, his chin coming down. He said abruptly: "Go and tell Limpy Smail I want him, Wiles. I believe he's in his bunk."

Valerie caught this, coming slowly out. "What is it, Father?" she asked.

"Trace seems to be away somewhere. Perhaps he left for White Oaks last night. Limpy will know."

They stood there on the platform, waiting. The slow steps which crunched forward to pause here were not those of the old watchman. Something nameless visited Valerie; she was suddenly cold as Buck Ewing looked up with his dark half-smile. "Good morning," he said quietly.

Jube answered him. They were still talking early morning routine when Limpy stumped forward with Wiles, the camp boss. Ewing fell silent and moved unobtrusively aside, and Smail lifted his vague face inquiringly to Pickett.

"Limpy, did Trace tell you he was going to leave for somewhere last night?"

Something flashed across Limpy's face and was gone. It left him serious, his gaze blank. "Why—seems to me he did, now," he stammered. "Where was it he went?" he asked himself.

"Come, come! Surely you remember a little thing like that." Jube was urgent.

Limpy hung back. His eye darted to Valerie and then to Buck Ewing, and he reddened. "Wal, now; it was—" He attempted to brighten. "That's right! He said he'd maybe take a ride over to that old place on Mescalero Crossin'." He looked candid and obliging. "I didn't ask no more."

Jube's expression was amazed. "Lesant's! What on earth for?" he barked.

Limpy didn't know. As to the time, he thought it might have been nine-thirty or ten o'clock; he wasn't sure.

A constriction crawled up Valerie's throat at these revelations. Her brother Trace heading for Lesant's saloon on the Standing Stone! The significance of this crashed through her. It seemed the world at large had suddenly got wind of the clandestine meetings at Mescalero last night and begun to converge on the spot. What had Trace learned to send him there?

Jube guessed none of these things; he remained mystified and testy. He told Wiles: "There may be something in this. Have a man saddle my horse at once. Half-a-dozen of us will ride there. Ewing, you'll come too; pick out another four men to go with us."

Limpy Smail quickly declared his intention of going, and even Bill Wiles had a sober look as he set off on his errand; but Valerie turned back into the car hastily. A new aspect of the situation suddenly sprang at her: It was incredible that Trace should go to Lesant's remote saloon late at night unless he knew the truth. And he had not come back.

Glancing out of the window a moment later at the sound of hoofs, Valerie saw her father, Ewing, and four of the Jingle-bob riders starting away. Limpy's shrill desire to go had been overridden; and Bill Wiles had seen fit to remain behind also. She did not want to follow the men in her thoughts; something told her to refrain, to stamp out Mescalero Crossing from her remembrance; but during the several hours of tense waiting, she could conjure up nothing else, and she started expectantly at every sound she thought heralded their return.

When they did come back, she heard nothing until she was attracted by a number of voices outside the car. She went to see, and found her father, Ewing and the others standing there while two men unfastened a tarpaulin-wrapped bundle from a jaded horse. Valerie was outside in a moment.

"Father—where is Trace; didn't you find him?" She did not know what to think, and the steady timber of her voice was a defense.

Jube put a comforting and protecting arm around her, and with the other hand gestured toward that object being taken off the horse. "Trace has been killed," he said, simply and huskily.

Valerie went utterly pale, and an inward-turning vagueness came to her eyes. "Trace—killed?" she faltered. "But how did it happen?" A dread she did not care to identify overshadowed her shocked thinking. She had a fleeting vision of Kincaid and put it from her. Surely some explanation of this thing would be forthcoming. She stood here with her face unchanging, gazing at her father's grim visage.

Jube did not answer her question. He patted her shoulder and quietly directed the two men to carry Trace's body into the car until it could be taken to White Oaks for burial. As it went up the steps, Limpy Smail appeared once more, his weathered face dismayed.

Jube said to him: "Limpy, my son has been murdered. I believe you know more than you've told about this affair. What is it?"

Valerie fastened her eyes on the little man fascinatedly.

Limpy swallowed. He swiftly measured these stern faces in a supplicating way, and his glance touched last and longest on Valerie herself. He was under the greatest reluctance to speak. Finally he managed: "Major, I—I'd rather not say!"

"Nonsense! You can't hold anything back now, man!"

Limpy moved restlessly, under some secret compulsion; it came to Valerie wildly that he was edging away from Buck Ewing—he was afraid of Ewing.

"What did you and Trace have to say to each other last night?" Jube bored in impatiently.

"I—well, we . . ." Limpy got desperate, his eyes white. He blurted: "I told him Miss Valerie wasn't in yet. I wish to God I'd kep' my mouth shut!"

Jube's gray face was unchangeably firm. "And what was said that sent him to Mescalero Crossing?"

"Aw—" Smail foundered; then flashed: "I told him Miss Valerie was meetin' somebody up there."

Valerie saw the net inexorably tightening. She exclaimed: "This is impossible!" in a small voice; and instantly she perceived with a touch of horror just how possible it all was.

Jube had fixed on Limpy with unshakeable intent. He said sharply: "How did you know that any such thing was the case?"

Limpy's spirit seemed to crouch in the shadow of Buck Ewing's bland and dark and waiting face. Only when Pickett rapped out, "Tell us!" did he manage to mutter: "Ewing told me."

Valerie's breathing stopped for this moment; she felt stifled and hemmed in. She had, she knew now, expected all of this; and a flash of deep-reaching indignation against Buck Ewing came to her support.

Jube's slow glance, fiery now, and not to be gainsaid, found its way to Ewing. "Ewing," he asked, "is this true?"

Buck said unequivocally, "It is;" and Valerie's heart sank. Her father turned to her.

"What have you to say, daughter?" His tone was gentle, but it was still commanding. "Were you with someone, up there in the hills last night?"

Wordless, Valerie nodded once. Her gaze did not waver. She was pleading silently and strongly with him; but for this time, he dared not see this. His level voice went on: "Who was it, Valerie?"

And now she was face to face with the thing she had feared. Buck Ewing's flat and unrepentant look was fastened on her; all these men were looking at her with a fixed and straining attention. She had to say something. She said, in an odd voice, a cold and unreal voice: "I do not care to say."

A pulse beat in Jube's forehead. He exclaimed: "Do

you realize your brother's been killed? You've got to speak!"

She only stared back, waiting for this mad moment to pass.

"I'll speak for her," said Ewing shortly, with a bold indolence. "It was Kincaid. If any further evidence is needed, Miss Sharp can supply it. She tells me she saw the man with your daughter at the ford last night, as I did."

This totally unexpected revelation of Valerie's intimacy with the man who stood at the head of 2 M floored Jube Pickett. His lean face went mahogany colored. Valerie, seeing that stark pain, cried lowly: "This is terrible! I can't stand any more of it!" But she stood rooted to this spot.

In the heavy silence, Buck Ewing proceeded suavely: "It's plain enough what happened. Kincaid is the man who killed your son."

Valerie said violently: "No, no, no!" and her sight darkened, her temples throbbed. She hated Ewing with her whole being.

"What makes you so sure, Ewing?" Jube's tone was heavy.

Ewing composedly told how he had reached the Crossing last night in the storm, and who he found there; how he had left with Valerie, and Kincaid had remained behind. "We didn't know about Trace, and didn't see him. He must have arrived later; they had words, and you know the result." He added shrewdly: "Kincaid is no fool. He knew what this would mean to the building of the railroad."

Haggard but stoic, Jube followed these words with

care. He realized their logic. His gray head shook. "This thing won't be dropped," he said. "I wanted to build this railroad and I'm doubly determined now . . . It will be impossible to swear out a warrant for this Kincaid in his own county, but I propose to get an arrest in another direction."

No one could miss the accent here of grim and unswerving purpose.

Sitting at Rusty Maxwell's desk, in the warm hour of early afternoon, Kincaid found himself musing on many things. He had completed the work he had to do, but he sat on; and there was with him, as always now, the full weight of his responsibility. It was a loyalty of mixed motives, he was aware; for not always were the land and the men the same thing.

Kincaid was still resolved that the South Western Pacific should not be built across 2 M. Thus far Old Rusty's tall spirit stood behind him. But there was no longer a secret feeling of dissent against Maxwell's course of action. It had come out into the open. Kincaid had made it plain to all that Rusty's harsh ways were not necessary.

The railroad was coming on again. The damage done by the flood had been erased; all danger of a repetition had been removed. The old wash was once more the scene of hectic activity as the rails retrieved lost ground with the inching inevitability of a boa constrictor.

Over all this in his mind, was Kincaid's knowledge that he stood accused of Trace Pickett's murder. Word of it had come back from White Oaks on the day of Trace's funeral; and it had been all that one man could do to prevent 2 M's retaliatory descent on the railroad gangs without delay. Kincaid bore the brand of false accusation without trouble, but many times he asked himself what had overtaken Valerie in the days since he had last seen her, and what was in her mind—whether she believed this of him. Siding it was the inward assurance that Jube Pickett would do something about the matter; that he had done something.

Accordingly it was without surprise today that Kincaid glanced past the office door to recognize the gray uniform of a state ranger. He got up at once and stepped to the door; this man was known to him.

Captain Ab Winters got out of the saddle easily. He came forward with a loose stride, a tall man, well set up. "Hello, Kincaid," he said without inflection.

They shook hands. Kincaid told him: "Come in and sit down."

Winters paused there at the door, and his eye took in without particular favor the half-dozen men ranged carelessly in the shade of the gallery. He told Kincaid, in a low aside, "Tell those boys to move on, Lance."

Kincaid glanced them over, his eye quizzical. "I can't see that they'll bother us, Ab. Let them stay . . . Have a seat. I guess I know why you're here."

Winters paused still, his visage inscrutable. Then he shrugged, coming in; and he responded in a matter-of-fact way: "I don't know whether you do or not. But I can set you right." He had iron-gray hair and firm, weather-roughened skin; but meeting that undeviating gaze and hearkening to the quietly decisive voice, no one ever thought to set him down for an old man.

"I've moved into this fight," he declared in his plain way, "with half-a-dozen men, Kincaid."

Kincaid's brows rose. His tone was soft, and he kept his eyes on his desk. "So that's the way of it, eh? Acting under the Governor's orders, I suppose."

Winters' face went a little set. He did not lose his aplomb. On the contrary. "If I know what you're thinking," he said, "you're entirely wrong. Don't make the mistake of explaining my actions to yourself by anything you've ever experienced before, and you'll save that much confusion. My men," he went on, "are not proposing to take sides, one way or another. But you can depend on it that we'll make certain there's no more lead-slinging from anybody."

Kincaid was still intent on his desk. He raised his eyes speculatively, letting them ride across the ranch-yard and beyond; but his mind was strictly on the job.

"Plain words, Ab," he said slowly. "I don't suppose anyone could misinterpret them."

"Not before me," Winters took him up. "What I do propose," he stated, "is to see that the law is observed. I have no interest and no concern in this feud Old Rusty saw fit to start. He was a big man, and my friend, but I can't follow him there; and neither will you, Lance. This range war foolishness has got to stop. If the railroad company stays within its rights, it will be okay with me, and it'll have to be with you." He broke off and put his direct glance on Kincaid in a waiting way.

Kincaid's faint smile was not humorous; it was more expressive than that. He spread his hands, and Ab Winters nodded briefly.

"Just so we understand each other," he murmured.

Kincaid, at least, understood only too well. It meant an enforced policy of hands-off as far as 2 M was concerned, and that meant eventual and certain defeat. The prospect of seeing the South Western Pacific come on without possibility of hinderance left him without a word to say that could convey other than his sense of overpowering chagrin.

"It looks like it will put us out of the fight," he said with an effort; and there rose before him a vision of the price 2 M had already paid—lives lost, even to old Rusty's. It was bitter.

"Maybe that's true," Winters said reasonably; "but in one way it isn't so bad for you. I've got a warrant here for your arrest for murder. It won't be like I was taking you out of a fight you had a chance to win."

So it had come—what he had expected. And yet Kincaid felt a leaden weight descend upon his spirit with the definite knowledge. He had failed, and he had failed greatly. Old Rusty would have turned over in his grave at the deep mark which Ben Sharp in one way or another had laid across 2 M.

He came back to the immediacy of these affairs in his steady way, saying: "Ab, I understand you've been having a look around Lesant's old place, the past couple of days. Have you any idea that I killed Trace Pickett?"

Winters was particular with his words. He didn't want to get into argument about a matter in which he had nothing to say, and he knew Kincaid too well to be brusque with him. He said: "It won't be my ideas that count. There's a pretty strong case of circumstantial evidence against you at the present time. How soon will you be ready to leave?"

Kincaid rose to do what he must do. He said, "It won't take me any time to speak of. We can start in five minutes." And he turned to an inner door and stepped through; and Winters, with a mien of alert gravity, rose to follow him and then sat down again where he was. But he listened with more than ordinary care to the casual sounds of this big ranch which floated in to him. The slow murmur of those men outside on the gallery ran on unchanged, but this did not reassure him. Smoke Givens' Southern drawl came through from deeper in the house, and the feeling of unexpectedness here was strong. Then the deliberate steps returning this way, and Kincaid stood in the door.

"We can start now," he said.

Winters got up with his briefly approving nod. Starting through the door with Kincaid at his side, he was not amazed to see these casual 2 M men standing in a loose semicircle with their guileless glances all turned this way.

Charley May stood here, his six-gun slanting at his supple hip, and Kincaid addressed him: "Charley, I'm leaving 2 M in your charge while I'm away."

Charley May said expressionlessly, "Okay, Lance." But Andy Stroud spoke with an inflection that made the ranger lay a hard and careful scrutiny on him.

"Where you figuring to go, Kin?" Andy said.

Kincaid told them all: "I'm under arrest for murder, and I don't know how long it will hold. I'm expecting you to look to Charley the same as you would to myself or Old Rusty." His voice held just a shade of sharpness.

Andy Stroud said: "Hell! Why let them get away with this, Lance?" There was a quick violence in him, and a suppressed anger. "We'll take you plumb away from this man, if you'll just say the word."

Ab Winters stilled and waited. This was in the line of duty for him, little as he liked it; he was prepared to carry it through. But Kincaid shook his head with a small smile.

"Don't make any play with Ab, boys," was what he said. "You wouldn't have a chance."

A minute later he and Winters rode away in this deep and sun-drenched silence.

XVII

SAM MILLS, the engineer Jube Pickett advanced to Trace's position as superintendent of construction, was a sound man, a business-like man. With the rebuilding of the track torn out by the floodwaters, Trace had been thrusting the work along vigorously; and Mills did not let up. This briskness of progress went farther to assuage Jube's bitterness of feeling about the death of his son than anything else could have done.

The work was not easy. The violence of the waters which Old Rusty had released had torn out everything, including the roadbed. Moreover, the right-of-way had been gullied deep; it presented problems for the scrapers which Jube himself oversaw, and for hours he had the tie wagons hauling dirt from the wash's banks.

Despite the strategic disposition of Ab Winters' rangers along the *barranca*, Buck Ewing's thirty or more gun guards were still on the scene. They paraded themselves with a certain insolence before other men, and by constituting themselves self-appointed camp police with extraordinary powers, they managed to bring unforeseen difficulties upon the broad shoulders of Bill Wiles.

It provoked Jube Pickett to disgruntled reflections on more than one occasion when instances of the overbearing conduct of Ewing's men were brought to his attention. The ceaseless grumbling of Wiles (who found himself in no position to do anything else about it) stung Jube like a cloud of gadflies. He saw Ewing as a parasite on the railroad's bounty, now; Buck by no chance did any useful work, nor, apparently, did he expect it of his men; yet they continued to eat heartily of railroad supplies and to draw handsome pay. The sharpest thorn in this posture of affairs lay in the fact that at no time had Jube approved of the gunmen. His son and Ben Sharp had procured them, and they had persuaded him of their necessity.

Matters were now in different case. Not only had the state rangers which Jube had asked for, superseded any private guards, but they had rendered them virtually impotent in any case, except in the instigation of trouble. A dozen times a night, some fight arose in the camp in which one or more of Ewing's arrogant adherents took a prominent part. And yet—if, indeed, not for this very reason—Jube hesitated before the impatient and even exasperated suggestions that he do something about it.

Things came to a head when, at noontime, Sam Mills accosted Jube on the way back to the cars for dinner. The engineer was a sturdy, sandy-haired fellow with a likeable, direct gaze. He said: "Major, I think we're laboring under an imposition. There are repeated complaints about excessive constructions costs from the Board, and Ewing's men are a dead weight on us. I spoke to Ewing this morning about a little work he could just as well take care of, and he was inclined to be surly. He turned me down, I scarcely need say. I thought you ought to know about it."

"All right, Sam," said Jube strictly. "You're right, of course. I'll take care of it . . . Bill!" he called to Bill

Wiles, who saw to the shunting of an extra tie-car on a nearby spur. Wiles waved to indicate that despite the snorting of the work engine, he had heard. Jube waited by the side of his private car for the camp boss to approach.

"You're coming right in, Father?" Valerie asked him, from a window.

"Yes. In just a moment," he responded, and turned to Wiles. "Bill, I want you to ask Buck Ewing to step here to the car as soon after dinner as possible. I want to see him."

Wiles, with a slow look, assented; and Jube went in to his meal. Over it, Valerie asked him suddenly: "Father, what is it you wish to see Mr. Ewing about?"

His reply was heavy. "His men are a drag on us, Valerie. Mills spoke about it. I've decided to give him some work that he must see done."

She gazed at him steadily. It was a moment before she found her words. "Father, you know how I feel about Mr. Ewing. I've told you I am convinced that Mr. Kincaid was not responsible for Trace's death; and Buck Ewing's actions are more involved than I believe he can satisfactorily explain. You are aware that he was at the old building at Mescalero Crossing. He walked in there while—Lance and I were together. But was he gentlemanly about it? He told Limpy; he got Trace to go up there. He is responsible for all that happened! . . . I hate that man. I want you to get rid of him."

Jube, impressed by her vehemence, admitted thoughtfully: "I've been thinking of doing just that. Since Miss Sharp removed her riders we've been at the mercy of his men. Maybe now that the rangers are here I can do something about it."

Valerie said no more; and when, twenty minutes later, Limpy Smail called from the car door to say that Ewing was here, she left her father and retired to her own compartment.

Ewing came in, tall and silent. Something of his bearing toward Jube was plain from the fact that he had not troubled to dispose of his after-dinner cigar. "Have a seat," Pickett told him; but Buck remained standing, his big frame darkening and making small this compact space. Not once did his saturnine eye leave Jube's countenance, nor did he speak. Pickett, busy with his own cigar, was wondering with some apprehension how Ewing would take what he was to hear. He got his light and cleared his throat.

"You are aware, Ewing, that since the rangers have stepped in here, there's a different set-up in our requirements," he said.

Ewing bored him, unmoving, as though daring him to proceed; and when Buck said shortly, "Go on," Jube's high cheeks flushed up with asperity.

"I am going on. Ewing, after the end of the week we won't need you or your men any more."

Buck absorbed that and saw that it could not have been averted. His long lips flattened. "That's about your size, Pickett," he rapped out sourly. "We pulled your chestnuts out of the fire, I don't suppose you'll deny. But now that you've got the rangers, we're through. That's the size of it, isn't it?"

"That's it," said Jube curtly, his cigar jerking.

Buck accepted the ultimatum with abrupt readiness.

Going out of the car, he stepped aside to avoid an opening door and came almost face to face with Valerie. She stiffened automatically, and her face went cold. Buck did not defer to her by so much as a nod, his strong face expressing a glancing contempt. Neither spoke; but in this instant of time, all that had hung between them for days, and all that had happened on the Standing Stone, was living and present. Out of the tail of his eye Ewing saw more than scorn and deep dislike in her brief, wide gaze; he saw suspicion as well.

Buck got down from the car more surly than ever. It had been against his urgent advice that Jube Pickett had sent out for the rangers; he had seen the rest of this coming, and he was not in the least surprised. But it was not wholly, or even largely, of the loss of an easy berth that he was thinking now. For his men he cared less than nothing. They might take care of themselves. What he regretted in a keen and urgent way was having to relinquish this strategic situation, from which the ride to Donita Sharp's Jingle-bob ranch was a matter of but an hour.

Matters were proceeding in relation to Donita which of themselves were enough to render him savage of mood. He could not understand it. For some reason unknown to himself, he could no longer get into the Jingle-bob house.

This was not what he had planned. It was, indeed, wide of the mark; yet where the slip had occurred he had no inkling. His careful plans, he told himself, had worked to perfection; why had they got him nowhere? What was it that Donita knew?

He went over the events of that night with a fine-tooth comb, and could find no flaws and but one minor regret: that he had been unable to follow Donita back to the Jingle-bob after her visit to Lesant's place, as he had watched her movements up to that point. Yet where could there have been any slip-up? Leaving the ford as she had done in a fevered state of mind and emotions, was it probable that she had done otherwise than to return home with the utmost haste? Time and again he conned this question, not once to arrive at an answer inimical to his own interests.

Donita's colored mammy could not tell him, or would not, why he was not welcome. She looked on him, at his successive visits, with the utmost suspicion, gave him unsatisfactory excuses, and closed the door as quickly as she could. The Jingle-bob men, who had been called home ostensibly to begin the fall work, were able to tell him nothing. And Donita herself, Buck was by no accident of chance allowed to so much as glimpse.

No persistence on his part remedied the situation. Several days later, when he and his men accepted their final pay with a signal bad grace and climbed aboard the White Oaks train, Ewing's temper was such that he would speak to no one civilly. It did not ease his mounting animosity to see Jube Pickett and his daughter get on the same train.

With Trace in his grave, Jube was under the necessity of transacting much of the business which his son had been in the habit of attending to in town. Valerie, for her part, evinced an increasing desire to get away from the scene of the railroad work for an occasional change.

At the White Oaks station, her father saw her down and across the street with his usual courtly attention.

Then he said: "All right, daughter? . . . I'll meet you at the hotel, after you've finished your shopping." He glanced at his watch. "Ten o'clock now. Dinner at twelve-thirty? I'm afraid you'll have to find some way to pass the time this afternoon by yourself. I'm not likely to be ready to go back before four."

"All right, Father." She gave him the benefit of her smile, simulating an ease she did not feel; and Jube, returning to his affairs, moved off. As soon as she lost sight of him, Valerie hurried down Cherry Street in the direction of the jail.

Miles Hudgin, the jailer, listened to her request with a vast politeness. "Mist' Kincaid?" he said. "Why, sure, Miss. Step right this way."

He led her by a dusky corridor which avoided the upper cells, where the murmurous droning of two drunks hollowly echoed, and at a wall of bars said, "Kin?" and then effaced himself.

Kincaid said "Valerie!" in a low, rich tone, and stood high and still with the parallel shadows over his lifting face.

"Lance, I'm sorry." Her words were impulsive; she put her hand through, and he took it in his, diffidently at first, and then enfolding it in both his own. She let it remain, gazing at him.

What was happening to him was obscure but powerful. He did not ask her the question which had ridden his broad shoulders for days now—whether she believed in his innocence; his answer was in her presence, and the pleasure he took in it struggled behind his dark eyes.

Valerie said: "I mustn't stay. But I had to see you— I want to do something for you. I want to go to Donita.

She may have seen something that night." Her voice was steady, and her gaze did not waver, but he knew sharply how much it cost her to say the words; to will the action they expressed. "Will she see me?"

He was struck again by the grave gallantry in this girl. It was more than a fine straightness of the shoulders, and an erectness of head. It was loyalty and unwavering faith. All this swept over him and he said quickly:

"Don't do that. I'm in no danger, Valerie. Matters are not as bad as that."

"But they are! They are every bit as bad. Have you seen your attorney?"

"Gavin?" Kincaid was strangely reluctant. "Yes, Fred has been here."

"And have you decided on your defense?"

"We talked it over."

She was watching him with a stillness on her. She burst forth lowly, then: "You have no defense! You left Mescalero Crossing soon after myself, and for an hour no one knew where you were!"

He said patiently, "Well—I think Gavin can manage."

She told him: "Lance, you are trying to keep me out of this, and I won't allow it. I know you are not—you couldn't have——" She broke away from that, but her eyes did not drop. "I want everyone to know you are innocent, as I know it."

"Thank you," he said simply. "That's the truth of it. It will come out in the end."

When she left a few minutes later, it was on a noncommittal note as to her intentions. Kincaid slowly strode the length of his cell and back, deeply meditative. He hadn't, he saw now, got out of her whether she was still fixed on visiting Donita; and he didn't know whether he wanted her to, or not.

"Donita is good-hearted," he mused. "I wish she could know Valerie as I do; but I don't believe she'll ever give her anything but a bad five minutes, and a resolution to stay away in future." He thought of Donita's blunt impulsiveness of nature and frowned. *Did* she know anything that would help? That Gavin had little to hold out, of a hopeful nature, was heavy in his mind. And the dusky shadows of this jail had nothing to offer.

So the afternoon came and dragged past, and evening found him in a frame of mind he was annoyed to find tense. But he was not so preoccupied that he failed to note Miles Hudgin's nervousness, when the latter brought him his supper.

"What's the trouble, Hud?" he queried.

Hudgin looked at him through grizzled brows. "Well, maybe nothin', Lance."

"That doesn't sound very promising."

Hudgin glanced past the barred window giving upon an adobe court. It was drowsy and quiet out there, under the pepper trees, but his tone was faintly querulous. "There's no reason why you shouldn't know that Ewing and his gun-slinging crowd have come in off the job and are in town. They've got money in their pockets, Lance, and liquor in their bellies, and they're feelin' mean." He hesitated. "You don't think they'd come and try to get you out of here tonight?"

Kincaid turned this over in his mind, his brows knit. His head came up. "What do you mean?" he asked, on a note of sharpness.

Hudgin said jerkily: "It ain't as personal as that between you and them?"

Kincaid said, "No," and afterwards he didn't know whether this was an honest answer or not.

Hudgin went away shaking his head dubiously. "I wish I could be sure of that," was the last of his muttering that Kincaid caught.

It was dark again when he came back, this time with two other men. He murmured, stopping before the cell, "I'll leave this here," and stood his lantern on the floor of the corridor; and then he went to answer the clamor of the drunks.

Kincaid said, "Hello, Dal . . . Quill."

Dallas Waidler looked at him steadily through the bars, his heavy face strong in the upward-slanting light. Quill Hoskins looked too, and then quickly turned his eyes down. He mumbled, "How are you, Kin?" in a self-conscious way, disturbed at seeing the man here and thus. Kincaid said directly:

"Dal, what's the railroad doing?"

Waidler intoned, "They're goin' on. They're out of the wash now, Lance; deep into the range." He looked tired and he sounded tired, at the necessity to report these things. "We ain't seen a move we could make to prevent any of it. Them rangers are on our tail day and night."

"I know." Kincaid let this silence run on, and it was Quill Hoskins who put in gruffly:

"You ain't been able to do nothin', Kin? Can't Fred Gavin think of no wrinkle, find no loophole for you to crawl through?"

"I guess not."

Kincaid shook his head, and Old Quill burst out: "Hell's fire; they done pushed you into it for fair! Charged with murder—in the hoosegow—the damn railroad crawlin' plumb into the gizzard of your land—and the rest of us with our hands tied! If this ain't a sweet mess!" He looked savage for a moment. "I dunno what the boys was thinkin' of, Kin, when Winters come out there for you. If I'd been there—or Dal, here, for that matter—you wouldn't be here now!"

Waidler breathed heavily amidst this pause, and then said: "Maybe it ain't too late to do something about it now."

His solid words were low; but an explosion of blasting-powder would not have brought the quiet of cell and corridor to a quicker sense of life. For a moment there lay here more than the suggestion of a hope, and Kincaid soberly considered it. He said:

"How many men rode in with you?"

Dal Waidler's lips seemed scarcely to move under the dark mustache: "Half-a-dozen."

Again that considering silence; and behind these bars, Kincaid's voice did not lose its gravity. "I expect you've already run across Ewing's bunch?"

Hoskins snorted: "We met 'em! They've took over the Maverick, lock, stock and barrel; lookin' for action!"

Kincaid said: "Stay out of that saloon . . . But I suppose Ewing's men are keeping a tab on all of you."

"They are that," Waidler grunted the admission.

Kincaid gave his decision on the proposal which they had brought here. His level voice was deliberate. "The sensible thing to do is to stay out of trouble altogether—all of you."

"Kin——!" Quill Hawkins protested, a resurgent and unconsidering violence on this man.

"No," said Kincaid firmly. "The first thing you know, more of you will be in my position—and with better cause. Let it alone. You hear me!"

The heavy silence of these two loyal men was his only answer, but it was enough.

XVIII

IT was early afternoon of a crisp, wine-like day between summer and fall; and though Donita Sharp's eyes had been open for hours, and the dulled homely sounds of the Jingle-bob ranch came to her during all that time, she was still in her room and in bed. There was no particular inducement for her to get up. For almost the first time in her memory, an overflow of natural energy did not drive her into mechanical activity.

She lay on her side with her glance avoiding the bright shapes of the windows, and her fevered thoughts were so busy that she did not note the indolence of her body. Her hands caught, and tore apart, and caught again; going through her mind were the eternal questions whose answers eluded her with diabolical persistence.

How could she bring herself to step forward and tell what she knew? It was impossible. They would put her on the witness stand and she must—if she told anything at all—confess that she had pursued Lance Kincaid knowingly to a rendezvous with another woman. No—it was impossible; her high and proud cheeks burned with the thought.

"But something must be done!" she half-moaned the anguish of her quandary. "If anything is to help Lance, it will not be this indecision . . . Why couldn't it have happened another way!" But bitter as the knowledge was that Buck Ewing had tricked her into her position, she had no thought of lying about her reasons for going to Mescalero Crossing on that stormy night. It must be the truth or nothing.

Her desire to help Kincaid in his extremity came straight from the heart. She had always admired him inordinately, and now that strong feeling rose to heights the consequences of which frightened her. For all that she could not put Valerie Pickett out of her mind and could not forgive her. What had the girl been thinking of—was she in earnest? But these things did not matter; it was Valerie who had dragged Kincaid into his terrible situation, Donita told herself; and she was sure of it.

It would not leave her, however much she tried to put it away, that, just possibly, if she were to step forward now to Lance's aid, it might turn him toward herself once more; yet if it should not——

These things were beating through her under the sledge of her emotions, when Old Effie, her negro servitor, stole ponderously into the room. Effie's loyal bulk was so heavy that she could move nowhere in silence; Donita sat up as she came in, her turning glance a little harried.

"Is you awake den, Honey?" The round black face was a picture of solicitude; the very whites of Effie's eyes were worried.

Donita exclaimed immediately: "If it's Mr. Ewing I won't see him. Tell him I never want to see him here again!"

"Aw, now!" Crooning, Effie fluttered about her mistress. "Doan' you fret like dat. It ain' Mist' Ewing,

Honey; it's a lady come fo' to see you. She named Pickett."

Donita abruptly paled. "Miss Pickett! Valerie . . . What can she possibly want?" Her hollow tone was almost a whisper.

Effie watched her in perplexed dismay. "Iffen you doan' want to see her——" she began.

"No, no! I can't," Donita persuaded herself; but she looked toward the door as if gauging a possibility. "Wait. Tell her——" She hesitated, and then fearing that something had come up which she was in danger of missing altogether, she plunged: "I will see her. Say that I will be down, Effie." And she slid her feet toward the edge of the bed.

"Honey, you doan' have to do a thing you doan' want to!" Effie protested cajolingly. But Donita was already slipping into her dressing-gown, digging with impatient toes at her mules. She said: "Go on, Effie. Don't irritate me now."

Effie knew that half-absent, wholly determined tone. With a sigh of feigned resignation, she waddled out of the bedroom and down the broad stairs.

Valerie Pickett, assured that Donita would see her, sank back into her chair in the parlor with a little shiver of anticipation. While old Effie retired (but not so far that she could not glance more than once, furtively, at the visitor through kitchen and dining-room doors, a seriousness on her dusky face) Valerie looked about her. The Jingle-bob house was like nothing she had ever seen on a ranch before. It had tasteful furniture, hardwood floors, rich damasks and Mexican-wove blankets on wall and settle. Most of this luxury revealed a woman's hand;

Donita's, probably, but certainly old Ben Sharp had been lavish for his grand-daughter.

Donita appeared. Valerie stood up at once. She was as collected, as reserved, as the other girl; the stiff quiet awakened only to Donita's steps as she moved forward. Her slightly remote glance was level, and her tone was cool:

"Why have you come?" she said, defensiveness shading her words, and the memory of their last meeting was heavy.

Valerie had not forgotten her pride. She did not wear it outwardly now; but it kept humbleness out of her supplication. "Miss Sharp, you must know about—Mr. Kincaid! I am trying to help him. He is in such a precarious position that someone must do something."

Donita said, with dry curiosity: "I take it that you do not believe this—this charge against Lance." There was a flicker of jealous questioning in her eyes.

"No more than you do," Valerie replied simply, slow with her talking. This speeded up, now: "Donita—I *had* to come to you and ask you if you know anything that would save Lance! Anything in the world. You must know things that I do not."

"Why do you come to me?" Donita's glance remained metallic, instinctively defending; but as she read in this girl's words and in her manner the gravity of Lance Kincaid's need, her tone was unsteady.

So they stood, half-a-dozen feet apart, with this man between them, and the silence built itself up. Valerie put out a hand. She said: "You were at that place that night. In God's name, what did you see? You know at least as much as most of the rest of us. You——" She broke off, perceiving the indirection of this plea, and then added lowly: "Donita, we both love Lance."

Donita's head came up. "You have lost a brother," she said clearly; "but I have lost something too." She said it proudly. A slow tear ran down her cheek, clung, and dropped. Of a sudden she folded into the chair beside her, her hands on its arm, her face against them, and she sobbed.

Valerie took two impulsive steps, held a compassionate hand above that tempestuous, honey-colored head, and then withdrew it. "I'm sorry, Donita," she said softly.

Donita's grief ran on. It was something she couldn't stop. Valerie had struck fairly upon an exposed nerve; and she knew that if this did not end shortly, she could not stand it any longer. She was fighting against involving herself, and at the same time she wanted mightily to talk, to unburden her heart. She raised her damp face, and her eyes had altered, the hardness and aloofness gone out of them. She said, wearily:

"You know what time I was at the ford. I—didn't leave, really. I went a little ways and waited, came back. I saw Buck Ewing walk in on you . . . Valerie, he knew you were there! He knew all the time. He hates Lance! . . ." She gazed away for a moment, hazily, through the tears; marshaling her pictures of that night.

"I saw you and Buck leave—I guessed where you were going. Lance remained for some time, standing on Lesant's porch. I think I know his thoughts . . . I waited while he waited. After a long while he put out the candle, and I crept closer. Lance mounted and rode up the canyon trail, slowly through the storm."

She sat with her head slightly tipped now, thinking

bitterly; and when she glanced at Valerie her eyes were wide. "I was about to leave myself, to go home," she said; "I had got a little ways off, when I heard a noise. It was a horse, and a moment later I recognized Buck Ewing. He was leading another horse. There was something on the saddle." The words were a whisper. "It was a man: a dead man." She put her palms to her face, and a shudder ran over her. Valerie stared at her.

Donita forged on: "Ewing was going—back to that saloon. He took a long time. Then I saw him again. He took the—man off the saddle. There was a flash of lightning, and I saw Buck's face . . . Valerie, I could have screamed. He was smiling! Carrying that body——"

"Trace?" Valerie queried huskily.

"Yes—— He took Trace inside. I heard a thump on the floor. And Buck murmured something. I—it struck a chill through me, a madness. I think I turned and ran . . . I don't remember—except that a long while later I was near home. My horse brought me . . ." She was speaking brokenly. Valerie had come to her at last, and they were in each other's arms. Old Effie, peeping in on that strange sight, shook her turbaned head and tiptoed away, muttering. . . .

In Valerie's mind there no longer was any doubt of Buck Ewing's guilt of the murder of her brother. She had left Ewing that night, gone on alone—like Kincaid himself, it left Ewing unaccounted for from that hour until the following morning. Valerie saw it all with a crystal clarity: Ewing and Trace had somewhere met; death had come to Trace; and Buck Ewing had determined, out of the depths of his hatred and his wild jealousy, to pin the crime on Kincaid. He had come so near to succeeding that Valerie felt an echo of the chill of apprehension that shook Donita's small shoulders. But Valerie knew what must be done. She stilled Donita, lifted her face.

"Donita, this will save Lance," she said, with a firmness and a steadiness she did not entirely feel. "Will you make a statement to Mr. Winters of all you have told me?"

All her resistance gone, Donita could only nod her head in assent. The tears came freely now, and there was upon her the ease of a decision put behind.

Evening draped White Oak's reviving Main Street with cool light. Along these walks, many boot heels struck with a brisk firmness, and saloons were beginning to send out trickles of laughter and music. Beyond the wooden awning of the Maverick, the strong glow of the sky falling across his lower face, Buck Ewing pulled on a cigar and watched the drifting life of this town.

For diplomatic reasons, Bill Wiles had always been familiar with Ewing in a casual way. He came across the dust now and lifted a greeting hand. Ewing's hard glance relaxed with recognition. He said: "What's doing, Wiles?"

Bill, smoothing the rumpled shirt over his portly stomach, knew what he was driving at. Ewing, for some reason unknown to the railroad camp boss, had not yet lost interest in the activities at the end of track. Wiles knew too, the man's interest in Donita Sharp. He lifted a placid glance to Buck's high face and responded: "Why, things are moving along. We got out of the seven-tenths grading at last, and are pushin' across 2 M land at a great rate." He had more to say of the actual construction work, and Ewing listened patiently, his eye running restlessly over the shifting faces along the walk. Finally Wiles cleared his throat easily and remarked: "Well, the rangers seem to be gettin' somewhere in that Pickett case, finally."

Ewing's smooth and dark face did not change. "That so? What have they dug up?"

"I don't rightly know," Wiles admitted. "But Ab Winters, and the old man and his girl set off for the Jinglebob yesterday, and was there most of the day. I smelled around out of curiosity," he went on; "but you know what rangers is. You can't get anything out of 'em." He looked shrewdly at Ewing, his own enjoyment of this moment and this discussion running away with him. "They can't fool me. I know they turned up something mighty important."

Ewing's brows rose, and Wiles continued:

"Why should there be all this mystery business, and runnin' around, if it was just a plain idea somebody's dug up. They'd be checkin' up on all hands, wouldn't they? But has anybody come to me, say, about anything— no; nor to old Smail neither." He shook a knowing head. "I guess I know what's what."

A moment later Wiles was accosted by a conductor off his run on the southern line; Ewing, looking neither to right nor left, his movements deliberate with an iron control, stepped into the saloon.

"Rye," he told old Kize, and tossed off a stiff slug the instant the glass reached his hand. He had a second one, and then turned, impelled by some insistent attention which struck through his powerful abstraction from one side, to glance down the bar. Quill Hoskins fixed on him an undeviating glower. Hatred was in it, and challenge, and plain and biting contempt. Ewing returned this look for that moment and then swung back to the bar and to his glass.

Of Quill Hoskins, or of any other man in the room, Ewing had no slightest fear. It was easy now to turn all these things off, to forget them, in the stress of his own anxious speculations. The truth was that a cold shadow was suddenly closing over him, rising from circumstances which had nothing to do with this moment. Bill Wiles' gossip had thrown a jar into him such as he had not experienced for long.

Ab Winters, Pickett, and Valerie—going to the Jingle-bob! He asked himself what they could have found out. The question was, Ewing amended, this: What could Donita tell? She knew nothing. Of that he would have been certain . . . Or had she come back to Mescalero Crossing that night?

"No!" his thoughts hurled the answer at him; and the very vehemence of his assurance gave him pause. There was more than the mere problem of what Donita might have discovered by accident to be answered. She had been at the ford that night, and through the one flaw in all his careful planning, he was unable to say with certainty that Donita had ridden straight away from there, after she had seen what he had wanted her to see. Beyond even this was the ominous pattern of her actions since that time. Not once had Buck been able to approach her. This in itself rang a warning bell in his brain.

A somberness and a forbidding mood rode Ewing's temper such as he had never experienced. No act of violence would have stopped him now if it would have gained him his ends—but he knew better. There was a net closing in about him which no tearing would remove. The aloofness of Donita put a blackness before him and honed his hunger to unbelievable rapacity. Rashness and an indifference wholly foreign to his coldly calculating nature poured through him.

All that had been warmth of sentiment turned to vitriol in his veins. "She knows!" his inescapable sense told him what to expect. "She came back, sure as fate. It wasn't inside Lesant's old shack that I had anything to fear, that night!" And he built up with lightning rapidity, what must be happening. Donita still loved Kincaid. He couldn't escape that. For days, knowing what she did, Ewing pictured her fighting out the question of whether to speak up. And she had spoken, finally. Ab Winters, the ranger, knew her story now. And only a counter accusation would save Kincaid—even she must know that. How soon would it be before the rangers came searching for him, Buck Ewing?

Ewing made up his mind with characteristic decision. He poured down a final jot of whisky and motioned to the proprietor. Len Riley pushed forward, his swarthy face lifted in inquiry.

"Len," said Buck abruptly, "how much money are you holding for me?"

Len's eyes were steady. "I got about three hundred that belongs to you, Buck."

"You better give it to me."

Riley didn't say anything just then. He went to his safe in the little office, and after a moment's figuring and counting of bills, closed the safe and came back with a roll which he slid across to Ewing. Then he grunted, his glance limpid: "Goin' away?"

Ewing's tone was colorless. "I may be taking a little trip, Len."

He counted the roll and stowed it in his clothes. After paying for his drinks he swung out of the saloon with his usual firm stride, and five minutes later found him getting up his pony at the livery stable. He paid his bill there too.

Nosing around for just such unconsidered trifles of information as this, Quill Hoskins watched Buck Ewing single-foot up Cherry Street and out of town, alone. Quill scratched his head, the battered Stetson canted, and muttered perplexedly: "Now, what in hades can that hombre be up to?"

Morning sifted into the White Oaks jail and the timeless sun laid a pattern on the packed dirt floor of Kincaid's cell. He got up from his cot to glance out into the court, where a dog slept under the nearest pepper tree. Nothing else showed out there. He sat down again, a restlessness on him. He expected Fred Gavin this morning, with the announcement of the date of his trial—and, Kincaid reflected soberly, not much else of any account. It might be that Gavin was constructing his defense step by step in his own mind; certain it was, that he took no one else into his confidence, and Kincaid found it a little wearing to the nerves.

He was thinking these things, with long patience, his elbows on his knees and his head down, when the sound of approaching feet came to him. He looked up expectantly. The boots came near, they stopped; and Kincaid was surprised to see the sheriff and Ab Winters at his cell door.

The former fumbled with the lock while Winters gave Kincaid an easy, matter-of-fact greeting. The door creaked back, and Ab stepped over the sill. He opened up at once:

"Well, Lance, we have no reason to hold you any longer, and this is your release. Miss Sharp has told and sworn to a story that bears on your case; and between that and a few things I've dug up myself, you are in the clear. It looks," he went on in his dry, explanatory manner, "like we've got a shut and closed case against Ewing for young Pickett's murder."

Kincaid studied the lined, regular face. He was deeply surprised, but his tone was level. "Buck, eh?"

"Yes." Winters was laconic. "And Ewing doesn't seem to disagree with us, either. I've had a man looking for him, and he seems to have pulled up stakes. He can't be found anywhere."

XIX

WHEN Kincaid walked out of the White Oaks jail, a free man, he was met by a small but grinning company, standing on the walk in front of the place, headed by Dal Waidler. Ote Burnett was here, and old Quill Hoskins.

"Wal, Kin!" the last of these had his say at once. "How does it smell to you, out here?"

"Quite a change," Kincaid smilingly admitted, as he surveyed them. "If I know you boys as well as I think I do, you're even more anxious to celebrate this than I am. Let's go down to the Maverick."

They headed down there, and stepped in in a body. One of Buck Ewing's discarded gunmen stood near them as they lined up at the bar. He stared a species of scorn and disgust, and a moment later moved ostentatiously toward the door. No one had anything to offer him as he took his leave.

"Not many of them fellers around any more," Dal Waidler volunteered, in a low tone. "Quill saw Ewing pull out last night, and didn't savvy his play till it was too late. Since then these hard mugs have been climbing aboard the trains, half-a-dozen at a clip. I expect we've seen the last of them."

Kincaid nodded his satisfaction with the intelligence.

He was putting his questions concerning the progress of affairs on 2 M, when Waidler, in the midst of his answers, said, "Uh—s'pose you'll be ridin' back to the spread today?"

"Yes." Kincaid's glance waited.

"Better step around to the Exchange before you go," said Dal. He had not wasted his time in town, and had got the story of Kincaid's raid on South Western Pacific's stock issue.

"All right." Kincaid turned to include them all in his talk. He said: "We'll ride in an hour. I'll meet you boys at the stable," and downing his drink, he turned to push toward the door. They gazed after him, but no one had any queries to put, and no one offered to follow.

More than one man stopped Kincaid before he got to the Stockmen's Exchange. "Well, Kincaid! Things have been happenin' pretty fast for you. Glad to hear you're gettin' the breaks at last." That was the burden of their greetings. He met Fred Gavin, 2 M's attorney, and a ten minute conference served to clear up the business which lay between them.

In the Exchange, Kincaid first of all scanned the stock board and noted that beef was steady. He nodded his comprehension of what Dal Waidler had been driving at, walked over and had his look at the quotation for South Western Pacific. It was way off—26. While he was standing there, pondering the meaning of this, the clerk made a change in the reading. The railroad stock had slipped another quarter-point.

For the first time in days Kincaid's spirits lifted. He knew what this would be doing to the railroad's credit. With such a low market, the sale of the rail stock would drop off—perhaps had virtually ceased, and he began once more to entertain the possibility of blocking the construction across his land.

Jube Pickett walked in a moment later. Seeing Kincaid, he nodded without surprise and even spoke. "Sorry there was a mistake, Kincaid," he said formally. "I'm particularly glad this affair of my son's death has been straightened out."

Kincaid said quietly, "Thanks. I know how you feel."

There was little enough for these two to talk about, and Jube did not try to find more. He went over to read the quotation on South Western Pacific, and standing there for some minutes, he was plainly worried. It confirmed Kincaid's belief that his own fight was not wholly lost. The problem was how best to utilize the situation created by the depressed railroad issue. Deep in his thoughts, he walked out.

Pondering thus, he might have been excused for passing an acquaintance or two unawares; but there was no such occasion when, passing the White Oaks Hotel, the strike of light and quick heels on the porch entered his consciousness. He saw Valerie Pickett before she saw him, and changed his course to reach the steps.

A smile sprang to those clear features, lighting her up from within. They met midway of the steps, and neither noticed it. Both Valerie's hands were extended toward him, and for a moment he took them in his own.

She said: "I knew. I heard a few minutes ago. It's wonderful, isn't it? Donita did a brave thing."

"Both of you," he said in his low, solid tone, "have done more than I know how to repay."

"But it was Donita who . . ." she began quickly.

"Lance, I had no idea she was so sensitive. I am proud to call her my friend."

"I too," he agreed sincerely.

They talked here lightly for a moment, finding a remembered balance. Again Kincaid was engrossed in the sense of impact she brought to him; of the fineness that life concealed until its sudden emergence was a discovery, profound and moving. Her creamy skin was something that his glance could not calmly accept, but must verify again and again, with a kind of wonder; her confiding and happy glance was a warmth which stole through him and remained with him.

"You are staying in White Oaks now?" he asked.

"No, Father brought me in from the camp. The railroad claims so much of his time that I should not feel myself his daughter if I neglected it."

Kincaid passed over that subject smoothly. He said, nodding: "We met, a few minutes ago. He looks as if he could do with a rest. But you," he added pleasantly, "remain as fresh as the day I first saw you." And he shook his head in amused puzzlement.

Valerie laughed, her blue eyes dancing appreciation. "I don't believe you have changed either . . . . I suppose you will go back to the ranch at once?"

"Right way," he assented. "Unless you have the day on your hands . . ."

Something crossed between them as Valerie glanced at him with a flash of gravity. "I am afraid——" She hesitated. And then, in a tone of casual suggestion: "Father expects to return at noon. A work train will be going out——"

It was as though Kincaid did not hear these references

to a forbidden topic; or else they reminded him strongly of other things. He brightened as he said: "I look forward to the saddle with so much pleasure that an overcast sky doesn't bother me in the least."

Indeed, a thin haze had gathered since the morning, until the bright sun paled to a faintly outlined ball.

Valerie said: "We shall have rain soon. Father remarked that he felt it, this morning, in his old wound . . . Here he comes now," she added a moment later, her glance running down the street.

Kincaid took his leave, sweeping his hat off with a lingering look at the smiling, faintly wistful eyes of this girl, and that erect head. Half-an-hour later, in a thin fine rain, the first of the fall rains, he was riding back to 2 M by a short-cut, with Dal Waidler and the others with him. Dal continued to study the murky and thickening sky as they jogged along.

"We'll get somethin' out of this," he predicted.

Kincaid bared his head to that damp coolness, and the peace of the open range flowed over him and in upon him: a balm under which he had always thrived and which he could never give up. He had come as near to losing all this as he expected ever to come again; the coldness of that escape still played on his nerves and bent his thoughts back to the problem of how he was to defeat the railroad. It seemed to him that in this rain he saw a promise and a great change; and when, two hours later, the ropy and subdued shriek of an engine whistle came to him from afar and he saw the low-hanging coils of smoke down the range, he knew that that train would within a little while be passing across his own land. It was like a stimulant under which, before ever 2 M came in sight again, his complete plan was formed.

He thought of Old Rusty. It would be a day darkened by more than rain for the old man if he could come back now; and Kincaid wondered what would have been Maxwell's answer to the challenge of the rangers. Rusty would have made some decisive reply, it seemed certain. The knowledge riveted Kincaid's purpose of persevering in his efforts to preserve 2 M as an inviolate monument to Old Rusty's indomitable spirit.

News of Kincaid's coming seemed to have run ahead of him when, in early and lowering evening, he finally reached the ranch. Every person of any standing on 2 M, and many who measured their standing in terms of personal feeling alone, turned out to meet him, whether along the feeder lane where the row of straw-bosses' homes stood, or at headquarters. Plain it was that they needed the bulwark of his steadfast and strong will.

Smoke Givens had ready a good meal for Kincaid, Charley May, Stroud, Gurley and the others whom Kincaid included in this council over Rusty's table. But little was covered beyond the routine reports which served to assure Kincaid that things had gone smoothly with the work of the ranch in his absence. Afterward he retired with Charley May to the office.

"Raining stronger all the time," Charley commented as he looked out.

"Yes, and I'm counting on it. How about the hills?" Kincaid asked. "Have you had any storms up there, to speak of?"

"Lots of water in the hills," May responded.

"We'll need a lot."

Charley May studied Kincaid speculatively as the latter gave concise instructions covering the work he desired started in the morning. "We'll put a crew on the Low Lake dam and run it up, and I want you to see that they push it. That dam, with head-gates, can be built up between the buttes another twenty feet—maybe more."

Charley said: "This is what you were driving at that day when you talked to Rusty on the way back from High Pond, isn't it?" And at Kincaid's level glance, he added: "Lance, will it work?"

"It's got to. And we've got to see to it that we give it all the chance there is."

Later, when he was alone, Kincaid's thoughts turned to other things. In the back of his mind, since the hour of his release from jail, there had hovered a picture of Donita Sharp's proud and yet supplicatingly soft face. Was it an accusing face also, or was that his own fancy? He well knew the debt he owed to her. He would have to go to her; and yet even in this act of simple decency he found a prospective discomfort which held him back. Thanks, he knew better than he knew many other things about Donita, were not the coin in which she would desire repayment to be made. Yet no more than ever would he be able honestly to bring her the only warmth of feeling she could accept. It was going to be a difficult half-hour for him at best.

In the morning, despite still-overcast skies, Kincaid saw to it that wagons and tools and men got off for Low Lake dam in the Basin, and later he rode down there himself. The Basin was a broad, gently-sloping area hemmed in by higher ground, and across the upper portion of which the South Western Pacific would lay its track. Already the survey-stakes had been driven; a ranger rode past Kincaid with a nod as he drew in to follow those stakes with his eye. Low Lake was a reedy morass which did not, at present, reach back within many yards of the right-of-way.

At the dam between the two buttes, a score of 2 M hands were busy under the direction of Charley May. Others drove up with wagon-loads of materials. The raising of the dam would be no easy task and no brief one, but May expressed his confidence that even with the spillway closed, his men would be able to keep well ahead of the natural rise of the lake.

"You'll have to do even better than that," Kincaid clipped off. "The railroad scrapers are piling up a road-bed only a few miles away; I don't propose to have that road-bed completed across the Basin."

He watched a while and then rode off, and when he was gone, Charley May again climbed the highest butte in the midst of anxious speculations, and from there surveyed the prospect as he saw it in Kincaid's mind. It would take a vast volume of water, he estimated, to back up and overflow the railroad right-of-way in an effective manner, and as yet the amount of water collected by the closing of the spillway, despite the steady contribution of the Standing Stone, remained negligible. A hard line-storm might do wonders; as for the present one, after an intermittent drumming during the night, it was already clearing. By midafternoon the sharp sun would be burning away the dampness which now jewelled sage and bunch-grass.

Would Kincaid's plan work? Charley May shook his

head in indecision, and strode back down to push the work along.

A day passed, and a second; the dam rose with celerity, since the men were shrewd enough to deduce of their own accord its connection with Kincaid's fight against the railroad, which he had assured them was neither lost nor dropped. It was on that second day that, leaving the ranch in early afternoon, Kincaid met Ab Winters jogging across the range with one of his men. The ranger captain's crinkled eyes as he came up told nothing. He began:

"I see you're doing some work on your lower dam, Kincaid. Kind of late to do any good this season."

Kincaid drew in, willing enough to spend a moment with the man. His tone was quiet as he responded. "Yes," he said. "Yes . . . I'll be working out one of my own ideas now, that Rusty thought was a bit irregular. We'll see."

Winters' gaze was steady, probing. He scrutinized Kincaid's lean face for a long moment, and when he spoke again it was on another subject altogether. Riding up toward the hills later, Kincaid smiled to himself. "He didn't know just what to make of that answer," he reflected, and not caring particularly what Winters thought. He well knew the rangers could have nothing to say in the course of action he was taking.

His ride took him onward and upward, higher and higher, the dry piny scent of these levels sweet in his nostrils. High Pond, at the head of the Standing Stone, when he came there, was filled almost to the level it had maintained before Old Rusty had knocked out the head-gates with so disastrous an effect. Kincaid nodded to his own thoughts. "If we get another good rain within the week," he mused, "it may just be that we'll have the water we need."

He turned away. His way now took him down the old trail which crossed the river canyon and climbed out again; and as he passed Lesant's tumbledown saloon with a slow glance for it, many associations arose to ride with him. Valerie Pickett's perfume-like presence was not absent from them; nor was Donita Sharp. It was toward the Jingle-bob that he was reluctantly headed now.

Drawing near the house which Ben Sharp had built here in the middle of Jingle-bob range, Kincaid felt sobriety settle over him. He pictured Donita pining in seclusion, and dreaded again the blow his inevitable manner would deal her. Sliding out of the saddle in the ranch yard, he was thinking that little evidence of the flood damage remained here now; the place was spruce and well-kept. As he moved toward the house on foot, coming across the porch toward him he saw Bert Hyde.

Hyde was a raw-boned and freckled red-head, Donita's second-cousin, who ran a spread over on the Rio Prado. An able man, good-natured and usually smiling, he came forward now with a great good will. They met below the steps, and Bert said: "I'm sure glad to see you, Lance. You're just in time to congratulate me." And he beamed all over him, like an overgrown and vastly pleased boy.

Struck by the unusual mood of the man, Kincaid asked smilingly: "How is that, Bert?" and Hyde threw out artlessly, all his teeth visible:

"Donita's just promised to marry me!"

Kincaid's jaw dropped. He stared. "No!" he ejaculated unbelievingly; and then catching himself: "By Jove, Bert,

I do congratulate you! Donita's a girl in a thousand, and you're a lucky man." He pumped Hyde's hand with an enthusiasm he would have found it hard to explain.

Hyde said, in a confusion of happiness: "I'm just going out to hitch up the rig. We're going to ride over to our place."

"Fine. And while you're doing it, I'll go in and speak to Donita." Kincaid turned to the house.

Effie let him in with a wide grin. As he entered the hall, Donita floated down the stairs, airily dressed, a lightness in her resilient body: a different girl from his picture of her. He stopped at the foot of the stairs and put his hands out; she put both of her own in them and poised there, her starry glance full on him. For perhaps the first time, Kincaid realized, they were whole-heartedly glad to see each other, and nothing else lay between them. Old Effi beamed on that sight and waddled away about her own affairs.

Kincaid said: "Bert just told me, Donita."

Mischief danced in her unaverted gaze. "You seem relieved, Lance."

Kincaid was taken aback, his confusion plain in his bronzed face. He attempted lightness. "I didn't expect to come over here and have you talk to me that way after what you did for me," he said. "It was splendid of you, Donita. I shall remember it always. And now . . . I honestly hope you and Bert will be happy," he ended.

"We will, Lance."

But as she looked at him, her eyes wistful, he seemed aware that it was not wholly of Bert Hyde that she was thinking with such a softness of face. They had this one long moment, during which Kincaid gave her all of admiration and warm liking that he could honorably proffer, and then it was broken by the sound of wheels as Bert drove the rig up outside. Suddenly, without the slightest self-consciousness, Donita threw her arms around Kincaid and kissed him on the lips. It was a wild second or two before he came to himself.

"And you are about to be married?" he exclaimed incredulously, searching her face.

Her low laugh was not wholly divorced from sadness, her steady eyes candid. She said: "How little you know of women, Lance."

XX

HIGH in the hills on the flank of Comanche Mountain, Buck Ewing lay in hiding. In a deep crevice in the rocks he had his little camp, where he dared light a fire only after darkness fell to conceal the spiral of his smoke. Much of the time during the days Ewing lay in his covert with his coiling thoughts. But even his iron command cracked under the severity of this confinement. Rifle in hand, he was wont to crawl to a point of vantage from whence he could look down over the tumbled pine-clad slopes. There was no anodyne for him in the fact that almost the full spread of 2 M lay under his smoldering eyes.

A part of Ewing's assurance of safety for the moment lay in the nearness of the State rangers. Through glasses he saw them down there, riding in authority where he had ridden; they would never suspect his presence here, and he was careful to show himself to no cruising 2 M hand. Haggard, unshaven, violent in his smoky impulses, Ewing no longer bothered to think beyond these things in the interests of his own safety. He did not dream of leaving. It was as if he were bound by a cord in this dangerous spot, a cord the other end of which was fastened securely at the Jingle-bob, where of nights he occasionally prowled, and whose faint smudge of buildings he could descry from his high vantage.

He saw also the shining steel ribbon of the railroad, twining into 2 M, like the outflung lash of a whip; and it did not escape him that Kincaid had set men at work on the low dam in the Basin. He spent hours conning the subject in a sullen persistence, without determining its object. Then came a night of heavy rain, during which Ewing's rocky crevice was a sodden misery; and late in the morning, crawling out with hard-bitten stubborness in his rocky face, he saw it all.

During the morning some 2 M man had climbed up to knock out the head-gates of High Pond once more. The Standing Stone spilled a strong tide into the Basin, and there the water backed out across the flats until Ewing saw an unbroken glisten lying across the path of the railroad right-of-way. The wheel-scrapers were drawn aside, and smoke no longer rose from the engines; work on the road had come to a halt.

The significance of this burst over Buck Ewing in a heated wave. Kincaid, it appeared certain, had won his long fight against the invading enemy; that fight whose opening gun Ewing himself had aimed and discharged, and in whose eventual outcome he had taken a vital interest. He saw Kincaid now in the bitterest terms. Like Rusty Maxwell before him, he dominated the country and men alike with ruthless decision; but beyond that, he was the immediate cause of Ewing's own downfall.

All Buck's venom for what had happened to him was directed in one growing knot of rage and hatred against Kincaid. The loss of Donita Sharp, this girl who had laid an imperious hold on his strong nature; involvement in the murder of a man who meant, in the end, less than nothing to Ewing; the crash of his far-reaching repute

for service to the law and his hard dominance of men—
in all this, without exception, Kincaid had played his part.
The knowledge was like gall on Ewing's tongue; it tor-
mented him to madness.

"He'll pay for it!" he gritted, his fury jerking him
about in his damp covert. "He thinks he's hounded me
to the end of my string; but it's a string that's fastened
to us both—I'll jerk him up short if it means both our
lives!"

Jube Pickett and Ab Winters got out of their saddles
in the 2 M ranch yard in the broad light of afternoon.
A bitter intentness informed every move of the railroad
man, but the ranger, tilting a glance toward the office
gallery, was as impassive as ever. Long years in the
service of justice had made him temperate.

It was not from the direction of the house that Kincaid, whom it was plain they were looking for, came
toward them but down the lane from the houses along
the *acequia* bank, where he had been visiting the con-
valescents. He strode out without hurry, and the three
men met beside the horses.

"Kincaid," Pickett broke out in harsh accents, "I'm a
patient man, I think. But there's some things no man
has got to put up with. I demand that you lower that
dam of yours!"

Kincaid looked mildly surprised, but only cursorily distressed, at this tone. "Why, I only just got that dam
finished," he said, his look undisturbed and steady. "How
can you have any interest in my improvements on the
ranch?"

Jube's visage darkened. "You know what I'm driving

at!" he exploded. "You did that flooding in the Basin deliberately to throw an obstacle in my way. Are you going to remove it?" There was the suggestion of an exasperated ultimatum here.

"No." Kincaid was brief. "I'm not concerned for your railroad. It's my cattle I'm thinking of; anything else is a waste of breath."

Jube whirled on Winters, who stood blocky and imperturbable through all this. "Winters, will you go down and order that dam thrown open?" he asked bluntly.

Ab shook his head. "I can't do it, Major. That dam's legal, far's I can see. It's on Kincaid's land."

"And I'll take the responsibility for it," Kincaid inserted calmly.

"You'll have to!" Pickett hurled at him, his eyes flashing with indignation. "And you'll find it's considerable of a responsibility by the time I get this into the courts. I'll slap a damage suit on you that will make you smart!"

Kincaid nodded agreeably. "It's quite possible," he admitted. "In the meantime, I don't see that there's anything else you can do about the matter. Do you?"

Jube didn't, and it made him fume. The conference ran to considerable length, with bitter acrimony on his part; but no developments transpired beyond what had been reached at this point. In the end Pickett rode away with Ab Winters in a high dudgeon, and they left Kincaid to all intents in possession of the field for the time being.

He asked no more. Perfectly aware of the inevitable action of the courts in favor of the South Western Pacific, he was content in the meantime to let events take their course.

But apparently Jube Pickett was not going to accept tamely this posture of affairs. The next day Andy Stroud came into the office to tell Kincaid in a gruff tone that the railroad teams were at work once more, hauling dirt down toward the Basin. Kincaid knew what this portended. He sat back with a serious mien.

"Putting in a fill, are they?"

"Sure. There's not more than three or four feet of water across that right-of-way."

They talked it over with waning confidence. Long after Stroud had gone, Kincaid sat on, pondering this new threat. Once the projected road-bed fill was proven successful, defeat for his ends was inevitable. Across the Basin and to the western boundary of 2 M, nothing but space stood between the steel-layers and their steady progress.

There was only one thing that would make 2 M's position secure now—rain.

Kincaid left the office and walked to the edge of the gallery, there to examine the skies long and anxiously. They were overcast and gloomy. But, frowning, he had to own there was no particular dampness in the air. With typical fall deliberation, rain might hold off for days.

It did. There could be little speed shown in the laborious construction of the fill across the Basin at any time; but daily it inched forward, little by little, until the earthen dyke reached the halfway mark and crawled beyond. Kincaid rode out to survey the progress made, Charley May with him. Neither spoke, but when they turned back their faces were long.

That night Kincaid sat up late in the office. He was virtually resigned now to defeat, having thought of everything, without avail. Getting out of his chair, weary to the bone, he threw the stub of his smoke in the direction of the fireplace and was about to turn toward his bunk when a softly stealing sound gave him pause. Gently at first, and then with more strength, rain was pattering on the roof. Kincaid stepped to the door, building another smoke, and he forgot his fatigue. When, an hour later, he turned in at last, the storm was drumming with heavy, business-like persistence.

The next day it rained steadily, an unbroken deluge. At noon Charley May stamped into the house, flirting the water from his Stetson, a broad smile on his lips. He said: "They seem to be having a little trouble with that fill today. I saw it wash away in two spots, and then I rode in to get dry." He ruefully regarded his damp doeskin vest, free to worry about his own concerns; and Kincaid knew then that he had won.

Leaving a general elation behind him on 2 M, he rode in to White Oaks to see his attorney. Before he reached Gavin's office he was stopped on the street by an old and broken-down cowboy whom he knew. Len Slagle was a process-server, at present, it was clear, in discharge of his duty. Kincaid opened the paper presented to him and found it to be a show-cause order from the District Court. He was ordered to show cause why the waters backed up by his Low Lake dam should not be removed from the right-of-way granted by Gubernatorial edict to the South Western Pacific Railroad.

"You knew you couldn't get away with this," Fred Gavin told him, when he laid the document on the desk between them.

Kincaid said: "I didn't particularly expect to." And

then, with apparent irrelevance: "What's the railroad stock stand at this morning?"

"It's off another couple of points."

Kincaid thought about it, and then spoke: "Fred, I know as well as anyone that my dam will have to come out. If we can stall that off for a while, I think, however, that the railroad will fold first. It's the play I'm making. Can you give me a month's delay on this show-cause proceeding?"

Gavin could and would. "I don't suppose there's anyone on the range who doesn't admire you for the game fight you've put up," he said. "Now it looks like you would have your way. But Lance," and Gavin's steady look was inquiring; "are you sure you're doing right?"

"Certainly, I'm sure." Old Rusty spoke for Kincaid then, without hesitation. "I'm protecting my own land. What is there about it that isn't right?"

Gavin only shook his head.

Kincaid stayed in town that day. Before the Exchange closed, he walked in to note that South Western Pacific was quite evidently on the toboggan. The road's financial back had been broken, its credit swept away.

Jube Pickett was in the Exchange when Kincaid entered. He had nothing to say this time, no punctilious nod to proffer; he just looked holes through Kincaid and then turned his wiry back. Kincaid neither smiled nor shrugged, but when he walked out he continued to think about it. For the first time a new aspect of the situation struck him: What was this defeat doing, through her father, to Valerie Pickett? It might not touch them financially; but the effects of these things, as he well knew, were infinitely more far-reaching than that.

It was for this reason that Kincaid spent more time in White Oaks now than was his usual wont. The fall rains persisted until Low Lake, on 2 M, was a vast deep hiding every evidence of the railroad's efforts to overcome it. Fred Gavin had succeeded in averting the immediacy of action in regard to the dam. Success, for 2 M, was driven home and clinched.

One day Kincaid met Valerie on the street. She saw him coming in time to have avoided him had she so wished; but she waited. The sobriety in her face as he greeted her was only exceeded by the gravity of her reply. She said: "Well, you've won, Lance."

He found something wanting in the recognition. "I'm sorry it had to happen to your father, Valerie. But it could be no surprise. 2 M's intentions were declared from the start; we have certainly been consistent throughout."

"I know." Valerie's smile was tempered, a little sad. "Old Mr. Maxwell's wish has been respected. But it is you, Lance, who must live to regret it." Her eyes studied his lean cheeks. "You will not think I am seeking excuses when I say that the country needs women and children, it needs settlement, and homes; and that yours is not the way to get these things."

Her hold on him was as potent as ever, he saw with a deep disturbance. It was not alone her words that had such a profound influence over him, but something within her that was compassionate and wise; something that told him that, although things were different between them, it was not she who had changed, but him.

She had been going the way he was going, when they met; but as they had their talk out, in a deep language which had little to do with the words they spoke, and found little reflection there, she stood fast; and he did not press her. When they parted, it was on a note of abeyance. More could have been said which neither desired to bring into the light, and so no direct mention was made of what either meant to do. But riding back toward 2 M in the endless, sodden rain Kincaid could not get out of his mind the thoughts or the mood which Valerie had induced in him.

At one point he had to cross the railroad tracks; and here he saw the slow trundling cars of a train piled with equipment, moving out. It was a flat confession of defeat, but there was no depression of spirit in it. To the defiant yells and objurgations which reached him through the rain from angry trainmen he paid no heed.

At headquarters the atmosphere of exultation was unmistakable. Along the *acequia* and at corrals and bunkroom door, groups of grinning men watched Kincaid arrive and raised hands as though in salute to a conquering hero. He appraised them all with a slow smile, but he found no infection in their cheer. Going to his office, and sinking in the chair behind this desk which Rusty Maxwell had so often breasted, he asked himself what was the matter with him.

It was not alone the effect of all that Valerie had said. Through his mind, all the way home, and on into this hour there passed all that 2 M had fought for, through hate and enmity and even death; and now there commenced at last to crowd in upon him the conviction that all along they had been wrong, terribly wrong. It was Valerie, for that matter, who was in the right, who had always been in the right; and this vast empire flung down across the prodigal skirts of Comanche Mountain was a barrier to progress. Plainly enough, that torn sheet of water which, by turning his glance, he could just see down there in the Basin, was the symbol of his colossal and growing error.

Kincaid unconsciously straightened; he got up, took a few steps and turned, hands behind him.

"Yes," he mused, and his tanned lean face was unusually bleak; "I can see it. My loyalty to Rusty has put blinders on me for too long; the need to keep 2 M as it was, died with him . . . I've been blind and stubborn. The wonder of it is that Valerie should have so much patience with me."

He broke out of his abstraction, decision in his movements. Stepping to the gallery, he called to the men at the bunkroom door: "Send Charley May over here as soon as he comes in."

Quill Hoskins signified assent for them, and Kincaid turned back into the office. Charley May found him there half-an-hour later.

"Charley," Kincaid opened up without preamble, "I want you to ride down and open the lower dam. Don't lose any time."

Charley remained absolutely still, arrested there, but his stare said that he believed Kincaid had suddenly and disastrously lost his wits. He said carefully: "Lance, you don't mean——"

"You know what I mean, Charley." Kincaid was patient but firm. "Go ahead and do as you're told; I know what I'm doing."

Charley May's lift of the shoulders as he turned wordlessly away said that he doubted it. But he went. An hour later, looking down there, Kincaid knew without seeing that during the night, the Basin would return to its original proportions, and he nodded to himself.

This complete about-face, which threw 2 M into consternation, left Kincaid curiously directionless. The work went on, the next day, but it scarcely appeared to; the ranch looked deserted. Thus it was that Kincaid himself stepped into the ranch yard at the sound of arriving hoofs. He was electrified to meet the gaze of Valerie Pickett.

"Valerie! I didn't dare hope—— Get down. Come in by the fire. How glad I am to see you here!"

He took her into the house and made her comfortable. She neglected the chair he dragged toward the fireplace, standing with her straight back to it, her grave eyes following him in an unreadable way. She read the puzzlement in his face as to why she had ridden here on so inhospitable a day.

"I've come to say good-bye, Lance," she told him, her long lips stirring. At his breaking small frown of protest, she added composedly: "We are going to leave."

"You don't have to," he said simply.

She looked at him for this long and groping moment, and then she asked lowly, "Why?"

"Because I have opened the dam. The Basin is no longer flooded."

With a small cry she sprang toward the window. And she saw that what he said was so. Her words, as she turned back and then moved toward him, scarcely reached across the interval. She whispered: "Lance, why did you do it?"

There was no pride and no expectancy in him.

"I saw that you were right," he said; and then, quickly:

"Valerie! You make me want you. Why do you look at me in that way?"

But she had no words, and she needed none. A light had come into her damp eyes, transforming her soft face. It dragged Kincaid forward with arms extended from which she did not turn away.

"Darling——!" he murmured. With the full hunger of his life in the act, he drew her to him; and for the first time that erect head was bowed as it lay, trusting and somehow at home, on his broad chest.

XXI

THE warm sunlight of a crisp fall morning streamed through the windows of the White Oaks parsonage. They were wide and high windows, lending a dignity to the cheerful old room, with its dark-beamed walls of high-country hardwood and its heavy oak furniture; their light fell over this double wedding party and brought brightness to the scene.

Gideon Wall, in his surplice, book in hand, was a solemn, benignant figure who brought a glint of appreciation to Jube Pickett's eye, and to that of Gail Childress; this old friend of Ben Sharp, who had given one of the brides away. But Charley May and the Jingle-bob foreman, Dab Fyler, the two best-men, were stiff and angular with responsibility. Even Bert Hyde's flaming hair, as he stood beside Donita and eyed Gideon Wall as though for the first false move, was rivaled in color only by the deep hue of his neck. Donita, fetching in her billowy wedding gown, was demurely pensive. As for Kincaid, he appeared to have retired into himself in his stalwart way. It was only Valerie, beside him with her confident hand in his, who avowedly looked the happiness she felt. The future lay broad and unruffled in her soft eyes and in her proud and gentle face.

"Dearly Beloved," Gideon Wall intoned; and his full voice ran through these beautiful and hallowed old periods to the stately conclusion of the ceremony. Silence fell, rich and golden, over the accomplished fact of these four young lives, linked two and two, for the duration of life. Kincaid bent reverently to thank his wife with his lips; and Bert Hyde, if less self-possessed, was equally as eager. Jube Pickett stroked his mustache with a quick, nervous gesture and turned aside for this one moment of deep feeling; then, with Gail Childress, he was beaming his large approval on the company and claiming his privilege of saluting the brides.

"I declare!" Donita exclaimed a mock protest at Gail Childress' smiling ardency; "Mr. Wall will think he's made a terrible mistake, marrying me to Bert, Uncle Gail!"

A ripple of laughter greeted her remark, but Childress carried it off with his usual aplomb. "I've been waiting for this hour since the day you first crawled astride my knee, young lady. You wouldn't deny me this last chance Bert will probably ever give me?"

All of them entered into the spirit of light-hearted gaiety; but Valerie, at her husband's elbow, would not at once relinquish the sentiment or the significance of the moment. She said, under cover of the jollity around them: "You are not sorry, Lance—that you have married a railroad man's daughter? There is nothing to regret?"

His eyes claimed her in this still faintly surprised and wholly gratified way, and he shook an assured negative. "Only my stubbornness and delay," he murmured. "It was you who saved me, in spite of myself."

"Darling!" Her lips formed the word. Her warm eyes were a benediction.

"Well, folks—" Gail Childress made his bid for their

collective attention. "Breakfast is served, from now until we've dealt with it in our usual competent manner. Shall we go down there and relieve Gabe's mind? I understand he's gone to considerable pains in honor of the occasion."

They drifted toward the door, finding many happy thoughts to express, and anticipating the fun of the wedding breakfast at the White Oaks Hotel. The sky on this October day was a brilliant blue, flecked with the fleece of sailing clouds; warmth and invigorating tanginess poured into the busy morning street to make vignettes of the passing horsemen in their easy freedom. The promise of all the world was here gathered for light hearts to claim.

There was no one to take note of a crouching dusty form, pressed against the wall of a sun-blackened shed, where Buck Ewing watched the passing of the wedding party with bitterly enflamed eyes, from the mouth of an alley.

On the porch of the hotel, Gabe Brandon, the proprietor, met them with an expansive smile.

"Just nicely in time, folks," he declared. "If you care to step into the parlor for just a minute——"

"Well, if you're sure it'll be for no more than a minute," Gail Childress consented for them all breezily, "I expect Bert, here, and Lance, can hold out that long. I wouldn't wonder if Charley May and Dab have taken advantage of a little snack beforehand; and the Major and I have our cigars to fall back on."

Standing in the furbished and spotless parlor, the party made a gay group. Even Charley May and Dab Fyler appeared to have loosened up. The murmur of talk rose and fell.

"Lance," Jube Pickett said heartily to his son-in-law, "I don't know when anything has given me so much satisfaction."

"Or I," Kincaid nodded. Conscious of the clear and steady gaze of his wife, he knew the impossibility of putting into words his contentment with the turn his affairs had taken. No longer a sore spot between them, the railroad crept into their talk. They were still discussing it when, with startling absence of any warning, a scream rang through the parlor which could only have come from Donita.

With one accord they wheeled, the shock of silence running over them all. In the door, an unkempt and gaunt figure, the skeleton at the feast, stood Buck Ewing, gun in hand.

His hard eye ran over them with imperious cruelty. Hatred and contempt rolled out from him and brought a premonitory chill to this room. Standing here in the full tide of his latent ruthlessness, the man was a potential menace to everyone present; the wild look in his eye said plainer than words that he was on the brink of violence.

In the midst of the immobility his appearance struck over them, Kincaid stepped quietly and decisively forward. He was unarmed. Without taking his eye away from Ewing, he extended a commanding hand toward Charley May.

Charley muttered, coldly level: "I'll handle this, Lance;" but in comparison to his tone, Kincaid's terse words were like the cleaving bite of a cold-chisel. He said:

"Give me your gun."

Under the saturnine madness of Buck Ewing's glare, the six-gun changed hands. Ewing's long lips twitched, and flat words spanned the taut gap here. "I once told you we'd go out of this fight together. That still goes, Kincaid!" He threw all the basilisk force of his will into the wicked statement.

"No—oh, no!" Valerie seemed to come to herself in this instant of her husband's peril. She started forward, driven by the fear of what impended. "Lance——!"

She flung herself at him, striving to get between before Buck Ewing's rock-like immobility should crash into fire and destruction. Kincaid swept her aside; but not quickly enough. In that instant Ewing ripped into action, his long arm jerking.

The flash and thunder of a single shot rumbled against these walls. With a cry, Valerie staggered and dropped to the floor; her swift movement had delayed Kincaid's gun arm for that vital second.

Something dark and unreasoning and deathless, the grim intent of his life force, was unleashed in Kincaid then. Standing full and square to this bitter enemy, he drove slug after roaring slug into the gaunt form. This was the man who had killed Valerie's brother and plotted against himself; and now he had struck Valerie down. Kincaid's merciless bullets hammered Ewing resistlessly sidewise and over and finally to the floor, there just inside the door; and when Ewing's sprawled form twitched once more, Kincaid hurled in the finishing shot without compunction.

He flung the gun aside then, and bent to gather Valerie in his wiry arms, a great fear in his stoic face. As if the act had broken the trance which held them all, the others were churning about; cries echoed and men came running in, a sharp excitement on them.

Kincaid laid Valerie on a sofa. And now, in a hastily anxious examination, he was able to identify the slight extent of her injury: a graze from Ewing's first shot, which had raised an angry welt across her temple. He straightened to meet the fearful glances of all these people, and said in a voice which disguised his own revulsion of feeling, of flooding relief:

"It isn't bad, thank Heaven. Just a graze that will require a little rest. She's had a bad shock . . . Will you," he asked Gabe Brandon, "tell the maid to hurry some water and a clean cloth?" Charley May had already hurriedly pushed his way out in search of a doctor.

The relief here was audible; everyone began talking at once. The sheriff had appeared, and in low and smooth tones was directing the removal of Buck Ewing's lifeless form.

The shades in this hotel suite were lowered. Valerie, ordered by the doctor to take a few hours' rest, lay on the bed. She had regained consciousness and was lying quiet.

Kincaid, outside the door of the room, his face marked with lines which had not been there an hour ago, turned swiftly as the doctor emerged, a question in the eyes he fastened on the man.

"Mrs. Kincaid," said the physician quietly, "is quite herself again, but she must rest."

Kincaid waited for no more. But his haste left him as he approached the bed; he moved softly. Valerie's face lifted from the pillow and he bent over her.

"My dear! I am so glad you are all right." All her love for him spilled through these words which were no more than a whisper. Her arms stole up, firm and white and cool. "For just a moment——" She shuddered against him, and her eyes were pleading.

"Everything is all right, Valerie," he reassured her steadily. "Buck Ewing will—molest us no more, ever."

"But——"

"The coroner took my statement," he explained gently, "and we will hear no more about it." Quick feeling swept across his bronzed face, of compassion for the violence done to her sensibilities on this, of all days. "I'm sorry this had to happen, dearest—to mar your memories."

She told him, her talking muffled by his nearness: "I shall remember nothing but what I most earnestly desire to, Lance—your strength, and justness, and bravery."